Y0-BZJ-665

The Truth about Faking

by Leigh Talbert Moore

To Neruyda ~
A great friend
to me ~ writers! ☺
Best!
Leigh

This book is a work of fiction. Names, characters, places, and incidents are products of the author's imagination or are used fictitiously. Any resemblance to actual events or locales or persons, living or dead, is entirely coincidental.

The Truth about Faking
Copyright © Leigh Talbert Moore, 2012
www.leightmoore.com
Printed in the United States of America.

Cover design by Jolene B. Perry

All right reserved. No part of this publication can be reproduced, stored in a retrieval system, or transmitted in any form or by any means — electronic, photocopying, mechanical, or otherwise — without prior permission of the publisher and author.

For Mom, who believes;
For JRM, who inspires;
For CGM & LCM, who motivate;
For KCB, who loves each one more than the last;

And for JBP, who said, "What are you waiting for?"

One

My phone whistles at me from my bag. I try to ignore it. Mr. Laraby's words are still in my head from driver's ed. class last week: *Distracted driving is the number one cause of fatal accidents among teens.* His words and that disgusting movie with all the wrecked cars and dead bodies everywhere. I keep my eyes on the road ahead.

It whistles again, and I rationalize. Only my best friend Shelly sends me a hundred texts at once, and it's usually something like she's trying turquoise eye shadow or her cat fell in their fountain again. It can wait.

Another whistle and my scalp tightens. My eyes flick to the speedometer. I'm only going 35, surely it can't hurt just to look. In front of me is a giant Lincoln Towncar. I'm stuck behind Mr. Bender, the slowest driver in Shadow Falls. And the oldest. And the grumpiest.

Again it whistles, and my jaw clenches. What if it's not Shelly? What if someone's in trouble, and I'm the only number they can text? What if they're trapped under something heavy, but not so heavy they can't text. And I'm their only hope…

Suddenly Bender slams on his brakes — at a yellow light, of course. I stop as well, and with my foot on the pedal, dive across the seat to grab my phone. My shoulders drop. It's Shelly.

Where are you?

Again Mr. Laraby's voice is in my head: *"Where are you" is the most common text sent before accidents...*

All of a sudden, *BAM!*

My phone flies from my hand onto the dash, and my torso is jerked back by the seatbelt. My foot slips off the brake, and Mom's Denali goes right into Bender's Towncar before I can find the correct pedal to push again.

"I wasn't texting!" I squeal, realizing my eyes are squeezed shut. My whole body is clenched.

Shaking, I try to get control. I inhale and open my eyes as I remember my foot had been on the brake pedal, so I couldn't have hit Bender. I exhale with the realization: Someone hit me! Oh, thank God. It wasn't my fault.

Wait. Someone hit me. Now what? I've never been in a wreck before, and I try to remember what to do. Exit the vehicle, check for damages... I force my brain to start working again. Shadow Falls is so small, Pete, one of our two local cops, will likely be here in less than two minutes. I unfasten my seatbelt and open the door. My legs wobble as I stand up, and I actually feel a little dizzy. The noise had been so loud and unexpected, I can still hear it.

"God—" A tenor voice cuts off behind me.

I turn around to see a guy in faded blue jeans and a t-shirt bending over the back of Mom's SUV. He looks about my age, but I don't know him, which is strange. Everybody knows everybody in Shadow

—

6

Falls. He straightens up and starts toward me, rubbing his forehead, which is turning pink. I wonder if he hit it on the steering wheel or something.

"Are you okay? I'm really sorry," he says to me. "I was looking at that car lot over there, and you stopped so fast..."

I look across the median and see a used car lot I've never noticed before. How is that possible? *Do I have amnesia?* But I remember Bender and where I live, so I must be okay. Then I check out what hit me. It's an ancient blue sports car with a long front-end like a duck. Only now the bill is pointed down. Sad duck.

The guy's staring at me. "Hey, you okay?" His voice has softened, and I can tell he's worried. "I'm really sorry," he says again.

"It's... I'm okay." I answer, trying to get my bearings. "The light had just changed..."

"I know," he says through an exhale. "I glanced away, and when I looked back, there you were. Not moving."

"It was Bender—" I'm not about to confess I was looking at a text, but I'm cut off.

"What tha HELL!" That voice is *not* okay.

Mom's Denali had just given Bender's Towncar a butt lift, and I can tell he's pissed—as usual. A veteran of two wars, Mr. Bender isn't exactly mean, but teenagers top his list of most annoying things on the planet. And don't even *think* about pulling your phone out in front of him.

"I'm sorry, sir," the boy starts again, this time a little nervous. "I was looking off, and—"

—

7

"You're right you're sorry!" Bender growls. "How old are you? Do you even have a license?"

"I'm seventeen, sir. Yes, sir, I have a license." The guy stutters, holding his hands up like Bender's got a gun on him.

"Then you should know. Ten and two. Eyes on the road!"

"Yes, sir. I just noticed that used car lot, and I need a new car…"

"More like you need driver's ed," Bender barks. "Gimmie your license."

The boy drops his hands and starts digging in his back pocket. I see the flashing lights pull up behind his duck-billed destroyer, and sure enough, Pete climbs out and starts slowly heading our way, silver-metal clipboard in hand. He spots Bender and immediately looks tired.

"We need to move these vehicles from the lanes of traffic," he says, beginning to write. "You okay, Harley?"

I nod. Pete's been friends with my parents since they were all at State College together in Glennville, the college town right across the river from us.

"Got your license, son?" Pete asks the guy.

Bender hands it over. He's just finished writing down all the information for himself, and I figure he'll be calling the poor guy's parents in a few hours.

"It's all my fault…" the guy starts again, but Pete puts a hand up. "Harley, you got yours?"

I slowly climb onto the running board and reach into my bag, still feeling a little off-balance.

—

"Tom, I'm going to need yours as well," Pete says.

"I'm not at fault here..." Mr. Bender starts. "I was sitting at the light, obeying the rules of the road, when Harley was shoved into my backside by this... menace."

The menace looks down, and I feel sorry for him. He seems embarrassed.

"I still need to fill out the report, so I'll need your license," Pete's voice sounds weary. It's the sound most people's voices get when dealing with Mr. Bender.

Bender huffs some more and digs into his back pocket, producing a sleek leather trifold from which he pulls his license. Then he stalks back to his Towncar and gets on one knee to examine his bumper. That leaves me standing in the median with the menace.

He shoves a hand at me. "I'm Jason."

Skinny. Shaggy brown hair and dark brown eyes. Not really my type, but a friendly enough smile. I reach out and briefly touch his hand before crossing my arms again.

"So, Harley?" He smiles and fumbles his hand into his pocket. "He's a little shaky, too, I notice. "Your parents bikers?"

"No." I pull my hair back in a band, ignoring a slight twinge as I do so.

"That a family name?"

I shake my head. "My mom thinks it's pretty."

I leave off the part where I've always been annoyed at being named after a motorcycle. Mom's also a little eccentric.

"Yeah," he nods and seems surprised. "She's right."

I look at him a second longer. He's not bad looking. Not that I'm interested or anything.

"We just moved here from Los Lunas," he says. "So I'm still learning my way around. You go to Creekside?"

I nod. "Everybody does."

"Then I'll say hey when I see you at school!"

"You don't have to." There's only one guy I want saying hey to me at school, and it isn't Teen Menace-Crash boy.

"Look, I'm sorry I hit your giant truck here." He pats Mom's Denali and makes an apologetic face. "But you'll be surprised what those body shop guys can do. It'll be back to normal in a week."

I slant my eyes. "You do this a lot?"

"No," he laughs. "I just like fixing up old cars. It's kind of a hobby."

"Well, this is my mom's truck, and she needs it for work. And I don't really know you—"

"Sure you do," he jumps in. "I'm Jason James. Just moved here from New Mexico, and you're Harley...?"

"Andrews."

He does a little finger-gun. "And I was going to guess Davidson."

"That's original," I say, looking around.

I need to get home and get started. Tomorrow's an important day. It's the culmination of Operation Luau, my big plan. The whole reason I was out here in the first place buying a dress, and everything has to be perfect.

"I guess not," Jason shrugs. "But I really am sorry."

I try giving him a warm smile and hope he'll take it as me letting him off the hook. Then I walk to the back of Mom's SUV. The doors are only pushed in a little, but when I pull the handle, they won't budge. I bite my lip. Mom needs the Denali to haul her massage table and equipment around, and she'll be pissed if she has to cancel appointments. I look impatiently in Pete's direction.

"I need to go," I say to myself.

"I've got my phone if you want to use it." Jason's followed me.

I glance up at him. "That's okay. I mean, I've got a phone. But thanks."

At last Pete starts walking back toward us. "Can you drive your vehicle?" He asks me.

"I think so," I say.

Pete hands us the papers to sign and then tears off our copies. I take mine and climb back into the Denali, turning the key as I watch Bender huff into his land-barge. Jason walks up to my door.

"Sure you're okay?" He asks.

Both hands are in his front pockets, and his dark eyes are very round. Puppy-dog.

I nod back at him.

—

"And I'll see you tomorrow?"

"Okay…" I say with a touch of hesitation. Then I shrug. "I mean, sure."

He lights up. "Later, then."

I resist rolling my eyes and instead do a little smile back before hitting the button for my window. As soon as Bender's clear, I turn the wheel toward the entrance to our neighborhood. I'll be home in less than two minutes.

Shadow Falls the neighborhood is neither shadowy, nor has waterfalls. It's basically the hub of Shadow Falls the town. Way back when it was built, graduates of State College wanted to get out of the city, with all it's crime and bad schools, but still live close enough to work there. Developers spotted this tract of land right across the river and got to work drawing out long, winding streets with cul-de-sacs sprouting off every curve. From the air, it must look like some giant, alien plant life.

Creekside is the only high school here. It's built on this trench the developers dug to look like a real creek running down to the river, and it's populated with kids who've known each other since before kindergarten. That includes me and my best friend Shelly.

My phone rings out again, and I grab it. It's her.

"Did you get my texts? Where are you?"

Shelly's voice is urgent.

———

"Ugh, wreck. Bender. Main and Spring. You would not believe."

"Oh my god! Are you hurt? Do you need me to call Mom's lawyer?" Ever since Shelly's parents got divorced last summer, she's been whipping out her mom's lawyer like she's a mob boss.

"I think I'll be okay," I say. "Pete was on it. The perp confessed his guilt."

"Well, good, because I've got the greatest idea, the solution to your problem. Mom got a new book— "

"Not another one," I interrupt with a groan. Shelly's mom turned into a self-help fanatic after the divorce, and she's always trying some new theory for finding happiness.

Shelly charges on. "It's all about how doing the same thing over and over and expecting different results means you're crazy…"

"Mm-hmm." I can't see where this is going yet or what problem of mine she's solving.

"Then it talks about the concept of Mr. Right, and how that's a myth used to keep modern women under control."

"Last time was religion." I glance out the window as I navigate the winding neighborhood streets. Our church is at the center of Shadow Falls, and everything sort of converges on that point.

"Whatever," she says. "This time it's about how *Mr. Right* is a myth."

A big hydrangea bush is growing where my street meets Shadow Falls Lane, and today it's bursting with bluish-lavender blossoms. As Shelly talks, I gaze at the huge fists of flowers and realize they're the exact same shade as Trent Jackson's eyes. He's my non-mythical Mr. Right, hottie future-husband. Well, I'm still working on that last part.

Last year, sophomore year, Trent started at Creekside High School and literally stopped every girl in her tracks. Unfortunately for me, I had no chance with him. My legs went up to my armpits, and when I smiled, you had to put on your sunglasses to block the reflection off my braces. But over the summer the braces came off, and my body got more proportional.

And Stephanie Miller got Trent.

A frown touches my lips, and I turn into my driveway just in time to hear Shelly's last words. "...put you through assertiveness training."

I jump. "What?" My name coupled with *assertiveness training* can *not* be a good thing.

"It's the whole reason he dated Stephanie all last fall and not you. Brian says he asked about you in August, and he watches you constantly —"

"Stop! *Who* asked about me in August?"

"Trent." She says it like it's the most normal thing in the world.

I almost drop my phone.

I can't swallow. It's possible I'm having one of those mini-strokes. "Oh my god, Shelly. What did he say? Tell me his exact words."

"You know, 'What is she like,' that kind of thing." Her casual tone is giving me chest pains. Maybe I'm having a heart attack. "With your dad being a reverend and all, guys don't know what to expect."

I shake my head. I'm sitting in my driveway and I cannot move. I'm completely paralyzed. Maybe it is a mini-stroke.

"What did Brian say?" I ask, trying to restart my breathing.

"I don't know," she says. "That's not the point."

"Shelly!"

"Oh my god! Chill. I'm sure it was all good things, you know Brian. But I'm even *more* sure Trent would've asked you out then."

My head is spinning, and the wreck, everything is forgotten. August? That was right after he saved me at the gym... we could be engaged right now. Okay, maybe not engaged. But promised?

"...of course, Stephanie came along and just swooped him right up." She pauses, waiting, but I'm imagining my wedding dress. It'll be white, of course, and floor-length. And with a lavender-blue sash to match his eyes. I'll wear my hair in a French braid. Maybe one of those four-stranded braids or an around-the-head, crown style...

"And *that's* my point," Shelly breathes loudly. "You're always so distracted and aloof, it makes guys think you're not interested."

"I am not aloof! I can't believe you're just now telling me this!"

"I'm telling you this because it's part of my great plan! Although I don't like encouraging obsessions-"

"Obsessions?"

15

"You've spent way too much mental energy on this guy. All last year it was nothing. Then he dates Stephanie six months, and you're still crushing on him. You're fixated."

"I am not fixated, and he just broke up with Stephanie. And clearly it could've been something, only you chose not to tell me."

"Like it would've made a difference."

"It might've." I'm finally able to move again, so I grab my bag off the passenger's seat and pull the keys from the ignition. I hop down and slam the door shut.

"Look, I didn't call to argue," Shelly continues. "I called to tell you I've decided to help you."

"Help me? How?"

"You never listen — with assertiveness training! I've observed your behavior. And whenever you're confronted with a guy you like, you freak and become closed."

"Is *freak* the clinical term?"

"I'm going to help you open up and Break the Cycle!"

That's probably the title of her mom's new book.

"Well, I've kind of been working on a plan already —" I smile at how Operation Luau is *so* in the bag now.

"First we have to set your goal," she interrupts. "What is your goal?"

"What?" I grunt as I climb over the backseat to get my dress now that the back doors are jammed shut. I drop back to the driveway and shake it out as I walk inside.

"Dating Trent? Making out with Trent? Marrying Trent?"

"Well, I wouldn't say marrying Trent," I lie. "That's silly!"

"So making out with Trent."

A million butterflies take off in my stomach at the thought of kissing him. "That sounds like a good goal."

"OK, then. You're going to model my behavior, and by the end of the week, we'll have you at the Spring Luau with Trent."

"Model *your* behavior?" I ask, but she keeps talking.

"After which, the two of you will proceed to an intense make-out session."

"Shelly!" My butterflies just had babies at that thought. "But I don't know." I balance the phone on my shoulder as I open my door. "I mean, I don't think I'll ever be able to you know. Model you."

"What's that supposed to mean?" She acts offended, but she knows it's the truth.

Ever since her parents' split, it's been really hard keeping up with Shelly. Last summer she went off the charts, dumping Brian, who'd been her boyfriend since middle school. Now she's been jumping from guy to guy like she's trying to set some Creekside record for most males bagged in a single year. She's starting to get a rep, and it's been taking all my creative efforts to keep it from my parents. That part kind of pisses me off. She knows how I feel about not embarrassing Dad. I hurry to the next problem as I drop all my stuff on my bed.

"And I'm not sure you're right about Trent picking me over Stephanie. I mean, seriously. Steph's a senior, she's cheer captain, she's got that long brown hair and... well... it all came together for her."

"I am your best friend, Harley." Her voice is suddenly serious. "I will not let you be intimidated by Stephanie Miller's boobs."

"Oh my god, I'm not intimidated by her boobs."

Still, it really isn't fair that Stephanie's never had an awkward phase as long as I've known her. She sailed straight from being the cutest little elementary school kid to being the first girl in middle school to—okay, get her boobs—all without even breaking a sweat. And she's not very nice about it either. My nose wrinkles.

"Besides, you're a cheerleader now," Shelly continues.

"Only because Trish got mono and had to drop out."

I'm literally the worst cheerleader. But I've got decent legs and blonde hair, and I can yell really loud—*Go Panthers!*

"We've got to teach you another jump besides The Banana. You look like a dork just jumping up and arching your back like that."

"Thanks," I frown, remembering how humiliated I'd been at tryouts last summer. Of course, it all led to my life-saving encounter with Trent—that day at the gym when our love became real. For me at least.

———

"Gotta run," Shelly's saying. "But I'll strategize more tonight."

Great. "See you in the morning." I toss my phone on my bed next to all the rest of my stuff. Then I exhale and flop in the middle of it all, remembering...

It all started last summer at cheerleading tryouts. I don't count sophomore year when I was completely invisible—at least I hope I was. No, it was a week before school started, and I'd just gotten my braces off. Shelly'd insisted I tryout with her, so we were all at the gym. The boys—Trent included—had been playing basketball on the half-court until Coach Taylor sent them outside. They'd pretended to be pissed, but we knew they were really there checking out the new recruits.

My turn went okay. I did some easy cheers, and then came the jumps portion. I did The Banana, and Stephanie nearly squirted cherry Icee through her nose. Meg leaned over and giggled, "What was *that*?" under her breath, and Stephanie'd shouted "Next!" like it'd been some sort of Broadway show from which I'd just been cut.

I kept my head down as I walked off the court, hoping my ponytail would hide my burning cheeks. I bit my lip, doing my best not to cry. Usually I'm not so weak, but that'd been about as humiliating as my stupid non-jump. I sat on the metal bleachers staring at my shoes until finally I grabbed my bag and decided to leave. I'd just opened the metal door when *Wham!*

Next thing I knew, I was laying on the ground with my head in somebody's lap. A voice was saying something, and my eyes flickered open. The sun was shining right in my face, and the first thing I was able to make out was... lavender. Trent's head was inches from mine. My stomach flipped, and I bumped our noses as I tried to sit up.

"Hey," he laughed, leaning back. "Harley, right? Can you stand up?"

"What?" I tried to stand, but my head felt like I'd run into a brick wall. I caught his shoulder. It felt really nice and firm.

"You ran into a brick wall," he said. "Sort of. David had just thrown the ball, and I missed it. It kind of knocked you out."

I reached up to touch my forehead, and as he helped me up, my face went into his chest where I caught a deep breath of the woodsy boy-smell coming off him. For a head injury, this could be worse.

"I was knocked out?" I timidly looked up at him, and he smiled.

The sun was shining all golden behind his head, and it made him look like a knight. Or one of those hot angels. Just then Shelly came outside.

"There you are. Sorry, just got my — what happened?"

"Basketball hit her in the head," Trent said.

I wanted to die. *What a dork!*

"I think she hit her head on the wall," he continued. "She might need to go to Urgent Care."

"Oh my god!" Shelly cried. "Bring her inside. I'll get Coach Taylor."

"I'm okay," I said. My knees were wobbly, but I couldn't tell if it was my head or Trent's arm tight around my waist. He was holding my hand even.

Shelly held the metal door open, and next thing I knew, David had joined us.

"Hey, Harley, I'm really sorry." He caught my other arm, and I felt Trent's grip loosen. His dark head was in the shadow of the gym, and he was definitely not an angel. *Go away, David.*

"It's okay," I said, trying to smile and scoot back toward Trent. "Really, I'm fine."

"I can drive her to the doctor," Shelly said. I tried to give her my most discouraging look. Just then Stephanie joined the mob.

"What's up? Harley? Are you okay?"

"We're taking her to Coach Taylor," Shelly said.

"What happened?"

"Harley might have a concussion," David said like it was the most exciting thing to happen all summer.

David was distracted by Stephanie, and I leaned on Trent's arm. He caught my waist again and smiled, and everything turned perfect. The humiliation of tryouts, the humiliation of being beaned in the head with a basketball, none of it mattered as I stood there with Trent's arm tight around me. Until Coach Taylor showed up and ruined it. She took me away and led me to the bleachers. Then she started shining her tiny flashlight in my eyes.

"Do you feel sleepy? Like you might vomit?"

Nice. I shook my head, and David started bouncing the dumb ball again. Coach Taylor shouted for all the boys to get back outside and told me to sit where she could keep her eye on me. I watched the guys leave, and just as Trent was going through the door, he stopped and glanced back. It was because he wanted to stay with me, I was sure, and I tried to catch his eye. David shoved him through the opening before he saw me, and I sighed, turning back to the court. Stephanie was watching, but she quickly flicked her attention back to her sheet and called the next name.

As I rested on the bleachers, everything felt sort of soft and glowy. It seemed like music was playing somewhere — and not because of my head injury. It was because I knew Trent was The One, my hero. I tried to remember if I'd thanked him, but it didn't matter. I was sure he'd ask me out.

A week later we all started junior year, and the next time I saw Trent, he was walking down the hall holding hands with Stephanie.

I press my lips together and come back to the present. Stephanie dumped Trent right after the Valentine's dance last month (so cold!), and ever since I've been waiting, carefully planning my approach.

Operation Luau begins with me giving him time to get over her. It also involves observation and strategic moves. Trent and I have the same algebra teacher this year, only at different times, so every day I've been running straight to class after second period and "accidentally" bumping into him as he leaves. He always holds the door for me, and then I smile, and then he smiles. Sometimes he asks about my head and we laugh, although I wish we could forget that part.

I've also been observing his taste when it comes to girls, and I've noted he has a picture of this blonde actress in his locker with her hair all braided in some Greek-goddess way. She's also wearing this long, white gown that would never work at school, although prom is a definite possibility. Response: I've been sporting fancy braid-designs in my hair every day for a month, and I just bought the perfect dress — it's flowy, but short and blue to match my eyes (bonus!). And here we are.

Shelly just confirmed he's interested, or was. Tomorrow I'll get Mom to braid my hair, I've got the dress, and I'll be wearing my best "ask me to the luau" face when I see him after second period.

Once I get past the wrecked Denali.

Two

I plan out my speech as I walk to the kitchen. It wasn't my fault, after all. There's no reason why I should be grounded or anything. I wasn't texting while driving or doing something dangerous like that.

My mom's massage-therapy student Ricky greets me when I get there, and I frown. Problem number two.

Since Mom graduated from the college in Glennville, every semester they send her a senior to help get hands-on training before graduation. Only this time she got the same student twice in a row.

"What's up, kiddo?" Ricky asks.

"Not much," I say, grabbing an orange from the bowl. "What's Mom doing?"

"Dispensing herbal wisdom," he says like he's reading a textbook.

Mom's in her office-slash-yoga room with Mrs. Bender of all people, and I can hear her saying *L-Glutamine* and *colonic massage.*

My nose wrinkles. "Gross. What're they talking about?"

"I don't want to know," he grins.

I drop into a chair and lean my head on my hand as I watch him dump white powder into the blender followed by a banana, thick orange syrup and ice. Ricky's super-hot in a *Men's Health* cover-boy kind of way. He's 23, and he likes wearing clothes that show off his well-toned body. He's also got a majorly obvious crush on my mom. He follows her around, hanging on her every word, and it's so inappropriate. Especially since he didn't graduate in December.

"What are you making?" I ask.

"Whey protein shake," he says. Then he walks over to me and slides the band out of my hair, raking his fingers through it. "Gorgeous. And you've never put anything in it?"

"You've met my dad, right?" I like reminding him of my dad, who happens to have the same platinum-blonde hair as me and clear blue eyes.

"Yes, but with your mom's coloring... It'll probably turn after you have babies."

"Don't be gross," I frown, pulling my hair back in the band again. Massage therapists are so earthy.

Just then Mom walks into the room escorting Mrs. Bender to the door. She's using what I refer to as her honey voice—soothing and sweet, it makes you feel all relaxed and sleepy. And ready to go home.

Mom's super-hot herself, in a dark and beautiful kind of way. The first time I saw that cartoon movie *Pocahontas*, I thought it was about my mom. She looks just like that Disney princess—tall and slim with long, silky brown hair and angular features. Except Mom has green eyes and she can't sing worth a flip.

"Well, I don't know," Mrs. Bender says. "I've had great BMs since I started taking your remedy."

My eyes widen, and Ricky snort-coughs.

"I'm so glad," Mom says, still using The Voice.

———

"And try to cut back on the caffeine if you can. I know it's hard, but it'll help."

"All right," Mrs. Bender agrees. "Bye, Jackie."

Mom does a little wave and then closes the door, turning back to the kitchen. The instant we hear the door catch, Ricky and I die laughing.

"Sorry," Mom says, dropping into one of the kitchen chairs facing me. Ricky hits the blender and it makes a loud, whirring noise. "Lois doesn't get the whole *Ew* factor of irritable bowel syndrome."

"No doubt," I agree.

I watch Mom twist her dark hair into a bun and then push it behind her shoulder. "I've got a small headache," she says. "I think I took too much glucosamine this morning. Or maybe I'm dehydrated."

Ricky immediately puts his spoon in his mouth and walks over behind her. I watch as he sweeps her hair aside and starts rubbing her neck. She closes her eyes, and I cringe. Massage is their specialty, after all. I just wish she wouldn't let Ricky touch her like that. Small-town gossip can be brutal, and they're custom-built for the rumor mill. It makes my stomach hurt.

"You should tell chicken-head to lay off the KFC if she's having IBS," Ricky says. Then he winks at me. I press my lips together and look back at Mom.

"I'm the one needing a neck rub," I say. "I was just rear-ended."

Mom's eyes fly open and she jumps up. "What happened?" She starts feeling the muscles around the back of my neck and shoulders, watching my face for signs of pain. "Are you okay?"

"I guess. This guy hit me from behind and then I rammed Mr. Bender."

"Do you have a headache?" She places her cool palm on my forehead. "I can make you some chamomile tea. Or maybe eucalyptus..."

"I'll be okay."

"You feel a little tight." She stands and rubs my neck again gently. "You should go see Alan tomorrow."

"I really think I'm okay," I say again. I'm not into chiropractors.

"And the Denali?" She frowns. "Should I even look?"

"It drives fine," I tell her. "But the back doors are jammed shut."

Her hands slide from my shoulders, and she walks to the back door to look out at it. I watch as she bites her lip and glances up at the clock. "It's already after six..."

"I can drive you around," Ricky says. "Or cover your appointments while it gets fixed."

So not surprising.

Mom walks back to me. "Did you at least get a number, honey?"

"Yeah, and Pete was there and everything."

"Let me see it," she says. I hand her the card. "I'll give them a call tonight and see how soon we can get it in the shop."

Ricky pours his shake into a travel mug and picks up his bag as Dad strolls in from his study. Dad's the exact opposite of Ricky—tall and skinny, wire-rimmed glasses and his nose stuck in a book. I see he's holding his favorite, *Issues in the Presbyterian Church*.

"Dr. Andrews," Ricky says as they pass in the doorway. He always straightens up when Dad's around. I give him credit for that at least.

"Ricky." Dad nods, glancing at him.

"See you tomorrow, Jackie," Ricky calls to my mom as he leaves.

She follows him out. "If you could take Mrs. Simmons at eight, I'll let you know about my other clients..."

Dad stops at the table and lowers his book.

"Hey, biker chick," he grins. "How's life on the road?"

"Sick of the bugs in my teeth."

It's our running gag, and it never bothers me when Dad makes jokes about my name. He's a reverend, but Dad's cool and we get along.

Mom comes back inside. "Harley was in a wreck," she says.

"What?" Dad frowns and walks over to me. He lifts my chin and looks into my eyes. "You feel nauseated? Dizzy?"

"I was a little dizzy at first, but I'm okay now," I say, gently moving my chin away. "They never see us bikers, you know."

"Let me check it out," he says, heading for the door.

"You can't really see it…" Mom follows him out, and I'm alone. I pick up Dad's book to see what issue he's studying. It's organized like an encyclopedia, with large headings followed by blocks of text, but I only see a big *H* before they return. I drop the book and slide back into my seat.

"They'll probably just replace the doors," Dad's saying. "It shouldn't take long."

Mom walks back to me. "I could give you a little valerian root if you're feeling tense," she says, concern lingering in her voice.

"I'm fine, Mom!" The words come out too sharp, and I wish I could take them back. I just hate being fussed over like a baby.

"Okay," she smiles, moving away.

"I mean… I'm okay," I say in a softer tone, looking down. Lately Mom and I keep having these communication *fails*, and it's so frustrating to me. Then she always retreats to Dad or Ricky, ignoring what happened. Or ignoring me.

"Bikers are tough," Dad grins, seeming oblivious. He picks up his book again, and Mom slips her arms around his waist. I watch him give one a squeeze.

"So. What should we do about dinner?" She breathes, resting her chin on his back.

Dad slides his hand down her arm and threads their fingers. "Maybe Harley'll run out and grab us something. Whatcha think, chick?" He glances at me, and I get the hint. He's trying to get rid of me.

—

It's unexpected that my parents are still so... affectionate. You'd think by now they'd be over it, and they're such opposites — Mom the earth-goddess, and Dad the gangly nerd. But sometimes I'll catch her looking at him like he's a chocolate-dipped strawberry and she's just come off a wheat-grass cleanse.

I grab Dad's keys. "I'll be back in a minute," I call as if anybody's listening.

I have no idea where I'll pick up dinner. I just know to make myself scarce for about a half hour and come back with something. Dad's Prius lights up and I look around. Without really thinking, I drive straight to KFC.

My eyes fly open before my alarm even goes off. My heart's beating faster than normal. Operation Luau-day has finally arrived. I throw back the covers and stride to the bathroom to wash my face. Then I start the hunt for Mom. I need her to do a French braid across the top of my head before Shelly arrives to drive us to school.

I find her in her giant office saluting the sun. Mom's office is a big space with her massage table behind a screen at one end. The whole room is dimly lit, and on hooks in the corner hang robes and towels. Another table holds candles, oils, and a trickly little wall-fountain. There's weird space music coming from two speakers hidden in the corners, and the whole place smells faintly of sandalwood. Magazines

---

and papers are scattered on her desk along with little packets of different herbal mixtures. On the shelf above are boxes of lotions and bath products she always gets in the mail to try. Apparently all the Earth businesses have learned Mom's sort of the green guru of Shadow Falls. She's just about to head into downward-facing dog, but I stop her.

"Hey, Mom?"

"Hi, hon," she inhales, and sweeps her arms over her head. "How's the neck?"

"A little stiff."

"Sure you won't see Alan?"

"I'll be okay," I say. "But I need you to stop that and braid my hair for me."

"What?" She releases a long exhale and lowers her arms again.

"My hair? Would you make a braid across the top of my head like this?" I motion in a headband way across the top of my head, and she smiles.

She steps over and cuts the music off, then I sit at her feet while she pulls out a brush and starts parting my hair. She's really good with things like braids and crafts and stuff like that, and I like having her help me. It gives us an opportunity to chat alone for once. In a good way.

"So Ricky's taking your clients this morning?" I ask.

"Yep, and I've got some of the ladies coming here." Then she laughs. "They were all more than willing to have Ricky cover for me if I needed him to."

"He's a rock star all right," I say.

"He's a sweet boy."

Ricky might have the hots for my mom, but she doesn't seem to notice. Last night when I got back with dinner, her shirt was inside out. Her hair was swept high in a pony tail, and around the temples it looked a little damp. She was elbow-deep in dish water singing a Peter Frampton tune off-key, and my dad was back in his study reading his book about issues in the church. He looked undisturbed, but something had happened while I was gone. I can always tell by the way they grin at each other when they think I'm not looking. It's reassuring, but at the same time, I don't want to picture what or where.

"Is it ever weird that he has a crush on you?" I ask, scratching polish off the skin beside my freshly manicured nail.

"What?" She frowns.

"Ricky? Mr. Hot for Teacher?"

"I don't know what you mean," she says, sliding a tiny row of my hair back from my face.

"C'mon, Mom," I groan. "It's so totally obvious."

She stops braiding for a second. "Harley. Ricky does *not* have a crush on me."

"If you say so," I sing-song.

"I know so. And I'm disappointed. You're being very stereotypical."

"I'm just saying how it looks." My head's resting on her lap, and I can smell the fresh eucalyptus lotion she uses after her bath. It reminds me of being outside in the springtime.

"Well, looks can be deceiving." She continues braiding, so I try another way.

"Don't you ever worry that people might... talk?"

I hear the frown in her voice. "Has someone said something to you?"

"No. I'm just thinking. Like what about Mrs. Perkins?"

Mrs. Perkins is the wife of one of the elders at our church, and I'm pretty sure she hates my mom, un-Christlike or not. The rumor is her husband applied for the pastor's job back when my dad was hired, and she never got over it. Then she met my mom and nearly lost her religion.

She openly states that massage therapy is unseemly work for the wife of a pastor. *Unseemly*, she likes to say. Mom just dismisses Mrs. Perkins's not-so-subtle insults as jealousy and ignorance, but I know that woman bugs the crap out of Mom.

"Harley." Mom's voice is firm. "You know I have no control over the students who're assigned to me. Are you saying I should give up my job because occasionally one of them might be... better-looking than the others? Is that fair?"

So she admits Ricky's better-looking than the others. "I guess not," I say.

"Well, I would hope not." Then she starts talking under her breath. "You can't live your life worrying about small-minded people with big imaginations."

"But the appearance... you know. Like Dad says." I try reminding her one of his favorite sermon texts.

Mom braids a few seconds in silence. "Harley, do you know what stereotypes are?"

"Yes." I roll my eyes. *Here we go.* Stereotypes are one of my mom's pet peeves. The other's eavesdropping. Oh, and gossip. But Mom has a lot of wild ideas about how people should act and what they should believe.

"They're tools ignorant people use to make sense of the world," she continues.

"I know."

"They're perpetuated by fear and a reluctance to learn and grow—"

"I know, I know!" I interrupt. *Jeez, now I've done it.*

"People see a young man like Ricky under my instruction, and immediately they assume the most stereotypical thing in the world," she continues.

"I was just saying—" I try interrupting again.

"Is it so hard to believe that I could actually teach him something?" Her voice is angry, and she's pulling my braid too tight.

"I wanted you to do my hair like this for a guy!" I blurt.

"What?"

Lecture effectively derailed. "There's this guy at school? Trent? I'm hoping he asks me out today."

Mom smiles and pulls my head toward her as she ties off the end of my braid. "Any boy would be lucky to go out with you." Her voice is warm now.

"So I gotta go," I say. "And I think it's wonderful that a nice young man like Ricky has such a smart, professional woman to instruct him in massage therapy."

She shakes her head and smiles, and I run back to my room to slip on the dress I bought yesterday, right before the collision.

Three

The bell signals the end of second period, and I realize I've forgotten my notebook in my locker. Precious seconds are passing as I stop to get it, and I'm so flustered, my hands are shaking. It's all been building to this. Operation Luau—the weeks of meeting him after class with warm smiles and encouraging hellos, the getting up early so Mom could give me Greek goddess braids, the dress I bought. And now Shelly tells me he asked Brian what I was like in August! Of course, that was a whole semester ago. Before Stephanie…

My fingers are trembling so hard, I can barely dial my combination, and my heart's just thumping. Right then, I hear a familiar voice behind me.

"Harley Davidson!" Jason.

"Hey," I breathe, jerking the door open. I push my other books out of the way and grab my notebook. I can feel the seconds ticking away.

"I think I'll just call you H.D.," he continues.

"Whatever. Bye, Jason." I slam my locker and take off toward Mrs. Gipson's room, glancing at the large clocks suspended throughout the hall as I run. Seconds make all the difference when we only have eight minutes between classes.

I dash around the corner just in time to see Trent walking toward the door, then I hop back and smooth my dress. I catch my breath and try to look cool as I walk casually toward our classroom.

"Oh!" I say as I almost bump into him. Accidentally, of course.

"Oh," he smiles. My heart does a little flutter. He really does have the sweetest smile. "Hey, Harley."

"Hey," I breathe. He always dresses like a model. Today, he's wearing cuffed khakis and a long-sleeved navy polo, and his hair's styled in a short, retro cut. *Stupid Stephanie Miller.*

We stand for a second in front of each other. I look around and try to figure out how to get us on the subject of the luau. I've daydreamed this moment a million times, and now I'm completely blanking.

"How's it going?" I stall.

"Okay," he says. "Basketball season's starting. Heads up!"

"Right," I laugh a little, seriously wishing he'd forget that part of our close encounter at the gym. How humiliating. "So did you have a fun weekend?"

He shrugs. "Sure."

"Me, too." I smile thinking... thinking... Then I look up and see a poster for the luau. *Yes!*

"Oh, look," I say pointing to it. "The luau's Friday."

His eyes literally brighten. "Yeah," he says. "I was thinking about that—"

But at that moment, a loud voice comes up behind me. "You know, it's not cool to walk off when someone's talking." I freeze. It's Jason again.

"Oh, hey. Trent?" he says, like he's trying to remember.

"Jason, right? Hey, man," Trent says. They give each other a fist bump.

"You two... know each other?" I look from one to the other.

"Met at the park Saturday," Jason says. Then he points at Trent. "Ultimate Frisbee."

"Yeah," Trent smiles. Then he motions to me and Jason. "Do you two know each other?"

"Oh, well..." I stumble, trying to think of a neutral response.

"Saved her life yesterday," Jason says, draping his arm across my shoulders. My eyes widen. "Now it's my job to keep her safe."

Trent frowns. "What? Another accident?" I'm about to die.

"It wasn't really that big a deal," I say, trying to slip out from under Jason's arm. *What is he doing?*

"It was," Jason argues. "And now, I have to keep my eye on you."

"What—"

"Ancient Chinese tradition," he interrupts me. "You save somebody's life, you become responsible for it."

At that Trent grins, clearly thinking Teen Menace is a great guy. "Oh, sure. I've heard of that." Then he starts moving away from us. "Well, I'd better take off. Class."

I panic. I've got to stop him, but my throat's constricted.

"Later," Jason says to Trent. Then he turns to me. "So you've got to go to the luau with me Friday. How else can I ensure your safety?"

I shake my head as I watch Trent leaving. My brain's spinning, and I'm grasping for anything to make him stop walking away.

"Wait... Trent..." is all I come up with.

He looks back and smiles, and I know he's conceding to Jason. But then...

"Oh, Harley." He stops and takes a step back toward me as if suddenly remembering something. My heart rises... "Does Shelly have a date to the luau?"

"Shelly?" *Oh. My. God.*

"Yeah. I was thinking I'd... well," he glances at Jason. "Maybe she'd like to go to the luau with me?"

"Go for it, Big T!" Jason is so encouraging, I can't wait to hit him over the head with my books.

"I don't think she has a date." I think I might cry.

"Okay." Trent gives me a small smile. Yes. Definitely cry. "Maybe you could put in a good word for me?"

"I'd love to..." I start, but I can't finish.

I'd been planning to say, "I'd love to go with you to the luau," but it's all wrong. He smiles and says something about being late as he does a little wave and walks away. I do a little wave back and turn slowly toward algebra, shoulders drooping.

"Are you in here next period?" Jason asks. I nod, unable to speak. My whole plan. Out the window.

"That's awesome! So am I."

—

"Awesome," I mumble.

He laughs. "Somehow, I don't think you mean it. What's the matter?"

I look up at him standing there all smiling and happy, and for some reason that does it. "You just ruined everything!"

"What?"

"You ruined it. All of it!" I storm through the door, Jason right behind me.

"I don't get you, H.D."

"I was trying to get Trent to ask me to the luau," I lower my voice. "And you just big fat came up and ruined everything!"

His smile disappears. "You wanted Trent to ask you to the luau?"

"You might be fascinated to learn that I had a life before you rammed me with your car yesterday."

"I figured that—"

"And you didn't save my life, you nearly took it," I continue, irritation surging through me. "I feel like taking yours."

He smiles and leans forward. "I love feisty women."

My lips clench and I try to shove him, but my bag strap falls and I trip over his stupid foot instead. He catches me. Strong arms. I quickly push away and sink into my chair.

"Just leave me alone." I drop my elbows on the desk and my face in my hands.

"Look," Jason's tone softens and he takes the seat right beside me. "I'll talk to Trent and tell him it was all a misunderstanding. Tell him to ask you to the luau... or something."

I think about that. Then I drop my hands and shake my head. "That would just make me look pathetic. Or desperate. Or not good enough for you of all people."

"I'd never say any of that about you," Jason smiles, glancing at my hair and dress. "You clean up real nice."

My eyes narrow. "Just let me think about it. I'll figure out something."

The bell rings, and Mrs. Gipson calls class to order. But I can't concentrate on algebra. I can't concentrate on anything but how Jason just wrecked everything again, and now I have to figure out how to fix this, to salvage my plan.

I plot out several different scenarios as I watch the second-hand tick. Somehow I have to go to the luau with Jason and appear to be having a super-fun time without also seeming like I like him too much. I watch Mrs. Gipson scribble out a formula she says we should memorize for the SATs, and it hits me. Stephanie dumped Trent because she's going away to college in California. She doesn't want a long-distance boyfriend, so she callously broke his heart. What if my heart is callously broken in the same way? It'll give Trent and me something in common, and since he's so wonderful, he'll naturally want to comfort me!

I take a deep breath as a smile spreads across my face. It's the perfect plan. I can't wait for the bell to ring.

Lunch follows third period, and of course, Jason and I have the same lunch shift. Sadly, Trent and I do not. But today it doesn't matter because we need to strategize.

"How great is it that we have lunch together?" Jason asks as we walk toward the cafeteria.

"It's a fluke," I say. My plan is awesome, but I'm still annoyed with him for making it necessary.

He ignores my tone. "So what have you decided about Friday?"

"Well, I've been thinking," I say as he holds the cafeteria door for me. "I've got an idea for how you can help me."

"Let's hear it."

He hands me a tray as I stop and swipe my lunch card, then I walk over to the salad bar while Jason grabs a bowl of chicken nuggets.

"OK," I say, once he's beside me again. I glance around to make sure no one's listening. "Here's the plan. We'll go to the luau together, then pretend-date for a few days, and then you'll dump me."

Jason snorts. "What?"

"You want to pay me back for nearly killing me — which is idiotic, by the way — you can help me get Trent."

"I saved your life," Jason corrects. "And how is dumping you going to help you get Trent?"

"Because," I motion with the salad tongs. "It'll put us in the same boat. I'm all broken hearted, he's all broken hearted, we turn to each other for comfort. It's perfect!"

"But why would I dump you?" Jason smiles as he watches me, and I mentally concede that he *is* cute. But that just makes it easier for me to pretend we're dating.

"It doesn't matter. You're going back to New Mexico once we graduate or something. You don't want any long-distance relationships."

"But I'm just a junior. And I kind of like it here." He follows me to the drink station.

"It doesn't have to be true!" I lower my voice again and get close to him. "You can change your mind later. It's just so Trent'll ask me out."

He looks down at me, and that silly smile returns. "I don't like it."

"What's the problem?"

"Well, what if dating you's fun? I mean, you might not be so bad to go out with."

"You're joking, right? I'm great to go out with, but more importantly, we are *not* dating. It's all fake."

"But what if you change your mind? I mean, I've heard I'm pretty great to go out with, too."

I see Robin waving at me from the cheerleaders' table in the center of the room. I always sit with them at lunch, but I can't today. I gesture towards Jason. Thank goodness he sees what I'm doing and steers me in the opposite direction. Robin's eyebrows pull together, but I shrug and follow him.

"OK. So fill in the blanks," he says. "How long are we dating?"

"Fake dating, and I don't know." I look around and spot an empty table in a far corner where no one'll overhear us. "Look, we can sit there."

We go to the table and put our trays down. Jason pulls up a chair, and I scoot close to him. He smiles again, and I notice he's wearing cologne that smells kind-of woodsy and a little citrusey.

"You smell nice," I say, opening my water. Then I notice he's wearing better jeans and a light-brown polo. His hair's also neater. It's like he planned to look cute today or something.

"Thanks," he says, but his voice breaks my distraction. It's too loud.

"Talk low. I don't want this getting out."

A sly look enters his eyes. "You spiked the Kool-aid?"

"What?"

"Sorry. I thought we'd moved on to the next harebrained scheme."

"Would you focus? This is all your fault, you know."

"How so?" He stabs a nugget with his fork.

"I've been working for weeks to get Trent to ask me out, and then you ruined it all in two seconds."

"I'm fast. But why the wait? Why didn't you just ask him to the luau yourself?"

"I had to wait because he'd just broken up with Stephanie Miller." I stab at my salad, remembering those miserable days. I could still see Trent holding her hand, her smiling blissfully back at him. *Ugh.*

"And anyway, I don't do that."

"Do what?"

"Ask guys out."

"Why not?"

"Not relevant."

Then he leans back in his chair, studying me. "Is this one of those 'nice girls don't ask guys out' things?"

I point my fork at him. "That's very stereotypical."

"Says the person doing it."

"I'm not doing anything. I'm breaking the cycle." That makes me think of Shelly. And Trent asking her to the luau. *Ugh!* again.

"Back to the blanks," I say. My perfect plan has got to work. "Two weeks?"

"What?" Jason looks lost.

"Do you think two weeks is long enough to fake date? That'll give us like, two Fridays."

"Oh. I don't know. I've never fake dated anyone before."

"Well, you're a guy. If there was a girl out there you liked and she was dating this other guy, how long would be long enough for them to date?"

His eyes travel around my face and hair before he answers. "Never."

"What?"

"If I liked a girl, I'd never want her dating another guy."

"Yes, but she doesn't *know* you like her," I explain. Jason can be so dense. "So if she dated another guy, say two weeks and he dumped her, would that effect your liking her?"

"I'm getting confused. This is a girl I like?"

"Yes."

"And she likes me?"

"Yes."

"Then why is she dating another guy?"

"Because some idiot walked up and asked her out before you had a chance to do it."

"So why didn't she tell the idiot no?" he whispers, and something in his tone seems to suggest he thinks *I'm* the idiot.

"Because he wouldn't shut up about saving her life and saying she belonged to him. He scared you off."

"That wouldn't scare me off."

Something about the way he says it causes a weird flutter in my stomach, which I choose to interpret it as maximum irritation. Or starvation.

"Would you stop?" I say too loud. I stuff a large bite of lettuce in my mouth and smile at our fellow classmates, who are now staring in our direction. I take a few more bites and wait for them to resume their conversations.

"So two weeks?" I whisper again after I've finished chewing.

"Sure," he says, still watching me with that look like he has his own plan.

"I don't think you're really thinking about it."

"Sorry," he breathes. "You're right. Two weeks is probably long enough."

"Right. Because less time might mean something's wrong with me, but longer might make him think I need a recovery period. And that could go on forever."

"I think you need a recovery period right now."

"And you should probably start driving me to school," I continue, ignoring his remark. "I mean, if we're dating and all. I'll tell Shelly."

"We're starting today?"

"Well, yeah! You asked me to the luau in front of everyone. We're clearly dating now."

"Sorry. It's only my first day."

"After a busy weekend. Jeez, you met everybody!"

"I was just cruising around. I'm a friendly guy."

"And a terrible driver. We'll just keep the driving me to school thing between us. My parents might not like it."

The bell rings, and we stand, collecting our things.

"Should I carry your books too?" he asks.

"Why would you do that? I'm not injured."

"I'm just saying, since you don't ask guys out and all."

I narrow my eyes at him. "I'll meet you this afternoon."

He smiles. "Later, H.D."

When I finally get to biology lab, Shelly is beside herself. She's going on and on about Trent popping the question, and my teeth clench as I make my way over to tell her about my alternate ride home.

"I never even saw it coming!" she gushes at Trish.

I smile less enthusiastic. Clearly my boy-crazy best friend had forgotten about her plan to help *me* get a date with Trent.

"I was just sitting there at lunch talking to Reagan," she continues. "And then there he was asking me to the luau!"

"That's really cool," I interrupt.

"And here I was trying to get him to ask *you*!" she shrieks, giving me a big hug like she's just won a trip to Paris. Then she sees my face. "Don't be mad. This is all part of the plan."

"Really? Which part?"

"It's the mentoring part. Where I model the behavior you're supposed to emulate."

"Oh, so I'm supposed to start dating the guys you like now? I'm not sure I can keep up."

"You don't understand at all. The deal is, if a hot guy asks you out, you say yes. You know, to Break the Cycle!"

"So that includes the ones your best friend's trying to date?"

Mr. Platt comes back in the room, and I know I have to get to my seat.

But Shelly catches my arm before I leave. "It's just the luau. And we'll probably only go out once. Or possibly twice. At the most."

I resist the urge to jerk her red ponytail. "That doesn't make it okay," I whisper, turning to my seat, but she catches me again.

"Think about it, if I go out with him, I can find out what he likes and stuff," she hesitates, then brightens.

"And you don't have to worry about him getting all serious with somebody else because I'm doing this for you!"

I just stare at her.

"Harley," she whispers. "Are you really mad?" Her expression is identical to the one she had the night her parents split, and I decide this must be one of those tests of patience Dad's always talking about in church.

"I'll get over it," I lie. She squeezes my arm, excited again.

"We can talk about it on the way home."

Then I remembered why I walked over. "Oh! I've got a ride home."

"What?"

"This guy… this new guy Jason? He offered me a ride."

"Jason? Who's he?"

"Well, he's uh…" His words after the crash fill my head. "He's Jason James. Just moved here from New Mexico."

"But what about Trent?" I struggle not to get mad at her all over again. Shelly can be completely clueless, but we've been friends since kindergarten. And after her parents' divorce last summer, I held her hand as she cried — it made us like sisters.

"I don't know. Jason asked me to the luau, and well…" I realize I don't have a believable reason for dating him yet. "He seems nice."

"Is he cute?"

"You haven't seen him?" She always has the latest on every noteworthy boy-event at school.

"No. I've been so knocked out by Trent asking me that I hadn't really noticed."

I can't hear her say those words again. "Well, you'll meet him after school."

Mr. Platt is walking down the aisle, and I have to get to my table before he starts deducting points. I also have to give this fake dating scheme further thought if it's going to work. People will get suspicious if I don't have a good reason for suddenly losing interest in Trent. I do not have my best friend's reputation for guy-hopping.

That afternoon in the parking lot Shelly's stuck to me like glue.

"I can't wait to meet this Jason guy. Anyone who could get your mind off Trent."

"Hey, over here," I hear him. "H.D.!"

I wish he'd quit calling me that. "There he is," I mumble.

"Oh my effing... how'd I miss that?" she giggles. "You know, I was feeling a little bad about the whole Trent thing, but not anymore. He's smokin' hot!"

I catch myself before I compare him to Trent. "Yeah. He is, right?"

I'd conceded earlier Jason was cute, but as we walk toward him, I notice the bizarre, triangle-shaped vehicle he's standing next to. It has to be 100 years old, and it's filthy. All his cute points are immediately cancelled out.

"What's that?" I say.

"That, my dear, is a Gremlin," he answers proudly.

"A what?" I can't believe it. He actually drives a car named after an old movie. What am I thinking? Of course he does.

"A Gremlin," he repeats. "Don't tell me you've never heard of a Gremlin."

"That must be why you never wash it," Shelly laughs.

"Huh?" Jason frowns, then his eyes light up. "Oh, right! Cause the water thing makes 'em mean! Good one, Red."

"I'm Shelly." She smiles and steps closer, and I decide it's a good thing Jason and I are only fake dating. Shelly is seriously abusing this new assertiveness-modeling thing.

"Yeah," I interrupt. "Shelly usually gives me a ride to school. She wanted to meet you."

"Making sure she gets home safe?" Jason smiles. "You're a good friend."

"I'm more than that." She blinks up at him.

"Okay!" I say, taking my friend's arm and pulling her back. "So this is Jason, and you're so excited because Trent asked you to the luau, remember?"

"Right," Shelly says still eyeing Jason as I steer her toward her car.

"He's going to pick me up in the morning, so I guess I'll let you know if I need a ride again, okay?"

"Damn, Harley!" She peeks back over our shoulders. "I guess I see why you weren't more upset about Trent."

For a moment, I'm confused, but I recover fast. "Oh, because Jason's hot. Right. Well, at least one of us got Trent."

It's a big fat lie. The last thing I want is Shelly dating Trent, even if it's only once. Or possibly twice. I completely agree with Jason on that point. When you like somebody, you never want them to be with anybody else. Not for any amount of time.

"I'd better go," I hear Jason start his freak-car's engine and walk over to get in the passenger's side. The door creaks when I open it and makes a popping noise when I pull it closed.

"Easy on the car," he says. "I just got her today."

"Where did you get this heap?" I ask, wrinkling my nose. "It smells like a wet cigarette."

"Carl." He leans over the seat to lower the back windows.

"The maintenance guy?" I can't believe it. Jason befriends everybody! "You bought this from the maintenance guy at school?"

"Sure! It's a classic." He drops back in his seat and cranks his window down. "You won't believe how great she'll look with a new coat of paint and some minor adjustments."

"It'll take more than that." I lean forward and grab the handle on my own window. "Are you sure we'll even make it to my house?"

"Have a little faith," he grins at me. "There's a six-cylinder engine under that hood."

"You lost me."

"Back in the 70s, when it came out, the big selling point was the Gremlin's got a six-cylinder engine. The Pinto's only got four." I watch as he turns the key and then leans forward, listening.

"Are you going to pick me up in a Pinto next?"

"No way." He taps the dash. "You're not listening. This has six cylinders compared to the Pinto's four!"

"Jason, I hate to tell you. Nobody cares." I lean forward trying to find a place for my bag. This car is ridiculous.

"I care. It's got more power, it's faster, heavier-"

"You're planning to ram somebody new?"

"That was purely accidental. Totaled my old Charger, though. I hated letting that one go. But it was time, I guess."

I look out the window and wonder who all's going to see me in this hooptie. Then I remember what I've been waiting to ask him all day.

"So how is it you twisted hitting me with your car into saving my life?"

"Huh?" he looks confused.

"All day long you've been going on about saving my life." I'm holding my hair back against the wind. "How'd you manage that rewrite of history?"

"Oh, well, I really did save it."

"Uh huh. Explain."

"I was probably going like 45 miles per hour when I looked up and realized you weren't moving. If I hadn't hit the brakes as hard as I could, I'dve probably knocked you into oncoming traffic."

"That's comforting." Now I wish my seatbelt had a shoulder strap.

"Yeah, it could've been bad."

I can tell he's embarrassed, and I look out the open window trying to think of a way to ease the sudden awkwardness in the car.

"It would've been Bender in the traffic, not me."

"Yeah, who is that guy? Ex-Marine?"

"How'd you guess?"

"I could tell by the hair and the super-starched clothes," he says. "We have a lot of those where I'm from."

We're almost at my house when I realize Mom might see me getting out of this strange car and with some strange guy.

"Maybe we should stop here," I say, reaching for my bag.

"Why?"

"Well, talking to Shelly today, I realized I hadn't thought through why we were dating all of a sudden."

"After all your efforts with Trent?" He grins at me, and I glance up at his smile, the wind pushing his golden brown hair in his face. Maybe I should go with Shelly's assumption and let everyone think I decided Jason was cuter. Everyone who doesn't know me, that is. No, my mind never changes that fast.

"And my parents don't know you, so I'm sure they'll ask a bunch of questions." I pull my bag onto my lap. "I don't like lying to them."

"What about Friday?"

"Friday?"

"The luau? I'm your date."

"Oh, right. I guess you're right. Nevermind, then."

He keeps driving and stops in front of my house.

"Thanks for the ride," I say, hesitating before I climb out. "Hey, I was just wondering. Why did you move here anyway?"

He pauses for a moment. "Well, Dad's from Glennville..." Then he glances down and his voice grows quieter. "After Mom died, he wanted to get closer to home."

For a moment I don't know what to say. That is not that answer I expected. "I'm... sorry."

He smiles back at me, but this time there's less sunshine. "S'okay," he shrugs. "She had cancer, so we had a lot of time to prepare for it. Say our good-byes and all."

"Still... I guess..." As I struggle for the right words, I imagine losing Pocahontas and my chest gets tight. "That must've been hard."

"Yeah. It's been fifteen months, but Dad and I are bouncing back." Jason tries another smile, but I'm still not convinced.

I pull the handle to get out. The door creaks and makes that popping sound again. There's no way I'm hiding this one.

"Tomorrow morning, then?" he asks.

"Sure." I smile back, feeling a little softer toward him. He really is easy to talk to.

"Bye, Jas."

"Bye, H.D."

I'm still thinking about what Jason told me when I open the front door and step inside. But when I look up, a scream flies out of my mouth. Mr. *Men's Health* is standing in the middle of our kitchen wearing nothing but a towel!

"Umm..." Ricky kind of laughs, then he says loudly, "Hey, Harley!"

Mom comes breezing into the room reading the label on a small pot of cream. "Here, see if this'll..." She freezes when she sees me. I haven't moved from my spot inside the door. My eyes are huge and my mouth is still open.

"You're home," she's smiling, but her voice is too high. "How was school?"

Then she glances at half-naked Ricky and does a little laugh.

"Why is he naked?" I whisper-shriek.

"No, honey, see," Mom's hand goes to her forehead and she rubs. I watch her long dark ponytail swing behind her. "Ricky had this mole on his glute he needed me to look at it, and it *did* look suspicious. So I offered to check the rest of his back. Just a quick visual screening—"

"You're not a dermatologist!" My voice is a high-pitched squeal, and my horrified eyes go back to Ricky on full display except for that little white towel. The light from our kitchen window highlights every line on his sculpted body.

"Well, no, but I know a suspicious mole when I see one," Mom says. "Skin cancer is very serious,

Harley, and those tanning beds accelerate the growth—"

Ricky interrupts in an amused tone. "I'm not *naked*."

I see his hand loosen on the towel, and I shriek again. "I don't want to see!"

Just then the door behind me opens. "Knock, knock!" a female voice sings out.

All three of us jump around to see a middle-aged woman in tight black pants and a low-cut top walking in carrying a slim plastic bottle. It's Trent's mom. I recognize her at once, even though I've only seen her at church.

"I got your message, and I figured I'd just come on by and... Oh, my!" Ms. Jackson looks up and stops. Her mouth drops open at the sight of Ricky in the kitchen. I literally can*not* breathe. Mom steps forward and takes her arm.

"Sandra! I'm so glad you came by," Mom says, trying to pull her into the living room. Ms. Jackson doesn't budge.

"You are?" she sounds surprised. Her eyes are glued to Ricky's bod.

"Ricky was just changing," Mom continues as if it's the most natural thing in the world for him to be standing around our house half naked. Like we live in the Playgirl mansion or something. "He'll be taking over your appointments for me... for now."

"He will?" Ms. Jackson looks like she might faint, and then a gleam enters her eyes. I grab my backpack and head to my room as Ricky slips into Mom's office and closes the door.

I don't even want to know what Trent's mom is thinking right now. Or who she's planning to tell the second she gets home.

After about an hour, when it's finally quiet again out front, I slip into the kitchen. I'm starving, and I'm hoping they're all gone. Mom's nowhere to be seen, but as usual, there's Ricky. At least now he's fully clothed and packing his gym bag to leave. I have no desire to speak to him. I can't believe Mom fell for such a lame stunt. Skin cancer on his glute. How obvious.

He looks up when I walk in the room. "I saw when you got home from school," he says with a smile. "Who was that in the monster mobile?"

I bite my lip, determined to ignore him, but he just keeps on talking.

"He drives a Gremlin?" Ricky shakes his head. "Throw that one back."

"He's not so bad."

"Was that Trent what's his face? Somehow I expected him to drive something... a little newer."

"No, that was Jason James. He asked me to the luau." I reach up and start pulling the French braid out of my hair. It's giving me a headache, and my neck is still stiff.

"Look at that." He walks over and starts combing the knots out of my hair again with his fingers. "Corn silk."

"Stop," I say, pulling away and going around the bar.

He goes back to packing, and I watch him place a few of Mom's all-natural bath products in his bag along with that little pot she was carrying when I walked in. "So what happened to Trent?" he says. "I thought all this was to land him."

"How'd you know about that?" I pull a bag of seaweed chips out of the cabinet and scan the label. I don't know why Mom can't just buy Doritos.

"Eavesdropping," Ricky glances up with a smile.

"Mom would not approve," I say. "She might even deduct points."

"Which is why we won't tell her."

"Where is she?" I look around. I'm hoping she'll apologize for embarrassing the crap out of me and for being so gullible. But secretly, after Jason's story, I really just want to give her a hug or something.

"In there with Dr. Hamilton," he says. "Lower back issues."

I've gotten used to the real doctors coming to my mom for massage and herbal remedies. They're all good friends, and she has a way of smoothing over any differences of opinion between the two approaches to treatment. I chalk it up to her honey voice.

"So why are you going to the luau with J.J.?" Ricky asks, like it's his business. "What happened to Trent?"

I tear open the bag and look at the papery green chips, frowning. "Trent asked Shelly."

"The silly redhead?" Ricky looks appalled. "He must need a little sexual healing."

"He does not." Now I'm officially ill.

"I don't know," he continues. "That girl is easy with a capital Z."

"How would you know?"

"Are you kidding? She was all up in my business last time she was over here. I know a party girl when I can't get away from one."

"Well, she's not easy. She just had a shock last summer, and she's sort of... going through a phase or something."

"Mm hm." His eyes narrow. "I hope her phase uses protection."

"Would you shut up?" I slam the cabinet. "They're not doing anything." *They'd better not do anything.*

"Okay, okay," he laughs as I head for my room. "Come on, Harley," he calls after me.

I go to my bedroom and slam the door. I'm sure Mom's going to say something later about the noise level when she has a client in the house, but I don't care. I flop on my bed. Everything is screwed up, and now I have to go through with this stupid fake-dating plan. I kick a pillow. I wish Dad would walk in on Ricky some time instead of stupid Trent's mom, who's probably telling everyone in Shadow Falls right now. I wish Mom would think about how things look and get a new student. I wish I was going to the luau with Trent. I close my eyes and see his model-perfect face. Those lavender eyes... I try to imagine kissing him, but all I can see is Shelly beating me to it.

Four

I spend the week tense, riding to and from school with Jason in his crap-mobile, and waiting for the news to break about my mom and her silly, half-naked student. But it never happens. Friday arrives, and the rumor-mill remains strangely silent.

Jason isn't such a bad fake boyfriend. I mean, we have good conversations, and he dresses well when he wants. Most of the cheer squad has their eyes on him, and I've even caught Trent checking us out in the parking lot a few times. I always smile and wave at him, and he usually gives me sad little smile back. I know it's because we were so close to being together, and then I imagine us holding hands, me smiling up at him, maybe he kisses my nose, slides his arm around my waist... A little shimmer moves through my middle, and my chest rises.

"...at seven?" Jason asks.

"Huh?" Lost in my daydream, I hadn't even realized Jason'd been talking to me.

"Seven o'clock? I'm picking you up tonight?"

"Oh, right. Better make it six-thirty. My parents'll want to meet you."

"Your mom's been talking to my dad all week, so she'll have an idea who I am," he argues.

"What?" I'm totally confused. "Why has my mom been talking to your dad?"

"The accident? She called my dad, and they've been working out payment for the repairs and stuff. Dad doesn't want to go through our insurance."

"I guess that's why you drive these old heaps," I say, patting the door.

"You know, you fix up a classic, and it can be worth twice what it originally sold for."

"So four dollars instead of two?" I smile.

"More like four thousand," he says.

"Ooo," I pretend to be impressed. "Yeah, so six-thirty, and remember it's a luau."

"What does that mean? For guys, I mean."

"Grass skirt, nothing else, of course."

Jason laughs. "Didn't know you'd go there, H.D."

"I don't make the rules." I shrug.

"OK, so grass skirt for the guys. What does that mean for the girls?"

"Oh, lots of things," I sniff, pushing my hair back. "Wrap skirts, blouses, halter tops, leis..."

"That doesn't seem fair." He grins like always as he watches me, and I have to confess, I kind of like it.

"Again, you'll have to take it up with the Hawaiians," I say, turning off to class.

Mom braids my hair for the luau, this time with two braids on each side just at the top, and I fluff out the rest, very *Vogue*. She's finishing up when I hear the doorbell and see Dad walking over to greet my... I guess this is a real date. But the only one. Dad opens

---

the door, and I yelp. Jason's standing there in what looks like only a grass skirt. Another half-dressed male!

"Uh..." Dad seems confused. "You must be..."

"Jason, sir," he grins, walking into the room. I'm afraid to look, but at the same time, I can't turn away. Jason's standing there shirtless in a long grass skirt with a lei around his head. He actually looks kind of hot.

"That's some get-up," Dad says. "Anything under there?"

"Yes sir," Jason moves the grass to reveal khaki shorts. I didn't see them in the darkness of the porch. "I have this, too."

He pulls out a Hawaiian shirt and slips it over his bare chest. I feel myself start to breathe again. It's not such a bad-looking chest he's covering up, actually. Strictly as an observation, of course.

"That was for H... Harley," he finishes, his eyes twinkling at me.

"What does that mean?" Mom's eyes are not twinkling. She's not smiling either as she approaches my fake boyfriend.

"Oh... Mrs. Andrews?" Jason looks startled, but he recovers quickly and sticks out his hand. "Jason James."

"Jason," Mom shakes his hand, then unceremoniously drops it. "Now why would you show up half-dressed for Harley?"

"Umm..." Jason looks confused, so I jump in between them.

"It's my fault, Mom. I told Jason the guys had to dress like that. I thought he knew I was kidding."

"I figured you were," he says. "It was a joke."

Mom doesn't relax, and I decide against pointing out the whole double-standard going on here. I'd been understanding about her ridiculous skin-cancer on the butt thing.

"Well, you're not to be out late," she says.

Dad puts his hand on her shoulder. "It's good to have a sense of humor," he says.

But Mom's still in hyper-protective mode. "Drive carefully."

"It's okay, Mom," I say. "Jason's been very ten and two, eyes on the road all week."

"Let's keep it that way," she says.

"Home by eleven, kids." Dad smiles and slides his arm around my mom.

"Yes, sir," Jason says.

I follow him out to his stupid Gremlin.

"What next, Jason? Jeez." I fluff my hair again. It's already getting flat. "Did you really *not* want to go to the luau after all?"

"Damn, Harley, your mom's a total babe!" he finally says. "You could've warned me."

"What?" He is so unexpected.

"And your dad had on a priest collar." He stops and opens my door. "What's that all about?"

"He's the pastor at First Prez," I say, getting in the Gremlin. "You didn't know that?"

"Nuh uh." Jason closes my door and jogs around. "I didn't know what to say when your mom walked over. I was thinking she looked just like…"

"Pocahontas?"

"No… I mean, Yeah! That's better," he says. "I was thinking of someone else. But Pocahontas is way better."

I really don't feel like talking about this. "Well, get over it. There's a line."

"What?"

"A line of guys waiting for her. Take a number."

"For your mom?" Jason glances at me. "I'm happy dating you, H.D."

"Good 'cause it gets old." I look out the window and don't even bother correcting him.

Jason's quiet for a beat. "But they say you should check out the parents of people you date."

"Fake date," I look back. "And who says?"

"The dating experts. That's what you're going to look like when you're old."

"Mom's not old. And it's not like we'll still know each other then anyway."

"We might. And it's good to be prepared."

"Don't get too prepared. This is only for two weeks."

He smiles at me. I frown back.

At the luau, Jason and I circle the gym talking to friends and carrying plastic cups with little umbrellas in them. I notice Trent and Shelly arrive and wave at them. Shelly's gone all out with leis around her wrists and ankles and a grass skirt. Trent's wearing jeans and a t-shirt, and he looks so great. I imagine it being me there holding his hand, whispering something funny in his ear and making him laugh. I picture him kissing my cheek, maybe that spot right beside my ear, and for a moment I melt.

"You okay?" Jason's watching me, and I almost blush.

"Of course. I was just thinking about... something."

He doesn't pursue it.

The luau's a sophomore-sponsored dance, so last year our class did all the planning and decorations. Reagan Smith and her little party-planning crew are all discussing whose version's better — ours or theirs. Reagan notes that last year, when she was in charge, we had a cochin de lait. I mentally note at least this year we have a limbo pole. She intentionally left that off last year's luau agenda.

Jason pulls me to the dance floor when a slow song starts. "Girls worry about the dumbest stuff," he breathes as we sway back and forth.

"Reagan's just afraid someone'll think this party's better than hers was," I say, resting my hands on his shoulders. "And she's working on prom now, so she's nuts."

"Prom." He exhales and makes a face.

I shake my head. "Don't worry. Our prom's pretty low-pressure, and finding a date's not hard. I mean, there's always somebody in need. Reagan just makes everything a bigger deal than it is."

I glance over Jason's shoulder at Trent, and imagine us at prom. Him in a tux, me holding his arm, wearing that white goddess dress…

"You all seem close," he says, catching my eye again.

I smile. "Well, except for you and Trent and a few other people, we've all gone to school together since kindergarten."

"That must be weird."

I look around the room at all the familiar faces. I wave at Shelly who's watching us dance, and I try to imagine being in a room with total strangers.

"I don't know. It can be nice. You know. Knowing everybody and what to expect."

We sway for a few seconds in silence. I notice Jason's hands resting gently on my waist and glance up again at his dark brown eyes. They're sort of deep like he's thinking about something.

"So, preacher's kid," he says. "You all wild and shit?"

"No," I frown. "And Dad's cool, but he would not like all the cussing."

"So you're not all wild and *stuff*?"

"That's a total stereotype. And stereotypes are how stupid people make sense of the world."

He laughs a little. "That something your dad says?"

"My mom."

"Yeah, about your mom…" I can feel Jason's fingers playing with the ends of my hair. The tiny pulls gave me little chills, so I slide it away.

"What's she like?" he says.

"I thought you weren't interested."

"I'm not, but… it seems like you were mad about her before. Or something."

I look at him for a second and then shake my head. "I shouldn't have said that before. Mom's great."

"So there's not a line of guys waiting for her?"

"No," I confess. "Just one."

"One meaning your dad?"

"One meaning her student Ricky."

Jason frowns. "Who's Ricky?"

I fiddle with the side of his collar, not meeting his eyes. "Her massage therapy student. He's always at our house."

"Your mom teaches massage therapy?"

I nod. "She coaches a senior from the college in Glennville every year. And she teaches yoga and prescribes herbal remedies. Stuff like that."

"We had a lot of that in New Mexico."

"I'm sure." I glance up at Jason's hair. It really is a pretty color, and for a moment, I imagine sliding my fingers through it. Just to see how it feels, of course.

"So you think this Ricky guy's after your mom?"

"Yes." I answer without hesitation. Then I pause. I've never told anyone how I feel about Ricky and my mom. I can't believe I'm telling my fake boyfriend.

"That's weird. What does your dad think?"

70

"Nothing," I shake my head. "I mean, nothing's going on. Ricky's just her student."

We're quiet a second.

"It just gets old sometimes," I say softly.

"I bet. It's like he's threatening your family or something."

"But he's not. Mom would never do anything like that."

Jason studies my face and our eyes meet. I didn't expect him to understand how I felt, or that it might matter to me. But I realize the song's over, and I lead us off the dance floor.

"She wouldn't," I say again. But for a moment all I can think of is Shelly's seemingly perfect parents, and how shocked we all were when it came out her dad had been sleeping with his secretary for three years. How it devastated her mom, turning her into a self-help addict. I notice Jason's still holding my hand. Our fingers are laced, and it feels really comforting. Just then Shelly runs up and pulls me away.

"Come with me," she orders.

She drags me to the bathroom, and as we go in, I notice Trent walking up to Jason. I wonder what they'll say to each other. I'm sure Jason'll help me with my plan, but for a split-second, I'm not sure how I feel about that.

"First, assertiveness training—pass! I am *so* becoming a life coach."

"What?" I'm confused.

"All that between you and super hottie." She looks at me, smiling. "Nice work."

"Oh." I cross my arms and lean against the sink. "That wasn't anything. I mean, he's my date, but that's all."

"You are so lying." She looks in the mirror and starts pinching her cheeks. "You two were totally into each other on the dance floor just now."

"We were not," I say, feeling embarrassed. "We were just talking."

"About what? It looked way intense."

"My mom?"

"Oh, shit! That's the other thing!" Her eyes are shining. "What's all this about your mom and half-naked Ricky? I heard Mom talking to Ms. Jackson after their divorce survivors support group. Sounds like somebody got an eye-full."

"Oh my god! Did she also mention I was there? And that Ricky wasn't naked? He had this mole on his butt, and he thought it was skin cancer." I cringe internally at how stupid that sounds.

Shelly giggles and smoothes my arm. "Calm down. You know Mom wouldn't believe anything bad about your mom. Even if he is crazy-hot. Did you get to see his thing? Is it… you know." Her eyebrows go up, and I think I might barf.

"I don't know! And I couldn't know because he wasn't naked. He had on a towel."

She does a little shiver and turns to the mirror again. "You are so lucky. It's *so* unfair."

"Nothing happened," I say. "Some women are just stupid."

She slants her eyes at me and then pulls out her lip gloss. "Well, Trent's about as fun as a pet rock."

My eyes fly to hers. "What happened?"

"Not a thing," she sighs. "I've been working so hard to get him to talk about anything, I'm absolutely exhausted."

"Define anything." I study her face. "Kool-aid stripes verses feather extensions? Is fringe too Boho? Is Boho even still in?"

"Hardly. I could talk to *myself* about those things and be happy." I watch her flick her bangs to the side. "Nope, I've tried sports, Shadow Falls, college... you name it."

"And what did he say?" I'm dying to know.

"That's just it! Nothing. He's all yep, nope and silence."

"But he's so sweet, and those eyes..." I look back at the mirror and think of the hydrangea blooms I saw earlier. "You're probably just overwhelming him."

"Thanks."

"I'm just saying. You've got a big personality. He might not—"

"Be able to get a word in?"

I bite my lip and try to cover. "That's not what I was going to say!"

"Yes, it was."

"I was going to say he might not know what to say." The truth is Shelly's right. I was going to say *get a word in*. But Trent is so perfect, he would never be rude to Shelly.

73

"Well, if you've moved on to Jason, maybe I'll try for an extra-hot make-out session," she says, glancing at me and gauging my response. "Anything to save this lame date."

I smile at her and try to hide my alarm. Now she's excited again. "Maybe he'll try something. I wonder if he has a move."

"What?"

"Maybe he's hiding a freaky side. He seems awfully tame, but I've been surprised before."

"Let's get back to the dance." I cannot think of Shelly getting freaky with Trent.

"OK," she says, and we both spot Jason at the same time. "But if you toss that one back, he's mine." Again she's watching my response.

"Sure," I say, with a small laugh. In two weeks, she can have Jason. But I can't let her know we're planning it.

Driving home, Jason's already organizing our next fake-out.

"I'm thinking we should hit the movies tomorrow night," he says. "What do you want to see?"

"I don't care," I say, staring out the window. Try as I might, I can't help but wonder if Shelly's out there making moves with my hottie-future-husband.

"Then *Roving Zombies Take Manhattan* it is," Jason announces.

"What?"

"Seriously, H.D. You gotta work with me here."

"Oh sure, I'll check online tomorrow and pick something." We're at my house, and I grab my sweater to go inside. "Thanks, Jason," I say, reaching for the door handle.

"Hang on…" He catches my arm and pulls me back. I freeze thinking he might try to kiss me. Fake kissing is not in the plan.

"What?"

"Don't look so worried," he grins. "I'm not going to kiss you."

"I didn't think that…" I lie.

"I was just going to say I had fun tonight."

"Oh, sure." I start to relax. "Me too."

"I mean, I don't really count tonight as a fake date. I meant it before when I asked you to the luau. For real." His voice is gentle.

"Right. Well, I'll see you tomorrow then?" I move to get out of the car before he changes his mind and *does* try to kiss me.

"Tomorrow," he says, releasing my arm. "The games begin."

Five

I text Shelly while I look at movie listings. I don't really want to know what happened last night between her and Trent, but I'm hoping she might give me a hint. She doesn't, but she does say Trent asked her to go to the movies tonight. Seems when we were in the bathroom, Jason talked to him about the four of us meeting up. I have to give him credit. It's a great way to make a fake date count. I just can't figure out why he didn't tell me last night.

Mom's standing in the kitchen when I walk in to wait for Jason. Dad's at the church preparing for services, and we're home alone, just me and her. I debate for a second whether to bring up the new gossip around town, but I know what her response will be. Another lecture on small minds and big imaginations. I just don't get how she can't see that she's fueling it.

"How was the luau?" Mom asks, glancing up from her book.

"Fun. Hawaiian. You know, same as last year." I sit down and look at the book's cover—something about magnets and menopause.

"So crash-boy's who you had me braiding your hair for all these weeks? I was expecting someone different."

"Oh, it was someone different. Jason just beat him to me."

"Beat him to you?"

"Well, Jason showed up at the same time and asked me out right in front of him."

"Oh," Mom makes a sympathetic face. "And the one you like…"

"Yep. Backed down."

"Well, I was wondering. You didn't seem too impressed with Jason after the accident. And I thought the other guy's name was Travis or Trey…"

"Trent. And yeah, Jason was sort of annoying at first, but he's okay once you get to know him, I guess."

"So you're going with him to the movies tonight? That sounds better than okay."

She sips her tea, and now I'm wondering what she'd say about my scheme to get Trent. Another lecture about using a stereotypically feminine trap to land a guy, I'm sure. She's just so perfect and beautiful. She could never understand what led me to take such drastic steps.

"Well, have a good time," she says. "Jason does seem like a nice young man."

I shrug. "What are you doing tonight?"

"Reading," she says, picking up the book again. "Magnets and menopause."

I poke out the tip of my tongue. "Ew."

"It's all part of life, Harley. I'm just not sure I'm buying this book."

"Where'd you get it?"

"Ricky loaned it to me. He's trying to get more into homeopathic remedies."

—

"He'd do *anything* to impress you."

"He's trying. Ricky's got a kind heart, if a little misguided."

"Misguided in that he's in love with a married woman?"

She narrows her eyes. "Misguided in that there's no way magnets ease the symptoms of menopause."

The doorbell rings, and I jump up.

"Church tomorrow," Mom calls after me.

"I know. 'Night, Mom!"

I open the door and there he is. He looks really nice actually, in brown cords and a dark blue shirt. Like this guy I remembered seeing in Shelly's *Cosmopolitan*.

"You look pretty," he says.

"Oh." I look down at my dress, wondering why my cheeks feel suddenly warm. "I talked to Shelly and she said Trent would be there."

"Right." His smile fades just a bit. "I meant to tell you I talked to him at the luau about meeting up tonight."

"And you acted like I could pick whatever movie I wanted to see," I pretend to scold as we walk to his car. "Of course, we'll see whatever they're seeing!"

"He didn't commit," Jason says, opening the door for me.

As we drive to the theater, I notice soft music is playing. He's quiet, and everything suddenly feels very intimate. Not at all like a casual friends-going-to-the-movies night. It almost feels like this is turning into another real date.

"Hey, I was thinking," I say, breaking the mood. "I really should pay for my ticket."

"What?"

"I mean, it's just a fake date after all. You shouldn't have to spend money on me."

"I don't mind buying your ticket." He seems annoyed by my suggestion.

"But it's kind of a lot. And I don't want any popcorn or anything."

"Look, H.D., just because we're faking doesn't mean I won't buy your ticket."

"I know. I just... I'd feel better about it if I paid for myself."

Jason looks at me a second. Then he shakes his head. His expression is a mystery to me as I hold out my ten, almost like he's about to tell me something, but at the last minute changes his mind.

"Just put it in the ashtray," he says.

I open the small compartment and stuff it on top of quarters and what looks like a rock.

When we get to the theater, he buys our tickets and leads me inside. I see Shelly and Trent waiting at the snack counter. Trent has on jeans and a plaid shirt with a blazer that I'm sure I've seen on one of those headless mannequins in the mall. Then he smiles, and I feel all squishy inside. Trent's teeth were so white, and they have the slightest tilt inward at the bottom. I imagine kissing him, and my eyes almost close.

"Hi, guys," Jason's voice snaps me back to attention.

"Hey," Shelly says, obviously checking out my date.

"Should we go on and get seats?" I say.

"We just ordered popcorn." Shelly seems even less enthusiastic about being with Trent tonight, and I figure the make-out session was a bust. *Oh, well!*

"Why don't you and Trent go," Jason says. "I'll help Shelly and get us something."

"Oh, you don't have to..." I start to say, but Shelly comes to life.

"That's a great idea!"

I do a double-take at her, but Trent steps over and lightly touches my arm. My pulse jumps through the roof, and I completely forget about stopping Jason or pretending to be miffed at Shelly's obvious interest in my date. My fake date.

"Our theater's Number 5," he says and smiles. I remember to smile back.

"Okay," I say, turning to follow him.

As we walk toward the big red five in the distance I hear Shelly talking to Jason.

"Your hair is the most amazing color," she says. "It's like dark chocolate with milk chocolate highlights."

I roll my eyes and almost laugh. Shelly does not miss a chance.

"What?" Trent's watching me.

"Oh!" I jump. I can't be amused by Shelly's tactics. Jason's supposed to be my *real* date, and it wouldn't make sense if I found her behavior funny instead of annoying. "I just thought of this funny story. Something Jason told me earlier."

"So you two are dating now?"

"I guess. I mean, we're just getting to know each other, so I don't know."

Trent nods, then he touches my arm again. *Zing!*

"This is us," he says, reaching to hold the door for me. I sigh inwardly. He's such a gentleman.

We go inside and pick out four empty seats next to each other. Then he and I sit beside each other in the middle two. Several minutes pass, and I try to think of something to say. All I keep getting are thoughts of Shelly making out with him and milk chocolate highlights.

"Did you have fun at the luau?" he finally asks me.

"Yeah," I say. "Did you?"

"Oh, sure."

Silence again. I looked around trying to find a subject for conversation. I don't know what Trent likes to talk about. Shelly covered everything that doesn't work last night in the bathroom, and we've never had a class together. We don't have lunch together, we didn't have lunch together last year, not that it would've mattered since I was hideous last year. We've never had the chance to really talk, come to think of it. Just then Shelly walks in with Jason. She's holding his arm and laughing like he just said the funniest thing on the planet. Jason looks up and his eyebrows rise slightly. My shoulders rise a hair in response. It's like we're using a secret code, only at this point I have nothing to report.

Jason slides into the seat next to me, and Shelly reluctantly moves across in front of us to Trent's other side. I wouldn't have put it past her to sit beside my date if the spot weren't already taken.

I feel Jason nudge my arm and look down. He's holding his hand in a position that indicates he wants me to take it. Suddenly I'm not so sure about my plan. Almost-talking to Trent just now, he seemed interested and maybe... just possibly disappointed that Jason and I are dating. What if he feels the same thing I do, that Jason does? That when you really like someone, you don't want them dating anyone else for any length of time. But I can't be sure.

Then Jason reaches up and laces our fingers. I let him pull our clasped hands forward so it's clear to everyone that we're holding hands. I see Trent glance our way, and my heart sinks. Maybe this is all a mistake.

The lights dim and the movie starts, but I can't concentrate on a thing happening onscreen I'm so worried. And when it's finally over, Jason releases me. I feel myself breathe again. Trent hasn't touched Shelly, and I'm willing to bet this'll be their last outing together. She doesn't seem to mind.

As we walk back to the lobby, I listen to everyone chatting about the film. I glance at Trent's lavender-blue eyes, and he smiles back at me. He looks sad again, and I'm about to say something, anything, when Jason takes my arm.

"See you guys Monday," he says and pulls me toward the Gremlin.

Trent turns and follows Shelly in the opposite direction.

Back in the G-ride, Jason sounds happy. "That went really well, I think," he says.

"I guess." I'm looking out the window, lost in thought.

"Well, I think this was a great first date… first fake date… whatever."

"I've been thinking. What if I was wrong?"

"About what?"

"Remember how you said that about not wanting someone you like to date anyone else ever."

"Yeah?" His eyes flick briefly to mine, then back to the windshield.

"What if Trent feels the same way?"

"I don't get you." Jason's voice sounds like he really does get me, but he's stalling.

I turn in my seat to face him. "What if all this fake dating is a bad idea and it ends up pushing Trent to date some other girl?"

"You mean like Shelly?"

"Well, no. Shelly would obviously rather date you."

He laughs at that. "She's a trip."

"Mm-hm," I agree, but I'm still thinking about Trent's sad little smile.

"So how'd a tame preacher's kid get to be best friends with her?"

"What do you mean?"

—

84

"I mean she knows her way around the field. I think she grabbed my ass on the way into the theater."

"I'm sure she did," I sigh. "We've been friends since kindergarten. And she wasn't always like that."

"Interesting. I'm really impressed with your tolerance for her stunts. I guess that's part of those Fruits of the Spirit. Patience?"

He grins at me, and I squint back. "So you *have* been in a church before."

"I don't mind going to church. It's just been… different lately. And we're new here."

"Well, Shelly doesn't mean to be a jerk. She really is a good friend. She's just… her parents got divorced last summer and it tends to cloud her judgment sometimes."

"No shit," he says.

"And seriously with the language. I'm not getting grounded over some fake boyfriend's mouth."

"Okay, okay," he laughs.

We're almost at my house, and when we reach the stop sign on the corner, I notice a car parked just ahead. It's a familiar car—it's Ricky's! *Why is he at my house?*

I grab the door handle and jump out of the Gremlin while it's still stopped.

"Harley!" I hear Jason yell. "What are you doing? I'll drive you home."

"That's okay," I say, slamming the squeaky, poppy door. "I'll talk to you tomorrow."

I run the half-block to my house and then dash up the walk. I notice Dad's Prius is still gone as I fly through the door, and I have no idea what to expect inside. But whatever it is, I'm about to bust it up. I'm surprised when I find the living room and kitchen dark and empty. Voices are coming from Mom's office, and I jog on tip-toes over to it, leaning my head toward the door.

"You just have to be patient." Mom's saying. "Things have a way of working themselves out."

"You say that, but it's hard to believe." Ricky's voice is quiet. He sounds like he's crying.

"I know," Mom says. I hear bodies moving, and I imagine them embracing. *This is not happening! Where's Dad?*

It's quiet a few seconds longer, then Ricky speaks.

"Thanks for letting me come over," he says. Sounds of movement again. "I felt like I had to talk in person."

"Don't worry about it," Mom says. "But you do need to go now. It's late and Harley could be home any minute. She might not understand."

"How is it possible I got sent to this tiny town and found you?" His voice is warm.

"Predestined?" Mom's voice has a smile in it, and I feel sick.

"More like my angel…"

The office door starts to open, and I jump and scurry back, trying to make it look like I just closed the front door. But not before I see my mom shake her head and smile back at him.

"Harley! You're home," she says. She sounds surprised, and I feel my eyes grow hot. "Ricky just stopped by to… discuss something."

I nod, but my heart is racing, and I can't meet her eyes. His angel? What wouldn't I understand? What were they doing in there while I was gone? While Mom was supposed to be home. Alone. Reading about magnets and menopause. Menopause! She could be his grandmother.

"Hey, biker chick," Ricky says.

"Only my dad calls me that." I won't look at either of them.

"I was just teasing." Ricky says, and I glance up. His cheeks appear damp in the dim light, and as usual he's wearing a tight polo. It stretches over his chest as he reaches to touch my mother's arm.

"I'd better go," he says.

"I'll walk you out," she replies.

I don't move as I watch them leave. In my mind I put together the timeline. Jason picked me up a little before seven, and the movie was two hours long. Did Ricky know I'd be gone? Was it just a coincidence? How long could he have been here? Maybe I got home just in time. Finally Mom returns.

"How was the movie, honey?" Her voice sounds tired and she lifts her hand to rub her forehead.

"Fine," I say, watching at her.

"That's good." Then she waves to the door. "Ricky just had… this thing. It was nothing really."

"Nothing?"

"Yeah, just something he's dealing with... but nothing for you to worry about."

I bite my lip and decide against asking if it was another suspicious mole. Instead, I internally freak out. What I saw was way too intimate to be nothing. My stomach feels both sick and crampy, and I wish she'd tell me more.

She just smiles and walks over to me. "I don't know about you, but I'm dead. I'm gonna hit the feathers."

She pecks my cheek, and I can't help checking for any sign something might've happened. Her shirt tags are all in their proper places, her hair isn't messy or swept into a high, damp ponytail. She isn't singing anything off-key...

"Where's Dad?" I ask.

"Hm?" Mom looks up and then glances at the clock. "Oh, wow. It's after ten. He probably just got tied up at church or something. Don't worry. He'll be home soon."

"I wasn't worried," I say. At least not about Dad.

"See you in the morning."

I stand motionless as she walks down the hallway to her room and closes the door. My stomach is still churning as I go to my room and lay across my bed. Then I get up and go back across the hall to the bathroom to wash my face. When I come out, I still don't hear anything from her room, so I go back to mine and change clothes.

I get under my covers and pick up a book, but I can't read it. I lean back and close my eyes for a

—

second. After a few minutes, I look around. It's strange because I don't remember how I got here, but I'm swimming in the creek. It's dark, and I'm alone in the black waters. At least I thought I was alone. There's a voice on the shore, a male voice. It sounds like Jason, but it's too far away for me to tell. I start to swim toward it, but something grabs my legs and starts pulling me under. It's scratchy like tree roots, and I struggle and kick. But it keeps grabbing me and pulling me down. My heart's beating faster, and I can't breathe. I try to cry out, to move my arms, but it's too late. The dark water is pouring into my nose and down my throat. I'm drowning. I can't lift my arms as I start to black out...

I sit up fast. I'm in my bed, and it's light outside. Sunday morning.

Six

I can't shake the dream as I prepare for church.
Slipping into my dress and brushing my hair, I can
still feel the scratchy whatever it was pulling my legs,
still feel the water running down my throat, and I
shiver. Anxiety tightens my chest, and I worry it was
an omen or something. Our quiet house isn't helping
either. I want to turn on the television or blast the
radio to fill up the silence. Instead I wander into the
kitchen and find Mom pouring a cup of coffee.

"Coffee?" I raise my eyebrows. "What happened
to the green tea regimen?"

"Hm?" She frowns, distracted. Then she smiles.
"Oh, I needed a little kick this morning."

"What's wrong?" I ask.

"Oh, nothing. Just didn't get enough sleep last
night."

She walks into the living room and sits on the
couch, staring at the black face of the silent television.

"Maybe you should've gone to bed earlier," I say,
watching her for any sign of a reaction.

She takes a sip and shakes her head. "It would've
just been more time lying awake."

I can't believe she missed my meaning. "Worried
about something?" I ask. Then I hold my breath,
waiting to see if she'll tell me anything more about
last night. Why Ricky was here or what "thing" he's
dealing with.

She glances at me, and for a moment I think she might. But she only smiles and shakes her head again. "Just trouble sleeping," she says. "I probably should've taken some melatonin."

I frown, but she turns back to the dark television screen again. I decide to try another approach and go to sit beside her on the couch.

"Let's see what's on," I say, picking up the remote. "Maybe they're touring another little village on *Sunday Morning*. Like that time when I was sick?"

"Harley," Mom breathes, standing. "You know Daddy likes it quiet before church. He needs these last moments to pray and mentally prepare."

And with that she walks back to her room, leaving me on the couch frowning at her half-empty coffee cup. I've never thought of my mom as a great actress, but she'd win an Oscar for her performance today. She's behaving like last night was the most ordinary Saturday evening of all time, and Ricky hadn't been here crying and pleading with her when I got home. The pressure in my chest grows worse.

During every church service there's this part where we "Pass the Peace." Basically we all greet each other and shake hands right before Dad gets up to deliver his sermon. As I shake hands with the lady sitting behind me, I spot Trent. He's always in church with his mom, and he always looks amazing in a coat and tie. Our eyes meet and he smiles, and in spite of it all, my heart flutters. I give him a little wave and then catch Stephanie Miller watching us. I smile at her but she quickly flicks her eyes away. Then I see Trent's mom watching my mom with a sneaky smirk on her face, and all my peace vanishes. But I also notice Ms. Jackson doesn't seem to have a lot of friends at church. That explains why her story's been so slow going. I wonder if Trent knows what his mom saw at my house. I wonder if he believes it.

I look at Mom, and she's making a point to shake hands with Mrs. Perkins. Mrs. Perkins stiffly nods and then follows with her evil eyes as Mrs. Bender waddles over to embrace Mom. Mrs. B's been Mom's closest ally for years. Ever since my mom convinced her not to leave her husband.

We all sit, and I watch as Dad takes his position behind the pulpit and begins to speak. Dad's been the pastor here since I was a baby. Our church is part of the Presbyterian Churches of America, but I didn't even know that meant anything until a few years ago. Basically it means our church falls into the most conservative category of Presbyterians, which doesn't surprise me. In my house it's always been no cursing, drinking, wearing certain clothes, watching certain movies and TV shows. Even me being on the cheerleading squad is just borderline okay because of the short skirts and high kicks.

So a few years back it came out that Mr. Bender'd had an affair with this Cambodian woman when he was on duty in Vietnam. He confessed to my dad that he practically had this whole other family in the South Pacific and Mrs. Bender almost left him over it.

But my parents saved the day—with God's help, of course.

Dad reminded everyone that Bender was a war hero and said what had happened was one of those "in love and war" types of situations. He said what mattered now was saving their marriage, that it was a mistake, and forgiveness was a gift. Mrs. Bender wasn't as understanding or ready to forgive, but after counseling with my mom for several months, she decided to put it behind her. I couldn't believe it, but Mom said I didn't understand the concept of building a life with someone.

Maybe I'm still learning, but I believe having another woman pop up with your husband's two long-lost kids seriously wrecks any life-building efforts. It's the exact opposite of how things went with Shelly's parents. Of course, once all that came out, Shelly's dad had been more interested in ending their marriage than trying to keep it together. That's what hurt my friend so much. But to be fair, I don't believe a marriage can be saved after something like that happens, and it's hard for me to understand where Mrs. B's coming from acting like it doesn't matter to her. Mom says I should wait until I'm older to decide.

As Dad continues speaking, I look over at my mom. Her eyes are glued to him like she's hanging on his every word. I chew my lip and frown. It's so confusing how she can go from a private huddle with Mr. *Men's Health* one night to gazing at my father like he's the Second Coming today. But it helps ease my dream-inspired anxiety, and it seems to subdue the gossip. For now at least. Maybe there's a chance I'm wrong. I mean, what I heard last night had sounded pretty incriminating, but there isn't any proof that anything bad happened.

I tune in to Dad just in time to realize he's giving me my cue. Every Sunday, he likes me to sing the Doxology to close the service. I did it once when I was five because the lady who was supposed to sing it never showed up for church. I was too little to be self-conscious, and I'd always liked the song. I imagined all the creatures were like the little mice and birds in *Snow White*, and I was the princess urging them to praise God with me. I thought it was pretty cool, and everyone else seemed to agree. So it became our regular way to end the service.

Now that I'm older, I know singing in church is kind of special, but I've been doing it so long, it'd be even more exceptional if I stopped. So that's the order. Dad brings the message, and at the end, he backs away for me to sing the Doxology while Mrs. Turner plays the large pipe organ. Then we all make a bee-line for the back doors and Sunday dinner.

Dad says his final words, and I stand to approach the smaller podium on the right. It doesn't matter that I hadn't listened to the sermon, I could do this in my sleep. But when I look up, I freeze. Jason's sitting in the last row of the sanctuary. He's wearing a suit and tie, and he actually looks... really handsome. Our eyes meet, and I see his eyebrows go up as the sound of the pipes burst out from behind me. I jump and move to my usual spot.

Mrs. Turner blares the last eight chords of the song, which is my introduction, and for the first time, my breath catches at the thought of singing out loud in front of everyone. In front of him.

Right on cue, though, my mouth opens and the words come out. It's the longest 30 seconds of my life. I worry that I might hit a wrong note. I worry that my voice sounds funny. I feel my legs tremble, and I want to turn and dash out the back door.

Praise God from whom all blessings flow.
Praise him all creatures here below.
Praise him above ye heav'nly host.
Praise Father, Son, and Holy Ghost.
A-men.

Finally the song is over, and as usual everyone breaks for the doors. I wonder if any of them even noticed the mini-panic-attack I almost had. Or that I actually cared for once that someone in particular was listening. As the crowd starts to thin, Jason waits at the back of the room. I tell Mom I'll walk home and go to meet him.

"You have hidden talents," he smiles. "And a really nice voice."

Warmth fills my stomach, and I feel wobbly again. I'm having one of those low-blood-sugar moments like that day at lunch. I'm sure of it. I mean, it *is* lunchtime, and this *is* just Jason. Jeez. What's wrong with me all of a sudden?

"Everyone knows the Doxology," I say.

"Not everyone gets up and sings it in front of the whole town." He turns to walk with me.

"I guess they would if their dad was the pastor." I stop as he opens the back door. "What are you doing here, anyway?"

"Just curious. You jumped out of the car so fast last night I didn't get to tell you I was coming."

"Sorry about that."

"Why did you?"

"What?"

"Jump out of the car like that."

I look over at him. I want to tell him what I saw, about Ricky's car being at my house and what I overheard. I want to tell him my fears and have him reassure me. Just like at the dance. I'm sure he'll understand and maybe even make me feel better, maybe tell me I'm being paranoid. But I decide to wait.

"I just remembered something I had to do."

"At ten o'clock?"

"I forgot to tell Shelly something, and I wanted to catch her before it got too late."

His eyes narrow, and I know he doesn't believe me. But he lets it go. "So what now?" he asks.

"Huh?" My eyebrows pull together.

"Last night you were having second thoughts about us fake dating. Did you want to change the plans or are we still together?"

I look up and see Trent helping his mother into their car. I've never seen his dad, since his parents are divorced. He glances in our direction before closing the door and then hustles around to the driver's side. I think about Jason's question and wonder what would be happening right now if he weren't standing here beside me. Would Trent come over and talk to me? I like the idea of that, but at the same time, I feel sad at the thought of Jason being gone. He's so easy to talk to, and he really seems to care about the stuff that's bothering me. I've actually started to like having him around. And it's so strange. I've never worried about how I sounded singing the Doxology in front of Trent.

"What do you think?" I ask. I stop walking and look at Jason, hoping his response will give me some clue about what to do.

"I don't know, H.D. This has been your game from the start."

And there he is, all dressed up in a coat and tie, and waiting for me to send him away. From the corner of my eye, I notice Trent's car drive off down the street.

"I think maybe we should give it a few more days. I mean, things have been going pretty well, and maybe you could talk to Trent and see how he feels."

"Like ask him if he likes you?"

"Maybe," I think about it. "I mean, yes! That would be perfect."

"But if we're going out, I don't think he'll tell me that he likes you. I mean, you're my girl. At least that's what he thinks."

I never thought hearing those words from someone besides Trent would make me happy, but when Jason says "my girl," a tingly little pulse moves through my chest. It makes me want to smile, but instead I frown and shake my head. What's wrong with me? This is all fake. I'm falling for my own scheme.

"You're right," I say. "Let me think about it, and I'll make a decision tonight."

"So if for now, I'm still your boyfriend. You should invite me over for Sunday dinner."

"Oh, really?" I glance up and smile. "You think I should do that?"

"Sure. I'm starved, and I did drop about forty bucks on you at the movie last night."

"I paid for my ticket! And I told you I didn't want any popcorn."

"Still," he takes my hand. "I deserve a free meal, too."

"OK." I slide my hand out of his. "But don't act like we're too serious. Then Mom and Dad'll be all weird when you dump me."

Jason's smile fades slightly. "Right," he says.

We walk over to where Mom's talking with Mrs. Bender. They're discussing her treatment for her "condition," and I'm thankful she has enough sense not to announce it in front of the group of ladies who are not so eager to move along. Mrs. Perkins walks up at the same time as Jason and me, all ready to make her weekly jab at my mom's job.

"Still dispensing voodoo potions, Jackie?" She smiles as if she's joking, but I know better.

"It's not voodoo, Crystal. Herbal treatments have been around for centuries." Mom's turned on the honey voice. "They're acknowledged by the church, and even doctors are recognizing their potential effectiveness now."

"I suppose if Ted were pastor, he might think it more godly to *pray* for Lois." Ted's Mr. Perkins, and it's such a joke that my mom's nemesis is acting so Christ-like. Everyone knows Mrs. Perkins is the biggest gossip in town.

"Of course Stuart prays for Lois," Mom smiles. "But finding ways to ease our suffering can be an answer to prayer, too."

Jason glances at me, and I roll my eyes. I've witnessed these "friendly" interactions before. Mom told me once you can learn a lot about people by the motives they project onto others. But I can't figure out what that means when it comes to Mrs. Perkins. Does she secretly want to be a voodoo priestess?

"Is that how Dr. Andrews feels?" Mrs. Perkins asks.

"Perhaps you should ask him." Mom's still smiling, but her eyes are sharp.

"Well, I've seen a world of difference since I started taking your special blend," Mrs. Bender jumps in trying to diffuse the situation. "And I thank the Lord for that."

I smile at Mrs. Bender. She can be a bit much, but she has her moments. Mrs. Perkins makes a little noise and turns to her car, her minions close behind.

Jason leans over to me and whispers. "GCBs."

I shake my head at him not understanding.

He whispers again, "Good Christian..." he sees mom turning to face us and finishes with a murmur, "witches with a *B*."

"Witch-bees?" I'm confused, but his eyes widen. Instantly I get it. "Oh!" I yelp at Mom, who's looking at us and smiling.

"What?" she says, and I can tell she's feeling victorious.

"Mom!" I motion at Jason. "Do you care if Jason comes over for lunch?"

She seems confused by my weird behavior, but she's immediately welcoming. "Of course not. There's plenty," she says, smiling at him. "You look very nice, Jason. Properly dressed."

He looks down, embarrassed. "That was just a joke."

Mom grins at him, and I feel a little better seeing her so light-hearted all of a sudden. "I'm only teasing," she says. "You're very welcome to join us. And I'd like to get to know you better if you and Harley are going out."

"Oh, we're just..." I stop short as Jason's eyes shoot to me. I'm not sure what to say to make it seem less serious. I guess we have been out on two dates for all Mom knows. And he has been picking me up for school all week.

"What?" Mom looks at me.

I breathe a laugh. "I don't know," I say, shrugging. "We're just, you know, happy to have lunch together."

Mom squeezes my arm and smiles before turning to walk to the car. Jason gives me a look behind her back like I'm acting deranged, but I just shake my head and keep walking.

It's nice having him with us at lunch, actually. Jason's a good buffer against what I've seen and heard between Mom and Ricky lately, and I've pretty much decided to forget trying to talk to her about it. After the way she acted in church, I've even started to think the whole thing might just be a big misunderstanding. Or me being paranoid because of what happened with Shelly's parents. And honestly, I don't want to imagine what else it could be. Just because *my* feelings get confused sometimes doesn't mean hers do. Right?

"Jason, is your family Presbyterian?" Mom asks, passing the mashed sweet potatoes to me. I take the bowl and ladle a blob onto my plate before passing it along to my guest.

"No, ma'am," he says. "Dad and I pretty much don't go to church now."

"Now?" Dad asks.

"Um... now that," Jason hesitates, taking the bowl from me. Our eyes meet.

"Jason's mom died last year," I finish for him.

"Oh, I'm so sorry," Mom's voice is pure honey. "Was it an accident?"

"She had cancer," Jason says. "It was about a year-long deal, but... you know."

"We're very sorry for your loss," Dad says.

It's quiet for a few seconds, and I can feel Jason squirm. I try to think of a new topic that won't seem too abrupt.

"I liked what you said this morning about finding answers, Dad," I say. That seems smooth enough.

"What's that?" Dad looks at me. I catch Jason's grateful smile.

"That part about how God's given us the answers we need, we just have to learn where to look and how to see them," I say. "That was pretty deep."

"Yes, well, I've been studying this book on seeking God, and it just came to me as I was meditating," he says. "People always want answers, and I think God uses a variety of things in our lives and situations to give us the answers we seek."

Mom's gazing at him across the table the way she did in church. Like he's just said the most amazing thing. I see Jason pause, and I know he caught her expression, too.

"It was exactly what I needed to hear this morning," she says.

They smile at each other, and now I feel squirmy. They sure can block out the world at a moment's notice.

"So," Jason jumps in. "Did you guys meet at church?"

My dad glances at him as if he suddenly remembers two other people are also at lunch. Then he stabs at his plate. "We met at State."

"What, you two had classes together or something?"

"No, Harley's mom introduced herself to me one day." He smiles, glancing at her again.

I know this story. "Mom was a stalker," I say with a giggle.

"I was not," Mom argues, smiling. "I just noticed your dad walking around every day with his nose in a book, and I wanted to know what in the world was so engrossing."

"That's about how it went," Dad says. "I was reading and the next thing I knew there she was in front of me asking about it."

"That must've been sweet," Jason says. Then he glances at my mom. "I mean, you know, like a nice surprise or something."

"I was very curious," Mom says. "And Stuart was very interesting to me. He was the first boy I'd met who actually thought about important things and wanted to talk about them."

"Important things?"

"Oh, our purpose. What life is really all about. Spiritual stuff."

"Well, I'd see my friends with their keg parties, and don't get me wrong, occasionally I'd be there with them blowing off steam..." Dad's eyes flicker to mine as if he's embarrassed I might learn some shocking truth about him I don't already know. "But at the end of the night, I just felt like there had to be more to it all."

"What were you reading, Stu?" Mom frowns. "Rousseau's *Confessions*?"

"Probably. Or something else I was too inexperienced to understand." He smiles at her.

I can tell they're about to launch into one of their "romantic" philosophical discussions, and if we don't dash, we'll be stuck. I check Jason's plate, and see he's as close to finished as I am.

"Hey, Mom? Dad? Would it be okay if Jason and I go for a walk? I can help clean up later."

Mom looks at my plate and then smiles at me. "Don't worry about cleaning up. Your dad'll help me."

I grab Jason's arm and we head toward the door.

"Thanks, Mrs. Andrews, Dr. Andrews," he says as I pull it open and jog outside.

The door closes behind me, and I let out a whistle. "That was close."

"What?"

"They were about to take Navel-Gazing Lane all the way to the Meaning of Life Superhighway."

"I think it's nice. Your parents really like each other."

"I know, but jeez. Try living with them."

We're walking down the sidewalk, and I watch him slide off his tie and unbutton his top button. He stuffs the tie in his back pocket, and it hits me. I haven't seen the Gremlin anywhere. Not even at church.

"So where's the monster mobile?"

"I left it at home. We're not that far from here."

I think about it a second and realize I have no idea where Jason lives. "Where is your house?"

"Down at the other end." He waves his hand. A cool breeze swirls around us, and although it's a sunny day, I cross my arms at my waist.

He frowns, watching me. "Are you cold? Want to borrow my coat?"

"Which end?" I press, ignoring his attempt to change the subject.

My house is almost in the center of the neighborhood, with the church a few blocks away as the actual center. At the front are the older homes that were built here first, and in the back the developers have recently expanded into what they're calling Shadow Creek. In that part they're building huge mini-mansions that have lawns backing up to the school's namesake.

"Oh, you know," he says. "That end. It's no big deal."

"Wait." I stop walking and catch his arm. "You're saying you live in Shadow Creek?"

He seems a little embarrassed. "Yeah."

"Jeez, Jas! You could've told me your dad was a zillionaire."

"He's not a zillionaire." He lifts the arm I'm holding and scrubs the back of his head, looking away from me. "He just, you know. Manages well."

"I'll say. Give me my ten bucks back."

"Okay." He laughs softly. "I told you I didn't want it."

I started walking again, one arm still crossed over my waist. Jason follows me and the soft breeze gently moves my hair across my cheek.

"And here I was feeling bad for Mr. I Drive a Hooptie Clown-Car and not wanting to take your money." I push my hair behind my ear.

"Does that change things?" He catches my arm and stops us.

"Yeah, it changes things," I laugh. "It means you're going to have to start buying your fake girlfriend better gifts."

He smiles and we start walking again. "I haven't bought you any gifts."

"Exactly!"

"So we're still fake dating?"

"You bet. At least for a few more days. I mean, there's no rush now that I know gifts are on the line."

"And what sort of gifts did you have in mind?"

"Oh, I don't know. Maybe something sparkly..."

"Sparkly, huh?" The breeze is ruffling his hair. He's smiling at me, and it's all very interesting.

I wrinkle my nose at him. "You know I'm kidding, right? No gifts. But you could've told me your big secret."

"It never came up."

We're at the end of the street, and I look back toward my house.

"You should probably keep going," I say. "I'll turn around and head back."

"Harley," Jason starts. His voice is gentle, and it's the first time he'd used my actual name in days. My stomach tightens.

"Yeah?" I brace myself. I'm afraid he might suggest we start dating for real, and I'm not ready to have that conversation with him.

I like our growing friendship, but Trent is my Mr. Right. Still, I've seen enough movies to know how this goes. If Jason wants to get more serious and I don't, that'll be the end of any kind of friendship between us. Or at the very least, it'll make things super-awkward—not at all like they are now.

"Please don't tell anybody where I live," he says.

"What?" I start to breathe again and almost laugh. "I mean, why not?"

"It's just, people act different if they think you've got a lot of money," he says. "And, well, I'd like them to get to know me for me first."

It seems like there's more to this story, something he isn't telling me, but I let it go for now. "Sure. I mean, of course I won't tell anybody if that's what you want."

"Thanks," he smiles, seeming relieved. "So you'll let me know tomorrow, right?"

"Tomorrow?"

"How much longer we're still together."

"Oh, right."

He starts to walk away, and I turn back toward my house. I don't even correct him about us just being fake together.

Seven

Not correcting Jason's fake dating error is the first sign my brain is betraying me. The second is I've completely stopped thinking about what my real Mr. Right likes when deciding what to wear to school. The next day I don't even consider the pictures in Trent's locker as I stand staring into my closet. All I'm thinking about are the outfits Jason's said looked pretty on me.

None of this is part of the plan! I've gotten completely off course. And in another five minutes he'll be here to pick me up for school! I change outfits three more times and wish I'd thought to get up early so Mom could braid my hair in that headband style he'd said he liked. I hear his voice in the kitchen and grab my book bag before running down the hall. But when I reach the kitchen, I see Jason standing by the table talking to Ricky.

Ricky. The sight of him makes me pause mid-step. Mr. Home-wrecker, Abercrombie-model is standing there smiling and chatting like everything's great and he hasn't done anything inappropriate.

"Hey, kiddo," Ricky says, but his voice sounds a little off today. "You look nice."

"Thanks," I mumble.

"Yeah, you do," Jason brightens, and I can't help feeling a little bit better. "Ready?" he says.

I nod and follow him to the door. Just then my mom appears in the entrance to her office.

"Harley? You didn't say goodbye," she says. Is she anxious, too?

"Sorry. Bye, Mom."

She can tell something's wrong, but she doesn't say anything. Jason does, though, once we get to the monster mobile.

"So that's the guy?" he asks, holding my door.

"Yep, that's Ricky."

"I get where you're coming from, but I gotta say. Your mom doesn't seem that into him." He closes the door and jogs around to get in on his side.

You didn't see what I saw Saturday night.

"It's more him that's into her," I explain once we're moving. "Mom just says he's a nice boy."

"He does seem really nice, but I wouldn't let that bother me."

"Oh no?" I glance at him. He's dressed in a white t-shirt and jeans again, and the wind's pushing his hair around. It's distractingly cute, and I look down at my hands, trying to refocus my brain back on Trent.

"Nope. I've seen your parents together," Jason continues. "Your mom looks at your dad like—"

"Like he's a chocolate-dipped strawberry?"

"Yeah," Jason smiles. "It's weird. But in a super-nice way, I mean. Since they're your parents and all."

"No, it's weird. They're the ultimate mismatch."

"Just on the outside. On the inside they really get each other. It's cool." Jason looks off for a second. "And I mean, sure your mom's hot, but it's not like your dad's a hamster or anything. You look a lot like him."

"Wow. Is that a compliment?"

"No, I mean... I think you look..." He's suddenly embarrassed. "C'mon, Harley, you know how you look."

In my mind, I'm still all braces and legs to my armpits, but I can tell from Jason's expression that's not what he sees. His eyes say I look very different, and the Gremlin suddenly feels both smaller and stuffier.

"Isn't there an A/C in this G-ride?" I complain loudly.

"Well, I hate to break it to you —"

"Jason! I might have to cut our fake dating period short if you can't at least drive a car with air-conditioning. I know your secret now, and this is just mean."

"Mean?" he laughs.

"Yes. You're going to dump me in a few days, and then next thing I know you'll be driving Shelly around in a Beemer."

"But she'll be my *real* girlfriend."

"So! This is too much."

We're at school, and I'm actually thankful to be getting out of the car and away from my fake boyfriend. For a second there it got a little too close to being true. I look up and see Trent in the parking lot, and I hurry to catch up with him.

"Hey, Trent," I say, breathless.

"Harley, hey!" He smiles and it all comes rushing back. Perfect teeth, kissing those lips. "Where's Jason?"

"Oh, he's coming." I wave my hand behind me. "We had a little argument, so I don't know."

"Argument?" he glances over my shoulder. I look back as well and see Jason leaning against the Gremlin. I decide he's seen me with Trent and is giving us a little space this time. Finally.

"It was something silly, but I don't know," I sigh. "Maybe we're moving too fast."

It's a stroke of genius, and it only took one dose of lavender to get me back on track. Trent doesn't say anything, and we keep walking toward the classroom building. As always he's dressed like a model in khaki pants and a polo shirt. It's a definite plus the way he takes such obvious care with his appearance.

We're at the first building, and Trent's class is inside. He stops and we're facing each other. *What to say?* I try to think...

"You know, sometimes things do get serious too fast," he says.

"You think?" I smile, blinking up at him.

"Yeah." He smiles and looks down. Then he glances up and reaches forward to touch my cheek. Everything stops.

"Look. An eyelash." He holds it out to me. "Make a wish."

I stare at the delicate brown hair on the tip of his finger as he waits for me to blow it away. But I can't do it. My only wish has always been to kiss him, to be here like this with him, to have him touch my cheek. I don't know why I'm hesitating.

We stand there a moment longer, but before I can recover, a soft breeze blows the lash away. He laughs once and shrugs. "Oh, well. Next time," he says. "See ya, Harley."

And with that, he turns and goes inside. My shoulders droop, and it takes all my effort not to collapse against the building. I can't believe it. Shelly's right. When confronted with a hot guy, the guy of my dreams, I completely flake out. I did exactly what I always do. I went all distracted and aloof. I look around, wondering what my mentor would say if she'd seen what I just did. Assertiveness *Fail!* Cycle Unbroken. As I walk to my first class, I touch my forehead, wondering if a giant, invisible *F* has been stamped there.

I don't see Jason again until third period, and he doesn't even look up when I walk into the room. I wonder if he's mad at me on top of everything else. I made up the story I told Trent about us having an argument, but now that fake story feels real, too.

"Hey," I say softly as I sit in my chair.

He glances up but doesn't smile. "So?"

"So what?"

"Making progress?"

I shrug and Mrs. Gipson enters the room to begin class. Jason turns his attention to our teacher, and I frown. Something's different, but I can't figure out what. He doesn't look at me once during class, and I don't hear a word Mrs. Gipson says. Could he possibly be mad about the Beemer comment? I was just kidding about that. Jason and I are always kidding with each other. Maybe I'm just being paranoid again.

But at lunch he continues his sudden withdrawal, and after ten minutes of salad chomping, I decide to get to the bottom of it.

"Okay, spill."

"Huh?" Jason looks up.

"What's going on with you?"

"I don't get you, H.D." He tries to smile.

"You're acting all distant and quiet and stuff. Did I do something to piss you off or something?"

"Language. Please." He tries to act offended. As if.

"Jason. What happened?"

He stabs his lunch a few times and stares at the tray. Then he glances up at me with those big brown eyes. I've never seen this look on his face before—like he's incredibly frustrated, but still hopeful. It causes a twinge in my middle, but I continue looking at him anyway, waiting for his answer.

"I don't know," he finally says.

I exhale. "What?"

"I mean, well, we were talking about your parents and all, and I was thinking about this... what we're doing, I mean." He pauses for a second and he seems the slightest bit nervous. "When we're together, it's like... it's really cool. And when we talk—"

Oh, God! How can I be so stupid? I've walked right into it.

"You know what?" I interrupt him and jump up. He looks startled. "I just remembered I was supposed to get with Shelly. We've got cheerleading practice this afternoon, and she'll have to give me a ride home."

"But I thought—" He's completely bewildered.

"See you tomorrow morning?" I smile as I back away. Now I'm the one who's nervous.

"Of course, but you haven't finished your lunch."

"It's okay," I wave. "I've had enough."

"But Shelly's not even—"

I turn away before he can finish his sentence and practically run. I only glance back once at Jason's frowning face as I push through the cafeteria door. *Ugh!* I can feel it as I hurry to the library to hide. Then I run to the bathroom just in case he decides to follow me. I know exactly what he was about to say. We both know Shelly doesn't have this lunch period, and I had to get out of there. Things are getting mixed up. Bad.

My heart's pounding, and I need to get as far away from him as possible. But something's wrong with me because the more I think about it, the more I want to go back and hear what he had to say. Hear the words that would ruin everything—a year's worth of dreaming and a solid month of careful planning. I looked up at the ceiling. *Why couldn't I have lunch or at least one class with Trent? It would really help, you know?*

115

After school I hang out in the bathroom a good fifteen minutes after the last bell—until I'm sure everyone's gone. I can easily walk home, but I don't want to risk running into Jason. There's no cheerleading practice this afternoon. Once football season ends, the squad pretty much goes on sabbatical until summer break and tryouts for next year. Sure, the basketball team still plays, but only half of us cover those games, and we alternate our schedules. I'm not on the schedule this week.

When I get home, Ricky's packing up to leave, and I hear him talking to Mom as they plan out the rest of their appointments.

"So the Denali's back, but I kind of like our new arrangement," Mom says. "Uses less gas, and I think some of the ladies prefer you anyway."

Ricky laughs. "So that means I'm keeping Ms. Jackson?"

"If you don't mind." Mom sounds like she's concerned he might mind.

"I can handle it," he says, with a groan.

As I slip through the door, I wonder what that's all about, but when I hear them moving my way, I continue scurrying quietly down the hall to my room. I don't want to see Ricky with my mom today, and coming in like this would have them both asking a ton of questions I don't feel like answering right now. Anyway, it's none of Ricky's business why I walked home instead of riding with Jason. He isn't my dad.

"And it's easy to take her," Ricky says. "Her house is on my way back to Glenville."

"Thanks." I can hear the warmth in my mom's voice. "All better today?"

Peeking from my room, I see him nod and give her a meaningful look. What meaning it's full of I can't tell exactly. But it means something, I'm sure of it. He goes to the door and leaves, and I watch Mom go into the living room and curl into her chair, exhaling deeply. I stand at my door and wait a few more seconds. I want to get to the bottom of whatever's going on with those two, but I don't know how to get on the subject without provoking a lecture on the perils of eavesdropping. A sudden burst of music nearly makes me jump out of my skin, and I grab my phone.

"Hello?" I whisper, ducking back into my room and closing my door quietly.

"Harley?" It's Jason.

"Oh, uh… yeah?" *Great.*

"You lied to me," he says.

I'm not sure how to respond. Is it possible he's joking?

"Um…" I force a little laugh. "What?"

"You didn't have cheerleading practice after school." He sounds annoyed. "And Shelly was in the parking lot looking for you when I left."

I decide to try innocence. "She was? Hmm. I guess I got my days confused."

"So how'd you get home?"

"Oh, I walked." I act like it's no big deal, but he isn't backing down.

"Why?"

I bite my lip. The tone in his voice is killing me, but I have to do it now. And at least we're on the phone, so I don't have to see his face.

"OK. Well, you see, Jason..." *Why is this so hard?* "I'm afraid things are changing between us. And that wasn't part of the deal. Remember?"

"So what do you want to do about it?"

"I don't know," I say, rubbing my forehead.

We're quiet for several seconds.

"Can I come over?" He finally asks, and I imagine his eyebrows coming together over his brown eyes. *Yes...*

"No," I say quickly. "I think maybe it's time we did the whole fake breakup thing."

"Really?" He sounds frustrated, and the fact that it bothers me is proof I'm right. It's time.

"Really."

"Dammit, H.D. Why? We're not even through the first week."

"I know, but I was talking to Trent this morning, and I think I overestimated the amount of time it would take."

"So that's it?"

"Well... yeah." I try to make my voice light and friendly. Why does this fake breakup feel so real all of a sudden? "I mean, that was always the deal, right?"

"Right."

"Okay, then. So no need to pick me up in the morning. I'll call Shelly."

"Okay," he says, and his tone makes me feel awful.

I try again to lighten the mood. "She'll be thrilled, I'm sure."

"I'm sure."

Things are not getting better, and after a few moments of silence, I decide I should let him go.

"Well... 'bye, Jas," I say quietly.

"'bye." He says.

We hang up the phone, and I walk over and fall across my bed. My stomach hurts, so I grab my pillow and pull it to me as hard as I can. I have the most overwhelming urge to cry myself to sleep, but that's silly. This was always the plan.

After a few moments of lying still, listening to myself breathe, I straighten out and reach across the bed to the small drawer under my lamp. It's the first time I've looked at the yellowed sheet of paper in ages, but I need to read it again, to refresh my memory. I carefully unfold the document, and there in my twelve-year-old textbook-cursive is the list.

"My Ideal Husband (a.k.a. Mr. Right)"
#1-A good kisser.
#2-Attends church (without complaining).
#3-Always dresses like a model.
#4-Always polite. (A perfect gentleman.)
#5-Blonde hair and blue eyes.

I close my eyes, and I can still hear Shelly's mom, my old Sunday school teacher, saying how important it is that we include things like "good communication skills" and "same goals for the future" on our lists.

But twelve-year-old boys are not known for their good communication skills, and none of us had any definite goals for our futures at that point. She laughed at all our blank faces staring back at her and said it was okay to include physical traits as well. Then we all joined hands and prayed, and for the other girls, that was the end of it.

I held onto my list, though, and last year when I saw Trent, everything else faded away. My Mr. Right was walking down the square, a slow-motion breeze pushing his blonde hair back and away from his blue eyes. It had all come true. And then when he rescued me that day at the gym, I knew we were destined to be together. Once these distractions got out of the way, like Stephanie. And now Jason.

I open my eyes again, and even though I still feel conflicted, I demand my heart stop trying to sabotage me. Jason and I were only faking—we both agreed. And now it's time to get back to reality. I get up and throw the pillow across the room. Then I punch up Shelly's number.

"Harley?" Shelly has to shout over her radio blasting. I hear the volume go lower.

"Hey, Shel, got a minute?"

She exhales loudly into the phone. "I can't believe you still *talk* on the phone," she says.

I'm so not in the mood. "Will I ever be as cool as you?"

"Probably not."

Ignoring that. "So you ready to start picking me up again?"

"Sure," she says. Then she gasps. "Wait. Does this mean?"

"Jason and I are no longer fake—" I catch myself just in time. "I mean dating. We're not dating."

"Jason's available?" she cries into the phone. "Wait, who broke up with who?"

"What?"

"I'm just saying, if he broke up with you that's one thing, but if you broke up with him—"

"It was sort of mutual."

"Hang up," she says.

"Shelly."

"No, seriously. Someone that hot requires immediate action."

"Are you picking me up tomorrow?"

"Of course! Now hang up!"

I growl. "'bye, Shell."

Click.

I refuse to be pissed at Shelly. That would also be ridiculous. I stick out my chin, swallow the knot in my throat, and reason away the pain in my stomach. I was never really dating Jason. It was all just a trick. To be mad would just make it more serious than it ever was. There's absolutely no reason why I should have this sick feeling like I've just made the biggest mistake of my life.

Eight

The next morning I find Ricky whistling around the kitchen. He even pats my head when I sit at the table to wait for Shelly. I didn't sleep well, but preparing to see Trent has taken my mind off last night's confusing emotional mix-up.

"Hello, pretty lady," he smiles. "You look amazing as always."

"Thanks," I say, ducking away. It's nice that he notices the extra time I spend getting ready, but he doesn't have to mess up my hair.

This morning I'd tried to recreate an instant-replay of last Monday, as far as my appearance goes. Only it's Tuesday, and there's no luau this weekend. Still, I have it all planned out. I'll dash over to algebra and accidentally bump into Trent. Then if he doesn't do it, well, I'm going to ask him out myself. I'm going to open my mouth and Break the Cycle. The thought makes me nauseous and panicky at the same time.

"You're mighty cheerful today," I say.

"It's true," Ricky smiles.

I frown at him. On Saturday night he was over here pleading with my mother and possibly even crying, although I'm not sure about that part. But even yesterday afternoon he was still down.

"So what happened?"

"Huh?" He pauses to look at me.

"The change. The out with the gray clouds, in with the super-Mr. Sunshine. Did you get into Mom's St. John's Wort?"

"Listen to you. I guess you're the up and coming little herbologist!"

"I've just been hearing about it for a while."

"Well, for your information, I have not been taking anything. I've just got a little dose of what's been brightening your eyes."

"What?" Compulsive scheming? Completely confused emotions?

"Let's just say, it's inspiring to see the world through fresh eyes."

I make a face. "What?"

"A change in scenery can be exhilarating!"

"Have you lost it?" I look around. "Where's Mom?"

"Oh, we traded up on some clients. She's off seeing Ms. Simmons, and I'm taking some of her afternoon appointments."

At this point, I'm so confused. He's acting like a giddy teenager, and Mom isn't even here. Has she managed to get him off her back? I replay yesterday afternoon in my head. Ricky went to cover Ms. Jackson's appointment, and then he said he was going home. Had he somehow gotten mixed up with Ms. Jackson?

"So you're here this morning, and Mom's out seeing clients?" I clarify.

"Yep."

"And who are you seeing this afternoon?"

I actually see his eyes sparkle. "Ms. Jackson."

"Ms. Jackson?"

"I am for reeal," he sings.

I hear a horn outside and go to the door. It's Shelly.

"Well, okay." I shrug. "Whatever. Bye, Ricky."

"'bye, biker chick." Then he makes big eyes. "Oops!"

I wrinkle my nose and go out to the car. Shelly's inside bouncing in her seat.

"Come on! Come on! Come on!" she's saying with each bounce. "We've got to get to school so I can see Jason!"

Everyone's bursting to see someone today, and I feel like I'm on a completely different planet. Shelly's gushing in particular makes me second-guess myself, so I tighten my smile and force my brain to think lavender thoughts. I remember Trent's perfect teeth, his pretty eyes. I imagine pressing my lips to his, his warm breath soft on my cheek... Yep. That helps.

Thankfully, we beat Jason to school, but when I look around, it appears we've beaten everyone else as well.

"Looks like we're the first ones here," I mutter.

"No worries!" Shelly sings. "They'll be here soon enough. We can wait."

I sit back in the passenger's seat as she blares her music. It's some dance song and she's wiggling around to it.

"Did you call Jason?"

"Yep!"

"And?"

"And he is soo hot."

"You've said that like a million times. Can you find a new word?"

"Harley." She stops bouncing and turns to me, concern on her face. "Will it bother you if I go out with Jason?"

"No," I say firmly. To both of us.

"Good!" she squeals, dancing again.

"Not that it would matter anyway."

"Oh, that's not true!" She pretend-pouts. "I'd feel bad every time I saw you."

I narrow my eyes at her but decide not to comment.

The song ends, and I choose to tell her my big news instead. "I'm thinking about asking Trent out today."

"No. Way."

"Yep. I'll give him one last chance after second period, and if he doesn't do it, I will."

"That's it! Assertiveness, Break the Cycle!" She smiles. "You're such a good little student."

"I was starting to think you'd forgotten about that."

She grabs my arm. "Here he is!"

I look up just in time to see Jason arriving in a newish-looking Passat. I knew it! Shelly takes a quick glance at herself in the mirror as I watch Jason park and get out of his super-nice car. In no time, she's at his side. I move a little slower and then hang back, feeling irritated with him. Yes, irritation! That's what I feel for Jason, I decide.

"Hey, Jason," I hear Shelly purr.

"Hey, Shell," he says. He glances in my direction. "H.D."

"Hey, Jas." That tightness in my stomach is me being angry with him. That's all it is.

"So where's that cute little monster mobile? Did you wash it?" Shelly teases.

"Nope. Got it in the shop," he says. "It's getting a new coat of paint and some... adjustments."

I haven't moved from beside Shelly's car, where I'm focusing on being irritated. But despite my best efforts, the sight of my best friend pressing her body against my ex-boyfriend makes my chest hurt.

Fake! Fake ex-boyfriend. Fake ex-date. We only went out twice and it was all for show. *Gah!*

"Hey, Harley," I hear a softer voice to my right and look around. I start to breathe again.

"Hey, Trent." I say, smiling. He smiles back, and even though his sweet smile doesn't completely get rid of the sting I feel seeing Jason with Shelly, I do feel a little surge of anticipation. Once I'm Trent's girlfriend, all of this Jason-confusion will be a distant memory, and nothing, not even my mom and silly Ricky will get me down. Cue the happily ever after music.

"So you and Jason?" he starts.

"Yeah," I say.

"Was it the thing from yesterday? Your argument?"

I shrug. "I guess."

We start walking together toward the building again, and I notice he doesn't seem as sad today. He actually seems a little happy. I was right! He wanted to ask me out, and the whole fake-dating thing worked! I'm a genius!

We continue walking in silence, and I notice he's humming a little tune. It sounds familiar, and I imagine us holding hands and smile. Soon I'll be the one gazing up at him blissfully.

"So I guess I'll see you after algebra?" I hope knowing that we'll see each other again so soon will give him plenty of time to start planning how he'll ask me out.

"Right!" he smiles. His lavender-blue eyes are so bright now. Hooray for love!

"And I just... I don't know what I'm doing this weekend." Did I actually just say that?

"This weekend." Trent grins and looks away. "Well, I'd better get to class."

"OK. See you in a few hours!"

"Yep."

Now I'm feeling a little bouncy, too. Everything is back on track. I'm finally going to go out with Trent! After all the planning and waiting and faking, it's finally going to happen. I trot to class counting the minutes to third period.

Trent's leaving Ms. Gipson's room when as usual I casually, oh so unexpectedly, happen to be walking up at the same time.

"Hey!" I laugh as if it's the most surprising thing.

"Hey," Trent smiles. He really does look happy. "So we meet again."

"Yep. Getting to be kinda regular," I say.

"Uh huh."

We stand there facing each other. Again. Me waiting, holding my books. Trent looking down, and then glancing up at me with those beautiful, bluish-purplish eyes. Such a pretty color. Like that hydrangea bush. Right before...

"Hey, H.D., Trent."

Jason. My jaw clenches.

"Oh, hey, Jason," Trent straightens up and starts moving away from me.

No! This is not happening again!

"Wait! Trent," I jump and move toward him. "I was thinking..."

"Huh?" Trent looks a little startled. I feel like an idiot. And I know Jason's back there watching the whole thing.

"Um... well... remember how I said something about this weekend?"

"Yeah?"

I wait a beat. Silence. Nothing's happening. Trent's just looking at me.

"Oh, well." I start. "I was just thinking..."

"Yeah?"

Oh my god! Why won't he ask me out? It's like he doesn't want to date me or something. But that can't be right. Not after how sweet he's always been and rescuing me and asking Brian about me. I summon my courage and press on.

"Well, would you like to catch a movie or something? With me?"

"Really?"

His surprise makes me pause. Maybe Trent isn't so smart. When I think about it, I have no idea what kind of grades he makes. He's never struck me as a dumb guy, and he always dresses so nicely. But still, he's awfully slow to catch on to things.

"Yeah. Like maybe Friday? You could pick me up?"

"Friday?" he seems to be thinking about something. "Friday... okay."

"Okay!" I laugh a little and start to breathe again.

"You want me to pick you up?" He smiles.

"Sounds great!" My voice has gone a little high, so I clear my throat.

"Oh, wait," he stops.

"What?" My heart lurches.

"I might not... would Saturday work for you?" His eyebrows come together over his pretty blue eyes.

"Saturday?" I start to wilt.

"Yeah, I just remembered I've got this thing. With my mom. On Friday."

"Your mom?"

"Yeah," he breathes a little laugh.

"But I thought, doesn't your mom get her massages on Friday?"

"Yeah." He seems confused. I guess he doesn't realize that it's my mom doing the massages. Or now it's Ricky, I guess. Whatever.

"She says driving makes her tense again. After her massages," he explains. "So I told her I'd hang around in case she needed to go somewhere."

"Oh. Okay." That makes sense, and it's very chivalrous. It doesn't bother me. Much.

"So Saturday? Yeah?" He smiles.

"Sure." I say.

That's actually better. Now it's more like he's asking me out, instead of the other way around. Like he's as excited as I am about us dating.

"OK." He gives my arm a little squeeze and walks away.

I wait a second and then turn around to see Jason leaning against the lockers grinning at me.

I narrow my eyes. "What?"

"So you *do* ask guys out."

"Shut up, Jason." I turn and walk into class, but I hear him chuckling.

"I'd like to think I had something to do with this evolution in your character."

"I'm sure you would."

He smiles as we take our seats. Last week established the unfortunate pattern of Jason sitting right next to me in class.

"Nicely done," he says. "Although I was a little worried about you for just a second."

"What? The Friday thing?" I pretend like that hadn't bothered me a bit.

"Yeah. I didn't want to see you crash and burn on your first try."

"And what would you have done?" I smile.

"Oh, nothing," he smiles back. "Unless you'd wanted me to, of course."

"Hasn't Shelly gotten to you yet?"

"I can handle her. Can you handle Mr. Personality?"

"Trent is very nice. Just because he's not all in your face like some people doesn't mean he doesn't have a nice personality."

"Uh huh," Jason nods, opening his notebook. "Very nice."

Mrs. Gipson walks in the door, and I say a little prayer of thanks. Now Jason has to be quiet. But after that exchange in the hall, I'm getting a little worried about my hottie-future-husband.

Nine

Even Mom's happier when I get home that evening. She's breezing around the kitchen singing one of her classic rock songs in her typical tone-deaf fashion. I like that Ricky's not hanging around in the afternoons as much now that they've traded appointments. Maybe Dad'll start coming home a little earlier, too. I won't even complain about having to make myself scarce a few times if it gets them back on track. Not that they're off track or anything.

"Hey, hon! How was school?" she asks as I walked in the door and drop my bag on the table.

"Perfect," I decide.

"That's pretty good. What made it perfect?"

"I got a date with Trent Jackson on Saturday. At last!" I do a little dance.

"Wait. What happened to Jason?"

"Oh. Well. We just decided it wasn't working out." I shrug like it's no big deal. Because it isn't.

"Really? You're kidding." Mom frowns and goes over to fluff the couch cushions. Then she flops on them. "I actually liked him. And you guys were so cute together."

That makes *me* frown. "You liked him? After the grilling you gave him before the luau?"

"Well, c'mon, honey," Mom smiles, twisting her long brown hair back into a knot. "He shows up topless to take you out for the first time. What do you expect?"

"I guess." I can't help a tiny grin when I remember half-dressed Jason shaking my dad's hand for the first time. He's so crazy. But in a very irritating way, I remind myself, putting the brakes on that train of thought.

"So Trent," Mom continues. "He was the first one you were trying to go out with?"

"That's him!"

"Well, great! Is he picking you up here?"

"Yes, Mom. You'll get to meet him." I roll my eyes and walk over to the refrigerator, reaching inside for a soda. "Hey, you've probably already met him. His mom's one of your clients."

"Who?"

"Ms. Jackson?"

"Oh. Really? They're the ones over in the new development." She releases her hair and picks up her yoga magazine avoiding my eyes. Very curious response.

"Right," I say, watching her.

"I do remember her mentioning her son, but I guess I didn't put you two together." Mom flips through the pages without really paying attention. "Ricky's taking her appointments now."

"He told me this morning."

Mom stops for a second as if she just remembered something.

"So Ricky seemed very... upbeat this morning," I say.

"Did he?" She doesn't seem impressed.

"Yeah. Except I guess you weren't here to see it."

"I haven't seen him at all today." She goes back to flipping.

"Well, he was *very* upbeat," I repeat, watching for any sign that it bothers her.

My phone interrupts our conversation, and I dig in my bag to find it. Mom motions to me and walks over to the front door, opening it and going outside. I look at the number. It's Stephanie Miller.

"Harley?" She says in her direct, head-cheerleader-giving-orders voice.

"Hey, Steph."

"Listen, Robin can't make it to the game on Friday. Can you fill in? I mean, I know you're dating Jason and all, but you're a junior. And you're sort-of the new person. So that means you have to fill in when a senior can't cheer—"

"Sure, Steph! No problem."

"Really?" It almost sounds like she's relieved.

"Yeah," I say. "And I'm not dating Jason. I mean, we only went out like twice."

"Oh. I didn't know." She sounds even more surprised. "You guys looked really tight at school."

God, high school is so dumb. Two dates, and everyone thinks you're engaged. "It's okay," I smile. "I'm actually going out with Trent on Saturday."

There's a pause. And for a second I worry I might've offended her, but that wouldn't make any sense. Stephanie dumped Trent. And it was almost two months ago.

135

"Really?" I can tell she's skeptical. "You're going out with Trent."

"Yeah."

"Trent Jackson."

"That's the one!" I say brightly.

"Well, have fun." It sounds like she means just the opposite. "But you'll be there Friday?"

"You bet!"

"Okay. Thanks, Harley."

We hang up, and I stare at my phone a second. Stephanie didn't sound mad that I'm dating Trent, but she certainly sounded surprised. Does she think I'm not good enough to date her ex-boyfriend? Just because she doesn't want to go out with him anymore doesn't mean I can't. He might not be right for her, but she's not the Queen of the World. Whatever. At least now I don't have to worry about being home alone Friday night.

"So it all worked out!" Shelly's beaming as I get into her car the next morning.

"What?"

"You're going out with Trent on Saturday and Stephanie says you're cheering for Robin on Friday!"

"Wow. News travels fast." I pull the visor down to check my face in the mirror.

"Steph called me first about Friday, but I told her to check with you and call me back."

"Thanks," I say, raising my eyebrows. Mom's health magazine said frowning causes premature aging.

"Harley! I knew you didn't have plans Friday, and I was hoping to be doing something with Jason."

"And are you?"

"Yesss! We're going to the game first and then after that, who cares! Sin City?"

"Shelly." For some reason, the thought of her being sinful with Jason makes me miserable. Which is ridiculous, since I don't care what Jason does now. Because he's just an irritant to me. That's all.

"He is so hot. I cannot wait til Friday. I can tell he's the best kisser."

I close the visor and look out the window. It doesn't matter what kind of a kisser Jason is.

Shelly glances at me. "So you'll have to let me know."

"Know what?" I look back, trying not to frown.

"What you think about Trent. You know, after your date Saturday."

"What do you mean, what I think about him?"

"I'm just saying. He was a total cold fish with me. I'm wondering if he gives you the same treatment."

"You know, he could just be slow to warm up." I think about how Trent is always polite. A perfect gentleman.

"Maybe." Shelly purses her lips and makes the turn into school. "But I've never had any problem warming guys up."

"You can be a bit much, you know."

She smiles and slants her eyes. "That's just your daddy talking."

"My dad would flip out if he heard you half the time."

"Which is why he doesn't. Ooo, lookie there. Yum!"

Jason's leaning against the Passat again, and the truth is, he does look good. Possibly even yum. But none of that matters to me now. He's in the past, a problem I don't have to think about anymore. Except for how I can totally predict his moves. Like for example, as I said, I had to ride around in the Gremlin and Shelly gets the luxury car. I get out and slam the door, walking straight to homeroom. I hear some remark directed at me, but I don't turn around. I'm not even interested in hearing his voice today.

And by third period, I realize I can't stand to sit next to him for an entire hour. It's simply too irritating. Or something. I wonder if I can do a quick visit to the nurse. Then I could just hang out in the library during lunch. Or the bathroom... I can't believe Crash Boy is forcing me to hide out at my own school. Aren't I lucky he came along and ruined my life ten days ago? God, has it only been ten days? Life changes so fast.

I manage to make it through the end of the week and Friday's the game. We all have to wear our cheerleading uniforms to school when there's a home game, and I have to stay after to help make the signs and get the gym ready for tonight. Cheerleading's as much a job as a sport.

My neck's still feeling stiff from the crash, and as I stand in front of my locker, I practice some of Mom's stretching exercises. I don't have to hurry to get to algebra now that Trent and I are going out, so I take a minute to close my eyes and lean my head to one side. I'm still stretching when two hands slid up my shoulders and started massaging my neck.

"Better?" Jason whispers in my ear.

Tingles race down my back. I jump forward and start grabbing my books. "Thanks. You don't have to do that."

"I don't mind. If it helps you feel better." He's standing too close to me, and his warm hands are still on my shoulders, making my heart beat faster. I'm trying to convince myself it's anger, but I've never felt this way angry.

"It's your fault, you know."

"What?" I hear him frown. "Why?"

"My neck's been hurting ever since the wreck."

"I'm sorry." He slides my hair to one side, and I feel his soft breath behind my ear just before his lips touch my skin. A sizzling charge shoots from my shoulder to my toes.

"Jason!" I spin around to face him, covering the spot with my hand. "What are you doing?"

My heart's flying in my chest, and I can feel my cheeks turning pink. I quickly scan the halls, but it doesn't look like anyone saw.

"We're not together anymore," I say.

He leans against the lockers and smiles at me like he knows his kiss felt amazing. "We never were."

I narrow my eyes and slam my locker door. He's doing it again. Trying to wreck everything. "And now you're dating Shelly," I say. "Keep up."

I push past him and take off down the hall. I'm almost running. I need to find Trent, and there he is, waiting outside class for me when I arrive. It's a nice change from before when I had to beat it to Mrs. Gipson's room in the hopes of catching him before he disappeared. Now he actually waits around to see me.

"Hi," I say when I walk up and see him leaning against the lockers. He's cute as ever, and so well-dressed. His faded jeans are rolled to the top of his boots, and he's wearing a tan-plaid scarf over a dark v-neck sweater. Very J. Crew. I exhale and will myself to calm down and get over my unexpected detour into Jason-land.

"Hey. I like your uniform." He smiles. Perfect teeth.

"Yeah, it's very popular." I smile back. "With at least half the student body."

Our cheerleading skirts are a bit short, I have to concede. But it isn't like we don't wear sport briefs under them. And mine are the boy-cut kind—my compromise with Dad.

"I hate that I'll miss the game. I always like watching you guys."

"That's sweet," I say, still smiling.

"So I'll pick you up tomorrow?"

"Seven o'clock!" I chirp and do a little bounce.

He laughs. "See ya."

I watch him leave, glowing with the knowledge that in just a few more hours we'll have our first official date. And he seems really psyched about it now. I told Shelly she's just too overpowering. Trent's one of those quiet types. You have to coax him out. Use a little patience. I'm so encouraged I do a little skip into class. But I stop when I see Jason's eyebrows rise. I narrow my eyes at him and slide into my desk. He leans forward.

"Now, see. You complain about the car, but why didn't you ever wear that when we were fake dating?"

"Shh!" I frown at him. "That's not to get out. Ever."

"I'm just sayin."

"There weren't any home games when we were together," I hiss.

"Well, shit, H.D., you could've given me a few more days!"

I frown at him. "You know, just because we broke up doesn't mean you can start cussing all over me again."

He grins and leans back in his chair. Mrs. Gipson comes in and starts class. I pull out my notebook and give her my undivided attention. I do not look to my left once.

I don't really mind cheering at basketball games. For one, I understand what's happening much better than I do at the football games. Football has so many odd penalties that are always changing, and the point system is so bizarre. I usually just watch my fellow cheerleaders during them and start yelling after everyone else does. But basketball is straight-forward. I know what's happening, and the games are super-fast. We're finished in less than two hours compared to football's four.

Mom drives me to the gym tonight because Dad has to do a hospital visit. She's only staying for the first half, and I tell her I'll catch a ride home with Robin or Meg. I do my banana jump, and she smiles and does a thumbs up from where she sits. I smile back and shake a pom pom at her. Then I notice Shelly arrive with Jason. They go high in the bleachers and sit. Her hand never leaves his knee, and his eyes never leave me. But I ignore them. Sort of.

Then I notice Ms. Jackson walk in with Ricky... and Trent! He made it after all! I skip over to where he sits.

"Hey!" I say, smiling, slightly breathless. "I didn't think you'd make it to the game!"

"Yeah," he says. "Mom had her massage, and then we were just sitting around."

"I thought she had something?" I guess he forgot he'd told me that.

"No," he says. He seems a little nervous tonight. Or excited. That has to be it—he's excited to see me and anxious like I am about tomorrow night.

"So you decided to come here?" I ask.

"Well, we were just sitting around."

"Yeah?" He already told me that part.

"And I suggested we go to the game."

Just then Ricky walks up.

"Hey, Harley," he smiles.

"Hey," I say. I'm not so glad to see him, even if it does appear he's moved on from chasing married women to chasing divorcées.

"Is your mom by herself?" he asks, frowning. Then again, maybe I'm wrong.

"Dad couldn't make it," I say. "But he comes to all the football games when I cheer."

"I'm sure." He turns and goes to where Mom's sitting alone in the bleachers. I watch her face brighten, and she smiles at him as he climbs up to meet her.

"Well, I have to get back," I say to Trent. "See you after the game?"

"We might not stay til the end," he says.

"Oh. Well, tomorrow then?"

"Yep." He smiles, and I look at his sweet lips. Tomorrow I'll get to find out what it's like to kiss them. *Go, Panthers!*

Trent walks to where his mother's sitting on the far end alone with a super-annoyed look on her face. I follow her eyes and wince. Ricky's parked right next to my mom, and the two are just chatting away oblivious to how they appear. Mom laughs and covers her eyes, and Ricky grabs her arm and shakes it. Wrinkles or not, I'm frowning as I clap my poms together. They look like two teenagers on a date. And right here in front of everybody! I can't believe it.

My eyes drift to Jason, who's still watching me. I only glance at him once, but I can see he isn't smiling either. He actually looks concerned. I just shake my head at him and turn back to the game.

After our half-time show, Mom and Ricky finally break it up, and he helps her down the wobbly bleachers. At the bottom he says something to her, and she smiles and squeezes his arm. Then she turns and walks to me. Trent and his mom are also collecting their things, and I recognize the look on Mrs. Jackson's face—like she wants to jerk Mom's ponytail. I could die.

Mom doesn't notice any of it, as usual. She combs a stray hair back from my face with her fingers. "Would you mind if I leave now?" she asks. "Those bleachers are killer on my back."

I'm still frowning, but I nod. "I'll come straight home," I say, just in case she's planning on having a visitor.

"I'll probably be in bed," she smiles, then she kisses my cheek.

I catch a ride home with Shelly and Jason after the game. I don't really want to, but Jason insists, and now that he has a nice, four-door Passat, how can I refuse? The whole ride I'm completely distracted thinking about Mom and Ricky and Ms. Jackson's face.

"You sure you don't want to go out with us?" Jason says to me. "We're meeting up with a gang at the Shadow Freeze."

I can feel the tension in the car rise as Shelly holds her breath waiting for my answer.

"No. I'm going home," I say, and I hear my best friend exhale.

"You guys looked great out there," Jason says. Our eyes meet in the rearview mirror, but I look out the window again. I can only deal with one problem at a time.

"You'll have to come when I'm cheering," Shelly says.

"Yeah. That's like next Friday, isn't it?" I try to back her up.

"Yep," she says.

"Okay," Jason sounds vague.

Thankfully when we get to my house, everything looks normal. I go inside and Mom's still up. Dad's in their bedroom.

"Did we win?" she asks when I walk inside.

"Yeah," I say. I look at her sitting on the couch with a book like it's been the most normal evening.

"You did a great job tonight," she smiles at me.

"I guess." I drop onto the sofa. "I'm not really the best cheerleader."

She grins and pinches my cheek. "Well, you're definitely the cutest."

"Stop," I push her hand back. She laughs, but I'm not in the mood.

"So you and Ricky seemed to have a nice time chatting," I say, watching her face.

"Oh." She looks back at her book. "He just had some questions about one of my clients," she says.

"Ms. Jackson?"

Her eyes meet mine, and she smiles. "It was just something unexpected came up and he wanted my advice."

I've got the feeling it was more than that, but I don't know what else to ask. We're quiet as she read another page. Then she closes the book and sits up.

"You have a date with Trent tomorrow?" she asks.

"Yep," I say.

She nods and for a moment I get that feeling again, like there's more she wants to say. But she doesn't. "Well, I'm tired. I think I'll go to bed now that you're in."

She kisses me on the head, and I watch her leave. And that's it, end of discussion. I take a deep breath and lie back on the couch, grabbing the remote. I flip through the channels a while, not watching anything, then I just leave it on a classic movie station. I stare at the obviously fake monsters and eventually fall asleep.

A strange tapping sound makes me jump awake. The movie's now some horror classic where people are bursting out of pods and eerie noises are playing as background music. I figure that's what caused me to wake up, but then I hear it again. Something's tapping on the window! My heart's racing as I grab a couch pillow. No good. I drop it and pick up Mom's book instead. At least it's a hardcover.

I creep over and reach with shaking hands to move the curtain back. Oh, god. I breathe. It's just Jason. I walk over and open the front door so I can step outside.

"Hey, you're still up," he smiles. "And still in uniform."

I look down. "Oh. I fell asleep on the couch."

"Let's go for a walk," he says.

I glance around and consider it. I'm wide awake now, and it's a warm night. "Where's Shelly?"

"I took her home."

"So why didn't you take yourself home?"

"Not tired," he says, reaching for my hand. "C'mon. Let's go down to the creek."

"That's at least a mile from here!" I slide my hand back. "I don't want to walk that far in the dark."

"So get in the car," he says, and I see the Passat parked at the street.

I sigh. It can't be much past twelve. "Okay. But not for long. Mom and Dad might wake up."

Jason drives us to his end of the neighborhood, where there are more empty lots than houses and the houses that are there are gigantic. Stephanie's family moved to Shadow Creek last fall. Right around the time she announced she was going to college in California. I look out the window and wonder what it must be like to be her.

Jason parks by one of the undeveloped lots, and we get out and walk down to the water. "It's nice here," he says. "Without all the construction."

"Yeah," I say, and I notice he's carrying something like a small box.

We stop under a big live oak tree that's branching out over the water. It's a nice creek, even if it is man-made and intentionally installed so they could name the high school after it. A faint scent of cut grass is in the air, and it feels like spring.

"What's that?" I ask.

He looks down and reads the box. "Wine coolers. Grabbed 'em out of the mini-fridge at home. Want one?"

I shake my head. "I don't drink. And besides, my dad would flip out if he smelled alcohol on me."

"Live a little, H.D." Jason grins. "Own your name."

"I own my name just fine, thanks."

He flops down on the soft grass and twists the top off a bottle. I sit beside him and listen to the water trickling downstream. It's a peaceful sound, and being here makes me feel relaxed and calm.

"So how'd it go with Shelly?" I ask.

"Eh." He takes a long drink and then frowns.

I watch him. "What's that supposed to mean?"

"Shelly's nice, but…"

"But?" I lean forward, trying to catch his eye.

"I don't know." He looks away.

"Maybe it would help if you hit her with your car."

He laughs and twists the top off another bottle.

"Number two so fast?"

"This one's for you." He hands me the cool, foil-covered glass.

"I told you—"

"I know. Just try it. Help you loosen up."

I slant my eyes at him. "I hope you're not thinking what I think you're thinking."

He laughs softly. "I won't even try to guess what that means."

I take the bottle from him, studying the fruit on the label. I have to confess, I am a little curious, and it's not like I'll have more than just a taste.

"It's okay, you don't have to." He reaches to take it back, but I pull away. I glance at him and take a tiny sip. My eyebrows raise.

"It's sweet."

"Yeah, it's basically crap."

"No, I mean, it's not what I expected. It's more like… punch." I try another, slightly longer taste.

Jason catches my arm. "Like spiked punch. Take your time."

"So what'd you want me for?" I ask.

He looks at me quickly. "What?"

"I mean… why'd you come to my house."

"Oh." He seems to relax. "I don't know." He looks down at the grass in front of him. "I miss talking to you."

"Yeah." I think about it a second. "Me too."

"And at the game… it seemed like you were upset. About your mom and—"

"I don't want to talk about that." The image of what happened at the game ruins the calm I'm feeling, and right now I just want peace.

"Okay." Jason nods, and we're quiet for a little while. I take another little sip and wonder what my big deal was with wine coolers anyway. They're not so bad. I'm starting to feel sleepy again when he suddenly jumps up.

"I know!" he says.

"What?" I jump, too, at his sudden movement.

"Truth or dare." The distant streetlight makes his eyes twinkle. Or maybe I imagined it.

I frown. "The game?"

"Yeah, let's play."

"Just you and me? Now? Uh uh. No way."

"What?" He drops onto the grass beside me again. "Why not?"

"I am not playing Truth or Dare with you... out here. Tonight. Drinking wine."

"That's the best way!" He smiles, poking my arm. "What's the matter? Chicken?"

You bet I am. "No," I lie. "It's just... that's just something stupid waiting to happen."

"Stupider than fake dating?"

"Yes," I nod. "Much."

"I'll go first." He positions himself right in front of me and stares at me for a few seconds. I stare back.

"What?" I finally ask.

"I'm first."

"I didn't agree—"

"Come on. Just one round."

I shake my head and sigh. "Truth or dare?"

"Dare."

"Really?" *Heck.* I look around. "You know, I wasn't expecting to play this game."

"Wuss."

"No, I'm just... thinking." I keep looking around. I don't usually play Truth or Dare. Partly because I can never come up with good dares, but mostly because I'm petrified of what the truth questions might be. Always something embarrassing or dirty. Or both.

"Time's a'wastin, H.D."

"OK. Um... I dare you... I dare you to..."

"The suspense is killing me."

"I dare you to go bang on the window of that house as hard as you can and then run back."

"What?" Jason frowns.

"Yeah." I push his arm. "That big one over there. I'm sure those guys have a house alarm. See if you can set it off."

"That is so lame."

"Well, I didn't want to play your stupid game anyway." I take another sip and turn away.

"Hang on," he breathes getting up.

Jason takes off running into the night. Sure enough, a few seconds later the entire oversized house across the street lights up like a parade with buzzers and sirens. I start giggling as I see Jason streaking back to where I'm hiding on the creek bank. He jumps down beside me.

"OK," he's breathing hard. "That wasn't so bad."

"Thank you!" I say triumphantly, rolling onto my back. There are a million stars out tonight, and for some reason, I keep wanting to giggle. We wait a few minutes for the house to return to normal. The owner walks out in a robe and looks around, then he says something about cats or kids and stomps back inside. I snort and Jason rolls onto his back beside me, looking up at the sky.

"Now it's your turn," he says.

I feel my throat go dry and sit up. "I didn't really want to play—"

"Too late!" He cuts me off, sitting up too. "I already did your dare. Pick one, H.D."

My stomach is tight, and I can feel my pulse picking up. Should I say truth or dare? No telling what Jason'll ask me. No telling what he'll try to make me do. And now I'm clear on the other side of the neighborhood. That's a long walk home in the dark.

"Come on," Jason demands. "Truth or dare?"

"You know, this really is the stupidest game."

"Pick one."

I grab the bottle and finish the entire thing in one gulp.

"This should be good," he laughs.

"Truth." I say. "No, dare!" Then I hesitate again. "No, truth."

"Listen," Jason leans over. "I know you're a little sheltered, but you can only pick one."

"I know." *Ugh!* "Truth."

"OK." Jason waits, looking at me. "You sure?"

"Just ask already."

"You have to tell the truth."

"I know." My heart's racing.

"Hmm..." he looks around.

"Get on with it."

"Patience, grasshopper. I gave you time to think."

"Well, you wanted to play this silly game. I figured you had it all planned out."

"Okay, I'll give you an easy one. Since you're inexperienced and all."

"Thanks."

"Truth. Were you at least a little sad when we fake broke up?"

I stare at him. This isn't the question I expected. It's quiet, and I can hear the trickle of the water flowing downstream in the creek. I think of that afternoon. The pain in my stomach, my urge to clutch my pillow and cry when we hung up the phone. I'm certainly not giving him that bit of information. Still...

"Okay," I nod. "Yes."

Jason laughs. "I knew it."

"So? It was fun. I mean... we had a good time together."

"Mm hm."

"Weren't you sad?"

"It's not my question." He grins.

"It is now. Truth or dare?"

"So we're going again?"

"Sure. Which is it?"

"Dare."

"Jason!"

He laughs. "What? You think I don't know how to play this game?"

"OK. Dare."

I look around again. *What now?* We're practically in the middle of nowhere. And I don't want to say anything too outrageous or personal because then it'll be my turn again...

"Go ring the doorbell five times on that house over there," I point at a different house slightly farther down the street than the previous one.

"Five times?" He frowns. "That's just mean, H.D. They could have little kids."

"Doubtful. I don't know anybody with little kids who can afford to live out here."

"That's very stereotypical."

"That's the dare."

He grumbles something and gets up. I watch him dash off into the night. The house is on the corner, so I lose sight of him briefly. My turn'll be next, and I'm not sure what I'll choose. Just then I see lights come on in the house and a slim, dark figure dash across the street and behind the neighboring houses. Moments later Jason's dropping onto his back beside me again, breathing hard.

"Shew," he pants, staring up at the night sky. "Too much running."

"You have to be in shape to keep up with me," I grin, leaning toward him. A piece of my hair slides into his face. He catches it and twirls it around his finger.

"Next house better be closer," he smiles giving it a little tug. "Truth or dare?"

I slide my hair back and straighten up again. "Um... Dare."

"Ha ha! Now you've fallen into my clutches," he evil-laughs, jumping up beside me.

"Jason. Nothing ridiculous."

"Uh huh," he nods. "Skinny dip in the creek."

I roll my eyes. "How did I know it would be something like that?"

"That's the dare," he smiles.

"No." I shake my head.

"You can't say no."

"I just did."

"So you're reneging?"

"I'm not getting naked in front of you."

"That's a nice image," he smiles, leaning back again. "You realize that gives me the next two turns?"

"I don't care."

"You don't have to undress here," he says as if I could be persuaded. "You could do it over there."

"No," I say.

"It's dark." He's still smiling at me. For some reason I think of his lips touching my neck and my stomach tightens.

"No," I say softly.

He seems encouraged. "Why not?"

I shake my head to focus. "Did you really just ask me why not?"

"I'm just wondering what your actual reasons are." He speaks like we're on the debate team. "I mean, I can guess what they might be, but I want to be sure *you've* thought this through."

"First, there's my stated reason," I say, matching his tone. "Second, because what's to stop you from running off with my clothes once I'm out there?"

"I'd never do that to you, H.D." He acts offended at the suggestion.

"Of course you wouldn't. Sorry. No."

"OK," he grins. "Truth or dare?"

I pause. Then I reach for another bottle and twist the top off. "Truth."

He watches me, still grinning. "Hmm... what would I like to know."

"This again," I mutter, taking a sip.

He looks around then brightens. "Who was your first?"

I cough and send wine through my nose. "Ugh!" I squeal grabbing his sleeve to wipe it.

"Now that's attractive," Jason laughs. "Nice. Do they teach you that at cheer camp?"

"Did you just ask me what I think you did?"

"Who was your first?" He repeats as if it's the most casual question in the world.

I sniff a few times and wipe my nose with the back of my hand. He's still looking at me, waiting. I sit back and push my hair behind my shoulder, trying to be cool. I look off at the creek.

"What makes you think there's been a first?"

Jason raises his eyebrows. "That answers two questions."

"So? My dad's a reverend. I'm saving myself."

"That's nice. I like it. I get another turn."

"Dare." I say immediately.

"OK." He thinks for a moment. Then he sits up again. "I dare you to say this."

I watch his finger trace letters on the grass. *F, U*...

"Seriously?" I say, catching his hand.

He laughs and laces our fingers. "What?"

I pull my hand out of his. "Are you just trying to be a jerk to me? That's not who I am, and you know it."

"It's just a game, Harley."

"But why do you want to play it with me? Why can't you just accept my choices and respect me for them?"

"I do respect you. But what if you're still deciding how you feel about your choices? And what if you decide to make different ones?" He looks down. "I'd kind of like to be there for that."

All those feelings for him are sneaking back, and I can't remember how I fought them off before. "I don't know what you're talking about," I say. "This is who I am. And if you don't like it—"

"I'm talking about, like with the wine coolers."

"I was just curious. I should've known you'd take that and run or whatever." Everything I want to say seems fuzzy. "That's just the kind of thing that makes it impossible for me to—"

I bite my lip. I was just about to say "to go out with you," but since when do I worry about going out with Jason? I'm going out with Trent!

"For you to what?"

"Nothing. Just nevermind." I move to my knees. It's got to be time to go home. "It's getting late, and I'm not staying up all night for this."

"So you'd stay up for something different?" His smile's back, and for a moment I glance at his lips and wonder...

"No," I say, shaking my head.

"Well, you're right, that was a pretty lame dare. And it's my last." He sits back on his heels again. "New one."

"I didn't mean—"

"Kiss me." His eyes lock on mine and hold them. My heart jumps, and I feel my cheeks grow warm.

"What?" I say, but my voice sounds funny to me. Too high or something.

He gets on his knees in front of me and leans in so our faces are very close. "Kiss me," he whispers. My stomach does a flip.

"No," I say quietly.

"Dammit, Harley!" He throws up his hands and leans back. "Why not?"

"Because I can't kiss you." I look down. I'm having a hard time breathing.

"Why not?"

"Because we were just talking about first times, and all that other stuff. It sounds like..."

"Like what?" His voice is soft, and he moves toward me again. That tingly warmth is in my stomach.

I push back and stand up fast. Then I suddenly feel like I might fall down. I look and see my second bottle's empty.

"Take me home," I say, reaching out to hold the tree. My head's spinning.

"Home?" He stands up beside me.

"Jason, take me home," I feel like I have my balance again and start walking toward the car.

"Slow down, Weavy." He trots down and takes my arm. "I'll take you home."

But when we get to the car, he turns me to face him and pulls me close.

"Just kiss me first," he says softly.

I push back. "I said no."

"I don't mean it as a dare," he says. "I mean it because I want you to."

I look up at his brown eyes. My heart feels like a little hummingbird caught in my chest. I can't kiss Jason. I'm hoping to be kissing Trent tomorrow night.

"No," I breathe, looking down and gently pushing him again. "Let me go."

He sighs and lets me go. I open the car door and get in, pulling my knees up to my chest. Jason goes around and climbs in on his side. He doesn't speak as he drives me back to my house. When the car stops, I reach for the door handle to get out, and in silence I walk to my front door. I've just gotten there when I feel him behind me.

"Wait," he whispers.

I turn around. "What?"

"Don't go yet," he pulls me back into his arms.

My hands are resting on his chest, and I'm looking at them. My heart is beating so fast. I really do want to kiss him, but I'm supposed to be kissing *Trent*, not Jason. What's wrong with me?

It doesn't matter. He leans forward and gently presses his lips to mine. I quickly slide my hands around his neck, and he pushes my mouth open with his. He tastes sweet like the fruity wine we've been drinking, and when our tongues met, electricity races to my toes. A soft noise comes from my throat, and he pulls me closer. My fingers clutch the soft fabric of his shirt, and his arms are tight around my waist. But through the haze I remember this is not supposed to happen. We aren't together anymore, and I'm supposed to be doing this with Trent tomorrow night. I step back out of his arms and turn toward the door, trying to control my breathing.

"Wait," Jason whispers, catching my hand. I stop. "Don't go out with him," he says.

I look back. "Jason—"

"I'm serious," he says. "I don't want you to go out with him."

His words send a pain through my chest, and my head feels dizzy. I don't know what to say. Trent's been my dream for so long, I don't know how to let him go. I don't want to. I can't. I have to keep my date tomorrow night.

"It's too late," I say. "I already told him I would. I mean, I practically asked him out."

"You did ask him out," Jason says, stepping closer again. His hands are on my waist, and I can feel his breath on my cheek close to my ear. "Call him and cancel."

His lips are so close, I can almost kiss him again. Instead I put my hand on his chest and gently push him back.

"I can't," I say, shaking my head.

"Sure you can," Jason smiles. He reaches up to take my hand from his chest.

"Jason," I sigh, trying to pull it away. But he doesn't let go.

"Harley."

"I'm tired. And my head feels... funny. I'm going to bed."

"I'll call you tomorrow," he says. Then he lifts my hand and kisses it. I watch his soft lips touch my fingers, and I struggle with the urge to pull us together again.

"I'm going out with Trent."

"I'll call you tomorrow."

I look down and nod slightly. Then I go inside and close the door. I feel like crying, but I don't know why. I go to my room and lay on my bed. I can still feel Jason's lips on mine and the sparkling electricity they caused. I can still feel his lips touching my fingers, and I pull my hand to my cheek. It's wonderful... But I'm supposed to be with Trent, and these feelings I'm having right now are supposed to be saved for him. This thing that's going on with Jason is not supposed to be happening, and I have to stop it.

Ten

But I can't stop Jason. The phone's ringing when I lift my face off my pillow and look at the clock. It's 9 a.m. and my head's throbbing. I'm still in my cheerleading uniform. *Gross.* I reach around to silence my super-loud phone.

"Morning, sunshine." It's him.

"Ooh," I moan.

"What's wrong? Is it the head?" I can hear him smile.

"Why did you do that to me?"

"Do what?"

"Shh! You're talking too loud," I say, covering my eyes. "And why is it so bright in here?"

Jason laughs. "I think somebody's a little hung over."

"It's your fault." I roll over and pull my pillow over my head. "You're a very bad influence."

"I'm coming to pick you up. Get dressed."

"I'm not going anywhere with you."

"Yes you are, and I'll be there in an hour."

"Jason…" The line's dead. I put the phone down and look at the clock. There's no way I'm going anywhere in an hour. I can't move. I close my eyes again.

Next thing I know, someone's sitting on my bed. I look up, and Jason's in my room.

"What are you doing in here?" I say, jumping out of the bed. "Where's Mom?"

"Don't know," he grins. "Front door was open, so I came in."

"Jason…"

"Hm." He looks me up and down and frowns.

"What?" I frown back.

"Still in your uniform?"

I look down at my outfit. "Look, I'm tired. My head hurts, and I really want to go back to sleep." I move to lie down again, but he jumps up and catches me.

"Nope. I'm taking you to breakfast." He pulls me back toward the door. "Hit the showers, party girl."

I stagger across the hall as Jason goes back to the kitchen. Once in the bathroom, I remove my uniform and turn on the shower. It's warm, and for a while I stand under the stream with my eyes closed. Finally, after a few more minutes, I start the process. Bathe, wash hair, wash face. At last all the remnants of last night are gone. Well, all except one. And he's waiting out in the kitchen for me to change.

I step out of the shower and towel-dry my hair. That'll have to do. I slip across the hall to my bedroom where I grab some old jeans and a t-shirt, but when I go into the kitchen, Jason's nowhere to be found.

"Hello?" I call. "Where are you?"

"Oh, hey," he pokes his head in from Mom's office.

"What are you doing in there?"

"Just checking out your mom's voodoo."

"It's not voodoo," I say. "It's herbal medicine."

"I know," he laughs. "I was just thinking about that woman."

"Ms. Perkins," I mutter as I walk into the room. I wonder if Mom might have any herbal cures for a hangover. Not that I could ask her, of course.

"You ready?" he asks, checking me out.

"Mm-hm." My head's still hurting, and my eyes aren't completely open yet. Jason takes my hand and leads me out to the Passat. We climb inside, and I pull on dark sunglasses and lean back in the seat.

"Ihop? Waffle House? Denny's?" He calls out the names like he's reading a list.

"What?"

"Where do you want to eat?"

"You haven't already decided?"

"Lady's choice." He grins at me.

"Jeez, Jason," I groan, turning on my side in the seat. "Why do you do these things?"

"What things?"

"You get all these bright ideas and make me think you've got some plan, and when it comes down to it, you're really just tossing stuff off. Just off the top of your head like that."

"What's wrong with that?" He's still smiling.

I'm quiet for a minute. My head's too thick to argue with him.

"Denny's is fine," I say. "Moons over My Hammy."

He laughs. "You do know your breakfast diners!"

"Just Denny's. Dad went through a phase when I was little."

"Denny's it is."

I'm starting to come around after the third coffee. The eggs and bacon on my pancake are arranged like a face smiling at me. I do not smile back.

"And I thought you were getting the moons," he jokes.

"Where was my mom?" I ask.

"Huh?"

"When you got to the house this morning. Where was everybody?"

"Don't know," he shrugs. "Front door was unlocked, so I let myself in. I didn't see anybody but you."

"That's weird." I try to remember if Mom told me she had something today, but it's hard. Yesterday's so foggy. Well, except for the kissing Jason part. I glance up at him and feel a little shy.

"I've gotta go," I say.

"Wait. I wanted to talk to you." He reaches for my hand.

Our conversation from last night's also on my mind, and I still don't feel like arguing with him.

"About what?"

"Tonight," he says, sliding his fingers through mine. Even that small movement sends a fizzy wave through me.

"Jason," I protest, but I can't bring myself to pull back.

"Just listen." I glance up at him, and his expression makes my chest feel tight. "I know we got off to a... well, a strange start. But I really like you."

"Jason—"

"Just hang on." He pauses a moment. "I really like you. And I think you really like me, too."

I can't answer. I do like him, but he has to understand. I have a dream. "That's really beside the point right now."

"How?" His eyebrows pull together. Another pain.

I look back at our hands, fingers laced on the table, and try to be firm, to reason with us both.

"You showed up here two weeks ago, and hit me with your car." I pause, considering my words. "And now you just expect me to drop everything I was doing and pick up with you."

"But you want to," he says softly.

"I'm not like that, Jason," I say, thinking of Shelly. Somehow the thought of her and her mom strengthens my resolve. "Maybe there is something between us, but there's also something between me and Trent. Something important to me."

I pull my hand back and look at him. "And I want you to stop trying to mess that up."

He stares at me, but I steel myself. If this thing with Jason is real, one date with Trent won't change it. And it'll help me be sure about my feelings.

He looks down. Then he takes out his wallet and drops some cash on the table.

"Come on then," he says taking my hand again. "Let me get you home."

I slip my hand away as I follow him back to the car. It's hard, but I know I'm right. This is something I have to do. I'm not boy-crazy. I'm deliberate and thoughtful. And I plan things out. Not counting last night.

We drive the rest of the way in silence, and when we get to my house, I open my own door before Jason has a chance to get out.

But before I close it, he stops me. "Harley?"

I lean down to look at him. He smiles back, and I almost decide to forget the whole Trent thing and give in. But I don't.

"What?" I ask.

He starts to say something, but then he seems to change his mind. "We can talk later," he says.

I nod and close the door.

Inside, I go straight to my room and close the door. Images of me with Jason are pressing on my mind, but I sit on my bed and try to refocus, to get my head back in the game. Today's the day I've been waiting for. I'm finally going out with Trent. I need to think about that. Be more excited about it.

Suddenly, I have an idea. I pull out my old list and read over it again. Then I take out a new sheet of paper and start to write:

"Traits of Mr. Wrong (a.k.a., My NOT-Ideal Husband)"
1. He crashes into me with his car.

2. He wrecks my personal life.
3. He's a bad influence.
4. He listens to me when I talk.
5. He refuses to give up…

…

I stop and sigh. Then I wad up the paper and lie back on my bed. Dad always says you should pray when confronted with a difficult decision. This seems kind of minor for praying, but maybe it isn't. I close my eyes, but I'm only able to think *God, I'm so confused…* before I fall asleep.

I open my eyes again and it's after four. The house is still quiet, and when I sit up, the piece of paper's still a ball in my hand. I walk to the kitchen and throw it in the trash. Where the heck is Mom? My head was so fuzzy before breakfast, I didn't feel like investigating, but now I'm starting to come around. I walk through the house looking for signs of anything. Then when I get back to the kitchen, I see her note. *Meeting with Ricky, back soon.*

Hmm. She never meets with Ricky on Saturday. I remember last night at the game and her strange comment about the client problem. I've been so preoccupied with Jason and Trent, I actually forgot to worry about her. Now I'm not sure what to think.

My phone goes off, and I answer it before I even look to see who's calling.

"Isn't it great to be in love?" Shelly gushes.

"Oh, hey, Shel." I'm not really in the mood for her right now. "I thought we didn't *talk* on the phone anymore."

"Don't be a pest. Are you going to ask me about last night?"

"Huh?"

"My date with Jason? Are you going to ask?"

I'd actually forgotten about that part, too. "Oh, right. How was your date with Jason?"

"Amazing!"

"Really?"

"He is so super hot," she says. "I've *got* to go out with him again tonight. We almost kissed."

"You did?" I try to sound impressed, but this is so far past awkward.

"What if we all catch a movie or something?"

"Oh!" My stomach does a clench. "No."

"What?"

"I mean..." I'm panicking but trying to stay cool. "I mean, what a buzz-kill. We'd all be out with our recent exes."

"Hmm, I guess you're right. I was just strategizing. So you excited about finally going out with the love of your life?"

"I don't know," I say, not really listening.

"What?"

"What? I mean yes! No, I can't wait."

"You're being weird, but I want all the details. Got it?"

"Yes. Details."

She hangs up and now I really think I'm going to vomit. I am not the kind of person who sneaks out in the middle of the night with my best friend's date. And Shelly would flip out if she knew what I was

---

doing last night — drinking wine and kissing Jason. A little charge of excitement hits me at the thought. As if I needed more proof! Jason is clearly a bad influence. And now I'm supposed to go out with Trent and be able to judge my feelings for him. But I don't have to judge my feelings — I know my feelings for Trent, right? Nothing's changed!

This is not happening.

Only it is happening. Trent texts me to say he'll pick me up at 6:45, and I'm still fussing with my hair. I look in the mirror, and of course! A zit's popping out on my chin. Perfect. I dash across to Mom's bathroom for concealer when she finally appears looking distracted. I don't have time, but I ask her if anything's wrong. She dismisses me with a wave and some comment about client business — her way of saying she doesn't want to talk about it — and I let it go. Dad's visiting at the nursing home in Glennville, so I'm left to myself, and by the time 6:45 rolls around, I've almost decided to call the whole thing off. But I don't, and Trent's very punctual.

"Hey, Harley," he smiles as I hold the front door open. Mom appears in the living room as usual to inspect my date, but I can't see a thing objectionable in the quiet boy standing in front of me in his khakis and short-sleeved polo. Trent's hair is done in his neat, short, almost-retro style that goes up on top. Nothing like Jason's long, floppy brown shag.

"Hey, Trent," I smile back. We're quiet a moment, then Mom walks up.

"Hi, Mrs. Andrews," Trent smiles, extending his hand.

She shakes it and then glances at the two of us. "Be home at 11," is all she says.

I follow Trent out to his mom's car. It's a nice, reliable, air-conditioned Accord. Music is playing softly as we drive, and it sounds like something my dad would play. I decide Trent must not be that into music. But that's okay, I reason. He can have other interests.

"I was thinking maybe we could catch a movie?" he says.

"Sure. What do you want to see?" I focus on leaving all that other stuff behind and enjoying on our date. My dream date with Trent. Yay!

"Whatever you'd like," he says, smiling.

We're quiet again, and the music switches to some new adult contemporary song. I wish I could change it, but somehow that seems pushy. I glance over at Trent again. His skin tone is really even, and when he notices me looking he smiles, uncovering those perfect teeth and crinkling those pretty blue eyes.

"What?" he asks.

"I was just thinking," I say, but I pause.

I can't tell him I've been dreaming of this moment since sophomore year, or that I believe he could be my future husband. He'll think I'm a nut job. Plus, I'm starting to feel like our future marriage has hit a rough patch, and I'm turning into Mr. Bender. Only without the whole family in Cambodia thing.

No, with all the after-hours sneaking, it's more like I'm turning into something worse, like Shelly's dad. I cringe at that thought.

"It's our first date," I finish.

"Yeah," he nods. "Gotta start somewhere."

I'm not sure what that means, but I steal one more glance at his soft lips. Just a few more hours, and I'll get my chance to kiss them. And then hopefully all this confusion over Jason will disappear.

We walk up to the theater, and I nearly turn and run back to the car. Shelly and Jason are walking up, or more accurately, Shelly's pulling Jason along behind her. I refuse to look at him.

"What? Hey, guys!" she laughs. "I thought you didn't want to see a movie."

"Hey, Shelly," Trent says, smiling.

I can't say a word.

"This is great!" Shelly's practically bouncing, holding Jason's hand. He's standing beside her with his other hand in his pocket. I glance up and meet his eyes for a split second. *Mistake!* I look away again fast. My cheeks feel pink.

"Which one should we see?" she continues.

"I don't care," I say. I want to get out of here. Now.

"That one's supposed to be really funny," Trent says, pointing.

He looks at me and smiles, waiting for my response, and mentally I shake myself. I have got to get control. Jason and I are just friends. But everything's different since last night. Since that kiss, and him asking me not to go out with Trent. *Ugh!* It's all too much.

"Well, my vote's always for a comedy," Shelly pipes up, oblivious to the whole situation. Trent's pretty oblivious as well.

"Sounds good," he says. "Okay with you?"

"Sure!" My voice sounds weird, so I clear my throat and smile.

I can feel Jason's eyes on me, and now I'm starting to get angry. He's doing it again. Barging in and wrecking everything. Well, I'm not going to let him ruin my date. I take Trent's hand and lace our fingers as we walk into the theater. Trent doesn't really grasp my hand back, which is disappointing, but he doesn't pull away either. I decide to take that as a good sign.

We find our seats, and Shelly and I sit beside each other in the middle with the boys on the outside. I reach over and clasp Trent's hand again and refuse to notice Shelly's hand on Jason's thigh. The whole film I try to concentrate on what's happening in front of us rather than what's transpiring beside me. Shelly keeps whispering in Jason's ear and giggling. At one point, I see her twisting her fingers in his hair. Assertive my butt, she's just plain pushy. Dark chocolate with milk chocolate highlights. Jason doesn't seem to be resisting too much. He's got a lot of nerve acting like I'm doing something so unbelievable when he's sitting over there allowing my best friend to practically undress him.

Trent's very sweet. He doesn't put his arm around me, but he does poke me in the ribs a few times at what I guess are the funny parts of this movie I'm not even watching. I smile, pretending like I'm having the greatest time. I study his mouth as he laughs. Maybe once I kiss him, my feelings will get back on track. He has to be the best kisser. He and Stephanie always seemed so into each other, and Stephanie isn't exactly a nun. I think about Stephanie. What would the head cheerleader do in a situation like this? Somehow I can't imagine her ending up in one. How do some people always seem to know the right thing to do all the time? I feel like I used to at least have an idea.

Finally the show's over, and we all get up to leave.

"That was nice," I say, smiling at Trent.

"Yeah," he smiles back.

"What are you guys doing now?" Jason asks, as if it's any of his business.

"Uh…" Trent looks at me.

"Maybe we can just go back to my house?" I say. Maybe if I get him on the couch watching TV in the dark, we can get things moving.

"Sure," Trent says.

"Sounds great!" Shelly gushes. "We'll see you guys Monday."

"Or we could come by?" Jason suggests.

I cut my eyes at him, but Shelly's on it.

"Oh, Jason, I'm so hungry," she says. "Maybe we could stop off for something instead?"

"Yeah," I agree. "And I can't really have a lot of people over tonight. You know. Church tomorrow."

Before another word can be spoken, Shelly's pulling Jason away, and I take Trent's hand to pull him to the car.

I try to chat about the movie as we drive the short distance to my house, but I didn't really watch it. I think about other things he might be interested in. The radio's still playing dumb ole parent music, so it can't be that. I'm racking my brains... what did Jason say they were doing? Ultimate Frisbee? But when we turn onto my street, I freeze. Ricky's car is at my house again, and this time it looks like two people are inside it. *Is my mom in Ricky's car?* I don't know what to do.

"Uh... Wait!" I'm scrambling.

"Huh?" Trent seems alarmed.

"Let's go to the creek instead!" It's the first thing that pops into my head. "I just... I'd rather sit outside and talk. I know a great spot."

"Oh," he seems to hesitate. "Sure."

I direct him to the place Jason and I were last night. He parks the car at the road and we walk through the grass to the tree on the bank. The water's rippling the same as before, and I remember it was a soothing sound last night. But I don't feel relaxed tonight. I feel anxious and flustered. Trent sits with his back against the tree, and I sit beside him.

"This is nice," he says. We look at the dark water. I think about my dream and wonder why Ricky's car is at my house late on a Saturday night. I wonder if that's my mom in it, and if so, what are they doing? And right there in front of the whole neighborhood!

"So I was thinking about your dad being a pastor," Trent says, interrupting my thoughts. I look at him confused. Is that why he's being so cautious?

"Yeah?" I say.

"What's that like?"

I think about my answer. "I don't know. He's gone a lot."

"Is he real strict and stuff?"

I shrug. "Not any more than anybody else's parents, I guess. I mean, most anybody else's." Shelly's mom is way less strict. Especially since the divorce.

Trent nods. "My mom's always searching my room."

"What? Why?"

"I don't know," he sort of laughs, but it isn't a happy sound. "I guess she thinks I'm hiding something."

"Well? I mean... are you?"

"Whose side are you on?" He pokes me in the ribs and pretends to fight.

I push his arm. "Yours," I say, with a smile. This is better.

We're quiet again, listening to the water. For a moment, I forget about Mom and Ricky, and instead I feel concerned for Trent. Why did he tell me that?

"So how do you know?" I ask. "Did you catch her?"

He shakes his head. "Sometimes I'll come home, and I can tell she's been in there. Looking under my bed and stuff."

"What for? Drugs? Dirty magazines?"

"Maybe."

"Has she ever found any?"

Then he laughs and says like it's an announcement, "There are no forbidden objects hidden in my room."

I smile. Now things are really better between us. But he gets serious again.

"I guess your dad doesn't do that."

I shake my head. "I mean… I don't think so."

A few seconds pass. The currents ripple by on the creek.

"I like my dad," I say. "But he's very… preoccupied all the time. With the church and all. The flock."

He nods. "I never see my dad now. Since the divorce."

I scoot closer to him and take his hand. "I'm sorry."

He looks at me and smiles. "It's not your fault."

"I know, but… I don't know."

We're quiet again, and he looks at our hands. He's really holding mine now, and with his finger he traces a line across the back of it. It feels nice, like we're making progress.

"So you must've really liked Stephanie," I say.

"What? Why do you say that?"

"I'm sorry!" I squeeze his hand. I'm an idiot! Why would I bring up Stephanie? "You just… you seemed so sad for so long after you guys broke up. I hated seeing you sad."

He's quiet, thoughtful. "We dated a while, I guess."

We're quiet again, and I bite my lip trying to think of a different topic. What moron brings up an ex-girlfriend on a first date?

"Remember that day at the gym?" I ask. "Last summer after cheerleading tryouts?"

"When you hit your head?"

Not that part... "You helped me after I got hurt?"

"Sure. I was really worried about you. We all were."

"I thought it was really cool how you made sure I was okay and carried me inside. Kind of like a hero or something."

"I think anybody would've done the same thing."

"Isn't that what all the heroes say?" I lean forward to catch his eye.

His face relaxes, and he squeezes my hand. "I'm not a hero, Harley."

"Well, you were very sweet. I was upset about tryouts and not making the squad, and you made me feel a lot better. I've always wanted to thank you for that. Somehow."

"You don't have to thank me. I'm glad I made you feel better." He pauses for a beat, thinking. "And I know what it's like to... well, to not feel good enough."

My eyebrows pull together. "You do?"

He exhales. "Yeah. I mean, I suck at football, and my dad was always making me play. It was humiliating..."

I bite my lip. I like that we're getting to know each other better, but if we keep going down this road, I'll never get that kiss. "Well, you helped me. And I've thought you were great. Ever since."

He smiles back. "You're pretty great, too."

Bingo. I scoot even closer and look up at him. Then I slip the tip of my tongue out to moisten my bottom lip. He seems puzzled, so I glance at his mouth. Then I blink my eyes back to his. "I was thinking we might... you know."

His mouth kind of twitches like he's unsure, then he leans forward and sighs before slipping his hand behind my head and pulling our mouths together. I'm so ready for electricity, but it doesn't come. Our lips don't part, and he just kind of holds me there as if he's counting in his head or something. My eyebrows pull together, and I try to open my mouth. But at that movement, he releases me and leans back. I look down quickly, completely confused. A hiccup-breath moves through my chest, and for some absurd reason, I want to cry.

"That was nice," he says.

I'm lucky my head's down so he can't see how my eyes just flew wide. There's no way he enjoyed that.

"You ready to head back?"

I nod.

We stand and walk back to the car, and I'm hoping with all my might Ricky's gone when we get to my house, because I'm ready to run inside and cry myself to sleep.

As we drive back, my mind scrambles for any reason I can find that makes sense. Somehow, someway, something must've gone wrong for our special moment to have gone so wrong. Something must've messed us up. I'm sure of it. He had to have been distracted. Or maybe I caught him off-guard. Or possibly he was nervous? Maybe he thought I wasn't the kind of girl who kisses on a first date. Maybe all that parent talk interfered with his game.

We get to my house and thankfully Ricky's car isn't there.

"Let's do this again sometime," Trent says as I start to get out.

I glance back at him. Does he want another chance?

"Okay," I smile and lean toward him. He leans forward and kisses my cheek. *My cheek?*

"Right," I say, getting back out of the car.

His phone buzzes, and he picks it up quickly. I watch as he glances at the text and for a half-second, he smiles and looks happier than he has all night.

It immediately disappears when he turns back to me. "'Night, Harley," he says.

I blink and then get out frowning. What was *that*? Clearly there's someone out there he wanted to hear from tonight. Someone whose lips he might've been more excited about kissing.

I walk slowly to the house thinking how this would just make Jason's day. This whole night would. That was the worst first date in the history of all first dates. I open the front door as tears are stinging in my eyes, but I stop when I hear voices in the living room. It sounds like my parents, so I wait and listen.

"It just doesn't look good, Jackie," My dad says.

"I know," Mom says quieter. "But I said he could talk to me whenever he needed to, and I guess he needed to."

"At ten o'clock at night?"

"He's dealing with a lot right now."

Finally! My dad's in on it. He'll put a stop to all this Ricky nonsense. I open the door and walk inside. My parents stop talking and look at me.

"How was your date, honey?" Mom smiles.

I decide to skip the gory details and just go to bed. Let them finish getting rid of Ricky.

"It was okay," I say.

"He looked like a very nice young man."

I shrug and keep walking. Too nice if you ask me. "'Night, guys."

I go to my room and close the door, hoping that by tomorrow Ricky will be gone and I can figure out what went so wrong with my Mr. Right.

Eleven

The future is never how you think it'll be. After church, Trent is waiting for me, and he even holds my hand as we walk to the back doors.

"I was thinking maybe Friday we could do something again," he says. I look up at his lavender-blue eyes completely confused.

"Really?" I can't believe it, but he does seem happier.

Boys can be so confusing sometimes. Maybe I misunderstood the whole evening. Maybe he was upset about something that had nothing to do with me at all. Maybe that text was from his mom offering to get him his own car. Or saying she'd never search his room again.

"Yeah," he says. "Mom has her appointment, but—"

"That's okay." I do a little laugh. "I'll be happy to drive this time. Mom's SUV is back."

"Oh, you don't have to drive, I just—"

"I don't mind. Really. Let me check with my parents, but I'm sure it'll be okay. I can pick you up at your house."

"Um, okay. Like after seven?"

"Sure," I say, smiling.

He holds the door open and says goodbye before trotting off toward his car. I start in the opposite direction toward my mom, but I notice there's a new addition to the group of ladies typically chatting on the lawn after church. Trent's mom has joined them, and she's standing right beside Mrs. Perkins.

"If it were me, I might feel it's a bit too... *familiar*," Mrs. Perkins is saying. Then she clears her throat and emphasizes her words. "Especially since you're giving him hands-on instruction?"

Mom's eyes narrow, and she seems angry. "Ricky graduates in four weeks. We've reached the point where he doesn't need direct instruction from me anymore."

I frown. Mrs. Perkins has never seemed interested in Mom's students before. I glance at Ms. Jackson and remember her attempts at starting gossip. I also remember how annoyed she was by Mom and Ricky at the game. Now she appears too cozy with Mom's nemesis.

"He seems very taken with you," Ms. Jackson's smaller voice says. "All he talks about at my appointments is how good you are. As a teacher."

I feel my heart beating faster as Mrs. Perkins raises her eyebrows. But Mom simply sighs and shakes her head.

"He was probably just a little nervous. He was having trouble mastering healing touches, and he did say he wasn't comfortable with end-feel..." She exhales and mutters. "This can't be interesting to you."

"Oh, you're wrong," Mrs. Perkins smiles her evil-witch smile. "I find this *very* interesting."

Mom glances at her, not smiling back. "I'm sure you do."

"And how does Dr. Andrews feel about you working with Ricky on, what is it? End-touching?" Mrs. Perkins' eyes are sparkling. She actually looks giddy. I feel nauseated.

"That's not the correct phraseology," Mom says, her annoyance apparent. "It's end-feel, and it refers to the joints and range of motion."

"I'm so sorry." Mrs. Perkins tries to act like it was simply an innocent mistake. As if anybody's buying that.

"Stuart is very supportive of my mentoring a student every year," Mom continues. "He approves of whoever the college sends me."

"That sounds convenient," Mrs. Perkins says. I wonder where Mrs. Bender is. She normally jumps in and defends Mom in situations like these.

"Well, I won't keep you from your lunch," Mrs. Perkins says. "Come along, Sandra."

Mrs. Perkins takes Ms. Jackson's arm, and the two ladies walk toward the car where Trent is waiting, looking at his phone. I turn to my mom and she's biting the inside of her cheek. Her eyes are somewhere else, thinking, and she touches my arm for a moment but doesn't look at me.

"Harley, I'm going to find your dad," she says.

"Sure, but I—" Too late. She's gliding back toward the front of the church clearly irritated and not listening to me.

I decide not to wait and start walking to my house alone. Now I'm really worried. The way Mom and Ricky acted at the game might've been overlooked by parishioners who've grown accustomed to Mom's annual student trainees, people who once upon a time saw no evil. But after the fallout from Shelly's dad and how surprised everyone was by his affair, it seems anything's possible now. Ms. Jackson's suspicions might've seemed outrageous before last summer, but now it won't take much for her insinuations to lodge in everyone's minds. And then what?

For that matter, what *is* going on with Ricky? Their behavior is suspicious and it isn't right for him to be at my house at odd hours alone with my mother. My phone goes off as I approach home. It's Shelly. I sit on the front steps to talk to her.

"Oh my god oh my god oh my god!" She's gushing.

"What?" I mumble.

"Jason kisses like… oh my god, I just can't even describe it," My stomach does a clench. This is not what I want to hear right now.

"So you kissed him?" I try to sound enthused and fail.

"Mm-hm and it was heh-van!" she sings.

I feel even more ill. "That's nice," I say.

"It was more than nice. It was hot."

"Okay! Well, great." I try to think up an excuse to get off the phone.

"So what happened with Trent?" she asks.

———

"Oh, we went down to the creek and sat and talked."

"That sounds about right." I can hear Shelly rolling her eyes through the phone. "And?"

"And he kissed me."

"What?" Shelly shrieks. "I don't believe it."

"Believe it."

"And?" she waits. "Were there sparks?"

"There was something." I leave off the part about having to work for it. Or about how it felt like he was doing mental math.

"Something like sparks?"

"He asked me out again for Friday!" I try to sound optimistic. There's no way I can tell Shelly what really happened. At least not until I understand what happened.

"Well, I've got to hand it to you. I'm very impressed. I tried everything."

"So are you going out with Jason again?"

"I don't know," she sounds discouraged. "He didn't say, and I figured I should let him ask me for once."

I look up and speak of the devil. "Well, you never know. Hey, I gotta run."

We disconnect, and Jason's standing there in front of me. He wasn't in church this morning, so while I'm in my Sunday best, he's in his usual jeans and a t-shirt.

"So?" he asks.

"So what?" I frown up at him.

He smiles then. "Doxology go okay?"

"Of course."

I get up from where I've been sitting on the front steps, and we walk a few paces in silence. I notice his car's parked up ahead.

"That was Shelly," I say.

"Oh, yeah?" He's just the slightest bit squirmy.

"Yes. She was very happy about last night."

"She's very… determined."

"Sounds like you got over me and Trent fast enough."

Jason stops walking and turns to face me. "Look, Shelly's okay, but you know how I feel."

I look at him. For a second I have the most overwhelming urge to kiss him.

"I'm going out with him again Friday," I say instead.

"So you think it's going somewhere?"

"What's that supposed to mean?"

"You and this Trent guy. You think something's going to happen?"

"I don't know. But I'm going to give him a chance."

"Fine," he says. "Good luck with that."

He turns and starts walking away, and I can tell he's angry.

"Jason…"

But he won't look back. He goes to his car and gets in, and I watch as he drives away. It hurts. He's never acted this way toward me, and for a minute, I fight the desire to call him and say I've changed my mind.

But I can't do that. I've got to give Trent another chance. I just do.

All week it's like I'm living out my Trent fantasy. He meets me every day before algebra, and every time he seems happier to see me. I round the corner for class to find his sweet, smiling face leaning against the lockers, and I walk over to have one of our interactions. I don't really call them conversations since they mostly consist of us smiling and looking at each other. It might not be witty banter, but it's a definite leap forward.

Jason avoids me as much as possible. I only see him in class, but even then he simply says hello and then focuses on his books or the lecture. It hurts to have him act that way, but I've decided it's for the best. I'm dating Trent now and everyone knows it. Soon he'll ask me to prom and then he'll give me his class ring, and eventually all that stuff with Jason'll just be a memory of a crazy night when I went off the radar. Like one of those lost weekends or something.

That's another thing. Dating someone who crashes into you and then causes you to act out of character is clearly a sign of emotional turmoil. Now that Trent and I are together, I've broken the cycle. I'm being both smart and assertive, and I'm no longer so easily distracted.

But while my personal life is getting on track, things at home have been strained between my parents. Ricky and Mom's flirty huddle in the gym at the basketball game was the icing on the cake for the gossipy church ladies. And that little pow-wow on the lawn Sunday caused a bit of friction between Mom and Dad. Understandably, if you ask me. I keep waiting for Dad to lay down the law—no more late-night visits from Mr. *Men's Health*. But he never does.

So the Ricky thing is not over and my anxiety has grown worse now that I know Mrs. Perkins is watching. And waiting. Ricky continues coming over every morning, and he and Mom continue their alternate schedule. Ricky takes the afternoon appointments, which includes Ms. Jackson, and every time I see him, he asks how Mom's doing. I wish he'd get over her and move on to Trent's mom already. If he showed her just a fraction of the affection he shows my mom, she'd probably back off. But maybe Ms. Jackson is like her son. Maybe she moves slower and wants Ricky to make the first move. Maybe that's why she's divorced—much like Trent had been dumped by Stephanie. Not everyone is as patient as I am.

Friday morning, I'm dashing out the door when I remember to ask Mom for the Denali. Ricky's waiting when I return to grab my bag.

"Got your wheels back, biker girl?"

"Mom's wheels, but yeah. I'm picking up Trent this evening. Maybe I'll see you at his house."

Ricky gives me a strange look. "You're going out with Trent again?"

"Yeah. Why?"

"I thought you were all into the crash boy now."

I can't believe Ricky's keeping up with my dating habits. Why is he always trying to be my dad?

"I just went out with Jason a few times. Trent's my guy."

"Right," Ricky seems distracted. "Well, see you later then."

Sure enough, Ricky's still at the Jackson house when I get there. He's unusually preoccupied and doesn't even make a comment about my corn silk hair or the fact that I'm wearing one of those dresses he says guys love. Not that I mind or anything, but it does make me wonder. Maybe he *is* nervous like Mom said. But why?

He's all business as Ms. Jackson leads me into the kitchen to wait for Trent, and when she goes over to Ricky, I see him tense. But he tries to hide it.

"Hi, Sandra," he says, smiling.

"Ricky," she oozes, and I realize Ms. Jackson is not at all like her son. She's more like Shelly. Hoping for a happy ending.

Ms. Jackson says she's going to change as Trent comes in and starts rambling around. He smiles when he sees Ricky and me, and he seems comfortable around the target of his mom's affection. I guess if your parents are divorced, you don't mind the idea of your mom being overly friendly with other men.

"Hey, Ricky," he says brightly.

"How's it going," Ricky walks over to where Trent's standing, and I watch as Trent reaches into the refrigerator and hands him a bottle of water. I smile. My future husband is always so polite.

"You want something, Harley?" Ricky asks as if it's his house or something.

"No," I say, and quickly add, "Thanks." Trent continues to stand by Ricky, and I start to wonder if I should suggest we leave when Ms. Jackson returns.

"Harley, that's the prettiest dress!" she says.

Trent looks up and smiles at me. "Yeah, it is."

"Thanks," I smile.

Ms. Jackson continues. "You can tell your mom her replacement is working out fabulously."

"Sure," I say. "She'll be happy you're happy."

"This one does amazing things with his hands," she purrs, running a finger up Ricky's toned arm.

Ew! I look at Ricky, dressed in black pants and a tank top that puts his hairless, muscular bod on full display. I feel bad for Trent. I know that kind of stuff embarrasses me, but he doesn't seem to mind. Maybe he feels like Ricky'd be okay to have around or something, like a big-brother type.

"You ready to go?" I ask.

He glances at Ricky's face and then turns to me.

"Yep," he says, and I'm glad he's finally moving in my direction.

"See ya, Ricky," I say, feeling a little more generous toward my mom's former stalker. I can deal with Ricky if he helps Trent out. Maybe keeps Ms. Jackson from searching his room all the time.

He smiles after us. "Have fun."

———

192

We walk out to the Denali, but suddenly Trent jumps back.

"I forgot my phone," he says. "Get in—I'll be right back."

I close my door and wait. I'm not even sure where we're going tonight, and despite it all, I can't keep my mind from drifting over to Jason. He always seems to have everything planned out when we're together. I smile, but then I stop and shake my head. That's not right. He just says a bunch of stuff, and then I have to make the final decision. Still… I wonder what he's doing right now.

Oh, right. Watching Shelly cheer at the game in her short cheerleader skirt and non-boy-cut sport briefs. I bite my lip. Will that tempt my fake ex-boyfriend? *Ugh!* I do not care! Jason can do what he wants.

Just then Trent opens the door and gets in. He seems unusually excited, and I'm encouraged. Maybe tonight will be special.

"I got us tickets to *Brown Bagging It!*" he announces.

Brown Bagging It? What? "Another movie?"

I can't hide my disappointment. I was hoping for dinner or even a walk in the park. The Shadow Freeze would at least give us a chance to talk, gaze into each others' eyes.

"I remembered you said comedies were your favorite," he says.

"That was Shelly."

"It was?" he frowns.

"I thought we might do something... where we could talk or something."

"But I already bought the tickets online."

"Oh," I look down. "Well, that's okay. I like movies, I guess."

I'm so frustrated. We arrive at the theater and Trent stops at the counter to purchase the biggest bucket of popcorn available. It is literally the size of an infant, and after we find our seats, he puts it right between us. No chance of us holding hands with the baby in the way.

I look straight ahead and watch the dumb actors say their dumb lines. And the whole time I keep noticing a light flicker as Trent checks his phone on the other side of his leg. I guess he thinks he's being slick hiding it down by his thigh like that, but it's like a spotlight in here. Who is he texting on our date again?

The movie finally ends and we walk outside. I don't even bother trying to discuss the film, since he obviously didn't watch any of it. We get in Mom's car, and I'm ready to take him home.

"Are you tired?" he asks.

"I don't know," I say.

"Well, maybe we should call it a night then. Don't want to wear you out."

"But we haven't really done anything."

"Well, and Mom might need me to drive her somewhere. Or something."

Seriously? I frown. Where is Ms. Jackson going at this time of night? Trent is majorly testing my understanding nature. How can he go from acting so into me at school to completely spacing out on our dates? We can actually *do* something now. It makes no sense.

Am I more attractive under fluorescent lighting? Is it possible he thinks I'm still into Jason? That's ridiculous. Right? Maybe being more open with my thoughts will encourage him, break the cycle-style. Like Shelly said.

"I was really happy you asked me out again," I say.

"Yeah. I like spending time with you."

"I like spending time with you, too." I smile.

We're sitting in front of his house, and I decide to go for it. I smile and lean across toward him. Maybe if we have a better kiss, he won't be so anxious to go home. Maybe he'll suggest we drive around some more. Maybe find a secluded spot. Our faces are an inch apart. I blink again, and he leans forward and kisses my cheek. Again with the cheek!

"Night," he says and jumps out of Mom's truck.

I exhale and watch him jog to his door. He goes inside and I sit there for a moment feeling like the biggest loser. Makes no sense.

Again, I wonder what Jason's doing. He's probably still at the game with Shelly, and here I am alone. Headed home. I look at my watch. The game's over. But it's still too early to be home alone on a Friday night.

After parking the truck, I drop my purse on the front porch and kick off my shoes. My bike's nearby, so I ride it out to the creek. I pedal hard to work off my frustration. Forget Mr. Right. I don't care anymore. Trent's a handsome, well-dressed, lavender-eyed dud, and I've pushed Jason straight to Shelly. My life is just perfect.

I hop off my bike and leave it at the road, running up the little rise to where the tree sits beside the creek. It's completely dark, and no one's here, so I slip off my sweater and unzip my dress. I've been thinking about this ever since Truth or Dare. I'm not actually going to skinny dip, but I'm definitely going for a swim. I want to wash all of the bad feelings and broken dreams away and start over as something new. What that means, I don't know, but maybe I can find out.

I hide my dress and sweater by the tree and jump in the water. It's warm, and the currents swirl around me. It feels wonderful, and I remember that time Mom and I went to a hot springs place that was supposed to be so great for natural relaxation. This is a little like that, only not so bubbly.

I'm just starting to relax when I hear voices and panic. It sounds like Jason and Shelly. I cannot let them see me here like this. I swim to the bank, but a dark figure is running toward me. I duck and try to hide in the shadows at the edge of the water.

"Come on, Jason!" It's Shelly. She's running, and I can tell she's planning to do exactly what I'm doing.

"You know, you shouldn't jump out of the car like that." His voice is a lazy complaint, and my eyes narrow. He's not fighting the peep show too hard. "You could get run over."

"How else could I make you stop?" Shelly says.

She's down at the creek bank now, still in her cheerleading uniform, and I watch as she slips off her shoes. *Crap!*

"What are you doing?" Jason says as she starts to pull up her top.

"Skinny dipping!" She smiles.

"Wait, wait." He says calmly. "Are you trying to get us arrested? It's too early for skinny dipping."

"It's dark. Nobody's going to see us."

"Shelly, this is a neighborhood. People walk their dogs..."

"What are you? Chicken?"

"OK," he says. I slide up in the water and watch as Jason pulls off his t-shirt. Mmm... I've seen that chest before. Just then I hear a sound. It's Mr. House Alarm across the street, and he's pissed.

"Hey!" He yells. "You kids better get out of here before I call the cops! I'm sick of you pranksters acting like you can disturb the peace all night!"

Shelly shrieks, scoops up her shoes, and runs to the car laughing. But Jason dashes in the opposite direction toward the creek. Toward me! I shrink back further into the brush.

"Don't leave. I'll be right back," he whispers loudly. I freeze. How does he know I'm here?

I watch as he pulls his shirt back on and jogs to his car. They drive off, and I stare after them unsure what to think. I wait until House Alarm goes back inside and creep onto the bank. It's a warm night, so I'm not cold in my wet underwear. Nobody's around now, so I wait a few minutes, letting myself dry some, before I put on my dress. I do pull my thin cardigan around me, though.

The currents are making their usual, soothing noise, and I try to do like Mom says. Clear my mind and relax. Not worry about things like Trent and whoever he's been texting that makes him so happy. The fact that he isn't interested in me, and the fact that I've spent a year building a fantasy-life around someone who only wants to kiss me on the cheek.

I lay my head back against the tree and think of nothing. Just then I hear the sound of footsteps jogging toward me and jump. That was fast! Where's my dress? I grab it and jump into it, jerking it up and pulling the zipper. It's strapless, so I don't have any problems getting it on before Jason appears.

"I thought that was your bike," he says.

"My bike!" Understanding washes over me.

"What's going on? Where's your date?"

I sit down again and lean against the tree. "I dropped him off at home."

"You guys have a fight or something?"

"No. I think it's just one of those things. One of those he's not that into me things or something."

"Oh." Jason sits beside me and puts his arm across my shoulders. I lean my head back on it, and I can't tell if it's being with him or the creek, but I feel warm and calm now. As if all the things that had been pressing on my mind can wait for little while.

"So what was all that with Shelly?" I ask, gently elbowing his ribs. "You bringing her to our spot?"

"Like you brought Trent?"

"What?"

"Yeah, I saw you out here with him."

I glance away, remembering Ricky's car parked in front of my house last Saturday.

"I didn't really want to go back to my house that night," I say. "But it wasn't like... I don't know."

"No Truth or Dare?"

I shake my head no, and we're quiet. My thoughts are on that night, being here with him.

"I saw your bike and slowed down. Next thing I know, Shelly's jumping out of the car."

"I almost saw you na-ked," I sing-song.

"I'dve kept my shorts on," he says. "So what are you doing out here?"

"Nothing."

"That how your hair got wet?" he lifts one of my damp locks and then lets it fall back.

"You gave me the idea." I look back at the water. We're quiet again, listening to the soft sound of the currents trickling by.

"I had this dream that I was swimming in the creek and something pulled me under." I don't know why I'm telling him this.

"And that made you want to get in it?"

"No. I just... I wanted to get away from everything, and it seemed like a good way to relax."

I feel his arm tighten around my shoulders, and I lean forward and put my other arm around his waist.

He kisses the top of my head and I look up. I want a real kiss, and I get one, too. Electric and tingly, his lips gently push mine apart, and I catch a faint taste of mint as his tongue touches mine. A warm pulse pushes through me with each heartbeat, and I drop my head against his shoulder to catch my breath. Jason's kisses are the best. We're quiet a moment, and I listen to him breathing and the water flowing past.

"So what did Shelly think about you living out here?" I ask, resting my chin on his shoulder and watching the water flow past.

"It hasn't come up."

I sit back to study his face. I have to get to the bottom of this mystery. "What's the deal?"

He takes his arm from around me and starts picking at his palm. "I told you," he says, looking at his hand. "I don't want people thinking I'm just some arrogant rich kid."

I slide my hand over his. "Why do you just assume that's what they'll think?"

He looks at the creek and doesn't answer. Very unusual for Jason.

"Tell me." I lace our fingers and notice him grasp my hand in return. "Was it a girl?" I'm actually not sure I want to know that.

He looks back and our eyes meet. Then he smiles. "I don't think I've ever met anyone like you."

"Is that good or bad?"

He laughs softly and looks down again. "It's very good."

Warmth fills my middle, and I squeeze his hand. He squeezes mine back, and I smile.

"But you still haven't told me. Why all the secrecy?"

"Harley," he groans.

"What?"

He glances at me a second, then he exhales. "Back home, it was like... Dad makes good money, right? So I got pushed into this group, and it was all about the money and the status. They didn't care about me." He pauses a moment. "Then the other kids, the ones who didn't have as much, acted like I was too good for them or something. But I never changed. It was messed up."

I think about how friendly and outgoing he is. "That must've been hard for you," I say.

"It sucked. I just wanted to have fun. Like I do with you. And then when Mom died... I didn't belong anywhere."

I look down, biting my lip. Now I feel like a jerk.

"I care about that stuff, too," I say softly. "At least the car part."

He laughs and tugs my hair. "You mean the Gremlin?"

"But it's just part of the act, right? To throw people off?" I smile, hoping his confession means the monster mobile is gone for good.

"No way! Those classic cars are the best."

I frown, watching him get all excited.

"You can feel the road so much better, and the engines are way more powerful. Not so much technological interference."

"You're a car geek."

He shrugs and looks down. "I don't know." Then he glances at me. "Does this mean you're gonna stop pushing me away now?"

I narrow my eyes at him. "I had a plan, you know. I was working on something else long before you showed up."

He slides the same piece of hair away from my cheek. "I know."

"And loyalty is very important to me."

"Mm-hm," he nods. "Just so long as 'loyalty' isn't another way of saying 'fear of something new.'"

"New isn't always better," I mutter.

"Sometimes it is," he says softly.

I smile and start to get up.

"Where're you going?"

"Home. It's late."

I start walking to my bike lying near the street, and he catches up to me, taking my hand, and lacing our fingers. It feels so good.

"Want to do something tomorrow?" he asks.

"What about Shelly?"

"What about Trent?"

I shake my head. "It's not happening. I think he's got some other girl. He kept getting these texts that made him all... happy."

Jason chuckles.

"What?" I stop and turn to him.

"Nothing," he says.

Then he pulls me to him. I look up and when our eyes meet, he leans down and kisses me again. His lips are warm against mine, and I slide my hand up to touch his soft brown hair. Kissing Jason makes everything else just go away.

I take a step back to my bike. "I gotta go."

"I'll call you tomorrow."

Twelve

But everything goes wrong on Saturday. I get up and Mom's left another note that says she's meeting Ricky. She writes that it's about a client again, but when my dad sees it, I can tell he's annoyed. Mostly by the way he crumples it up into a tight little ball and stares out the window with his lips pressed into a line.

Then he leaves the house without a word, and I imagine what he might do. Maybe he'll go find her. Maybe he'll walk right up and punch Ricky in the nose. No, I shake my head. I can't really see Reverend Dad, King of the Nerds, doing something like that. I wish he would, though. I mean, sort of. Okay, I don't really want him to hurt Ricky, I just want Ricky to stop trying to steal my mom.

Jason calls, but I let it go to voicemail. I'm too worried and uneasy to talk to him right now, and I don't want him here if there's going to be a showdown between my parents over Ricky. Instead, I pace the house. I go and sit on the couch and try to find something on television. No luck. I go outside and poke around in the flower beds. But I never know what's a weed and what's one of Mom's herbs, so I decide against gardening. I go back inside and lay on my bed, playing with my phone. I add some hairstyles and fashions to my pin boards, then I skip over to check my email. I mostly text everyone, so there's nothing but spam in my inbox. I play Feisty Hamsters a while. Finally, I hear my dad come back.

I go to my door and open it a crack. He walks in and goes straight to his study, so I creep out of my room and go over to his door and softly tap.

"Yes?" he looks up from his desk. I see he's reading that *Issues* book again.

"Hi, Dad."

"Hey, Harley." He looks back down, and it seems like he doesn't want to talk to me. I don't know what to say, but I try anyway.

"Where've you been?"

"I had to run up to the church. Some people wanted to see... me."

I nod and continue standing there, unsure what to say.

Dad lowers his book and looks up at me. "Do you need something, honey?"

I bite my lip and think about it. Then I say, "I wanted to talk to Mom about something." It's not exactly true, but I have to know what's going on. "Do you know where she is?"

He exhales. "No," he says, and looks down at his book again.

My shoulders droop, and I start to leave. But he stops me. "Harley?"

"Yes?"

"If you wouldn't mind, I need you to stay at the house today."

"Why?"

"Some people are coming over later, and well, you need to be here," he says. "They might want to talk to us as a family."

Talk to us as a family? "What's going on?"

"When your mother gets back, we can talk about it more. But I need you to stay here, okay?"

I nod, thinking how he almost never uses that tone with me, like he's trying not to show his anger. My heartbeat speeds up, and I take a breath and just blurt it.

"Is this about Ricky?"

Dad stops what he's doing and closes his book. Then he looks at me. "Yes."

I can't believe he said that. My throat gets so tight, I can barely speak. "Is it something... bad?"

He responds slowly, and I watch his eyes, the same color as mine, searching for the exact right words. "It's something that's, well, basically a misunderstanding."

"A misunderstanding about Mom and Ricky?"

He breathes and looks down. "Yes."

I wait a few seconds and then slowly say what I've been afraid to say for weeks. "What if it's not a misunderstanding?"

Dad looks at me quickly. "What do you mean?"

"I just... what if I heard something? Something between Ricky and Mom."

"What did you hear?"

My heart's racing, and it's hard to speak. "I don't know. They were talking, and it sounded like... well, like he was begging her for something."

I'm afraid I might start crying now. I can't finish the sentence. I can't say it out loud and make it real. Not to Dad. I don't want to hear it myself, not even in my head.

He puts his book down and stands up. Then he walks over and pulls me into a hug. I lay my head on his chest.

"Your mom's got a lot going on. You're going to have to trust her to know what's best."

"How can you say that?" I step back and look at him wide-eyed. "How can you just ignore everything?"

"I don't ignore anything."

"But you never stop her. You never say anything. And I know there are things you could say. Things you could do."

He sits down and exhales again. "That's not how we work, Harley."

"But what if she *has* done something wrong?"

He's quiet a few moments, thinking. "God puts situations in our lives to see how we're going to respond to them. If we'll make the right decisions, His decisions, or if we'll—"

"Stop." I cut him off. "You are *not* going to tell me God is somehow in what's going on with Mom and Ricky."

"God's in everything, honey."

I shake my head and start to walk out. "Thanks, Dr. Andrews."

"We can talk about it more when your mom gets home," he says. "Just try not to worry about it."

I pause to look back at him, but he's already returned to his book.

I can't believe it! He's seriously going to make some observation about God and not do anything! I storm into my room. I resist the urge to slam the door, but oh my god! My phone is going off again. Jason's texting me.

Where RU?
Home.

It rings in my hands.

"I called earlier," he says. "Why didn't you answer?"

"Something's going on here. Dad just asked me to stay put."

"Want me to come over?"

"No," I sigh. "Just wait. I'll let you know."

We're quiet again. Then Jason speaks.

"I'm glad..." he hesitates.

"What?"

His voice is lower. "I was going to say I'm glad I found you last night."

In spite of everything, I smile and warm tingles fill my stomach. Thinking about last night and kissing Jason has the power to make me a little less mad at my parents and stupid Ricky.

"Me, too," I say softly.

"Okay!" His voice brightens. "So. Later then."

"Later."

I close the phone and sit on my bed. It's a sunny

spring day outside. I should be running around holding hands with Jason. Maybe kissing him some more. Instead I'm sitting here waiting. Waiting to see what strange business is going to happen at my house. What strange people are going to appear and what they're going to say. Waiting to see what my mom is going to do. What my dad is clearly going to stand by and watch her do.

Mom finally comes home around lunchtime. I'm sitting at the table spooning egg salad onto a cracker when she breezes through the door looking distracted. She glances at me and smiles briefly.

"Hey, honey," she says. "Where's Daddy?"

I pointed to his study with my spoon. I wonder if she's even aware of what's about to happen at our house. And if she is, whether she even cares about how it affects me. Or Dad.

I watch Pocahontas glide down the hall toward his study, dark hair fanning out behind her. She goes in and closes the door. I can hear the noise of their voices, but I can't tell what they're saying. I stand and creep closer, hoping to make out their words. I don't care if it's eavesdropping. This involves me.

"Well, I'm going to have to tell them something," Dad says.

"I know, but it can't be that. I promised."

"So why has he been coming here at night then? Why couldn't whatever he had to tell you wait?"

That's what I'd like to know.

I hear movement. "Stuart. Do you trust me?"

More movement. "Of course, I trust you."

Silence. Then Mom again.

"Ricky's just young and everything seems so urgent to him. Perhaps it was a little my fault, too. I told him he could call me day or night."

"Calling is very different from showing up here," Dad sounds tired. "It looks like —"

"It looks like what they're saying is true." Mom interrupts.

I feel nervous, and my egg salad isn't agreeing with my stomach.

"Harley heard something," Dad starts.

"What?"

"She overheard one of your conversations, and she didn't understand."

"I'll talk to her," Mom says.

"Maybe I should get her now." I hear them moving toward the door and I jump, hurrying back to my seat in the kitchen. The door to Dad's study opens and he follows my mom to where I'm pretending to eat lunch.

"Harley," he says. "Now that your mom's here, we need to talk."

I nod, looking at both of them, wide-eyed.

"There's been a certain... development you need to know about," he continues.

For a second, it's like he just started speaking Portuguese. "Development?"

"Ms. Jackson went to Elder Bryant this morning and complained that Ricky has been, well, behaving inappropriately with your mother."

The spoon drops out of my hand onto the plate with a loud clatter. I jump up and tears fill my eyes. Trent's mom went to the elders?

"Harley," Mom rushes over to me, but I draw back from her.

"What did she say, Dad?"

"I don't know exactly what all she said," Dad says. "But I guess Ricky's car was here the other night—it was when her son brought you home. Do you remember that?"

Trent told his mom? I can't believe it. Even if he isn't my future husband, I can't believe he'd betray me like that.

"Yeah," I say. "But we didn't come here. We went down to the creek for a little bit first."

"Well, I guess he told her. And I think she confronted Ricky about it yesterday at her appointment."

I frown, remembering what Ms. Jackson looked like yesterday. I remember what she said about being so pleased with Ricky's hands. This doesn't make any sense. Then I think of Ms. Jackson's expression at the game, her nonstop staring at Ricky and Mom, and the way they were talking and laughing and touching each other, completely oblivious to how it looked. The ladies' pow-wow last Sunday after church.

"What did Ricky say?" I ask.

"I don't know, honey," Dad says.

"Mom?" I glare at my mother. This is all her fault. "You saw Ricky this morning. What does he say?"

"Oh, sweetie," Mom's trying the honey voice on me, but it isn't going to work. "Ricky doesn't know anything about this. I think they had some sort of misunderstanding, and—"

"Misunderstanding?" I interrupt. I'm so sick of all these euphemisms, these bizarre, substitute words. I know what this is about.

"Try not to worry about it," Mom says. "Daddy and I have to talk to the elders this evening, and we'll all decide how to handle it."

"The elders are coming here?" This is serious. Dad could lose his job.

"Just for a chat, honey. Everything's going to be okay. Your mom hasn't done anything wrong."

Avoid the appearance of evil. It's one of Dad's favorite sermon texts.

"Will they ask you to step down?"

"No," Dad smiles. "Nothing like that. We just need to decide how to address this, if we even need to include the congregation."

"Include the congregation!" I can feel my face turning red. Everyone will know my mom's been accused of doing something with her student. My mom! I want to crawl under the house and die.

"Sweetie!" Mom tries to come to me, but I step back again. She purses her lips. "Now, Harley. This is all just some silly misunderstanding like Daddy said. We'll discuss it tonight, and it'll be dealt with."

"Ricky has got to go!" I shout. "He's over here too much, and it's gone way too far."

"What's that supposed to mean?" Mom's green eyes flash, and all the honey in her voice is gone.

I look down not wanting to meet her eyes. I don't want to be on their side or believe their accusations. I want to believe her. But she's made it hard.

"He's just over here too much," I say with less fury.

"Well, I think you'd do best to keep that opinion to yourself this evening," Mom says.

Then she spins on her heel and walks back to her room, closing the door. I'm left in the room with Dad staring at me. I feel guilty and small, like I'm the one who's betrayed the family. How can he not say anything? And if he isn't worried, is it possible I shouldn't be either? But he hasn't heard what I have, and he didn't see them at the game. And he's never around when Ricky's here. Touching my mother or standing around in just a towel.

"Do I have to talk to the elders?" I ask softly.

Dad shakes his head. "I doubt it."

His expression is closed, but I can sense a slight bit of annoyance with me. I can't figure out why he's angry at me and not her.

"I guess I'll go to my room, then." I mumble and walk away.

This is all Ricky's fault. Everything is wrong, and it's all his stupid fault. I know Mom's way hotter than Trent's mom, but at least Trent's mom is available. Why couldn't he have just tried to not have a misunderstanding with her? Or whatever. Just give her what she wants. This is all just stupid and awful. And Ricky's fault.

The Session arrives at our house at 7 p.m. Besides my dad, the governing body includes Mr. Bryant, Mr. Bowden, Mr. Lloyd, Mr. Perkins, and Dr. Hamilton. The five men have supposedly spent the day meeting and evaluating whether Ms. Jackson's accusation is something the entire congregation should be aware of, or whether it's something that can be handled privately.

Of course, Mr. Perkins had his evil wife talking to him. She already has a big fat problem with someone like my mom being the wife of her pastor. She's been waiting for something like Ricky to come along. It's like the answer to her wicked prayers. The fact that Trent corroborated his mother's story means the elders have to take it seriously. But why would Trent tell his mom Ricky was here? He knows how suspicious she is.

Mr. Bryant starts the meeting. Mom and Dad are in the living room while I watch through a crack in my door. Dad says I don't have to be in the room if I don't want to, and I do not want to. It's all too medieval for me to believe.

"Well, Jackie, just for starters, Stuart's not going to be involved in these proceedings. That would be against the bylaws. He can listen, of course, but he can't speak for or against you in this matter. Do you understand?"

"Of course, Paul," Mom says. I can't tell if she's nervous or not. She doesn't seem to be. She almost seems bored with the whole situation.

"Are you aware of the accusations made against you by Sandra Jackson?"

"I guess," Mom says. "She thinks I'm sleeping with my student?"

Five throats clear loudly. "Well, I don't know if she's come out and said *that*," Mr. Lloyd answers. "I think she's concerned that you're headed down a dangerous path with this young man."

"Dangerous path," Mom repeats.

"Apparently he expressed… feelings for you while he was at her house yesterday." Mr. Perkins says. "And her son Trent says he saw you in the car with the young man outside your house here last Saturday night around ten?"

Silence.

"Do you have anything to say in response?" Mr. Lloyd gently prods.

I can see Mom's face in the lamplight. Something's going on behind her eyes, but I can't tell what it is. She isn't looking at any of the men. Dad's sitting next to her holding her hand, and I see her lips tighten.

"How old is Trent?" Mom asks.

"I'm not sure exactly," Mr. Perkins says. "Sixteen? Seventeen? Old enough to be taken seriously. Are you disputing his claim?"

"No," Mom replies.

Silence. I notice Dad squeeze her hand.

"Jackie," he says softly. "Are you going to say anything in your defense?"

I see her look at Dad in a way I've never seen before, as if she's evaluating him. As if there's a choice she wants to make, but the fact of him being here is making her hesitate.

"No." She says softly, still looking at him.

Dad's eyes lock on hers and the other men let out a collective breath. My stomach lurches. *What is she doing?*

"Jackie," Mr. Bryant says. "You're not going to let these allegations stand..."

"These allegations are ridiculous." Mom drops Dad's hand and stands up, walking to face the mantle. "And they're being put forward by an ignorant woman and a teenage boy who doesn't know what he saw."

"You can respond either yes or no," Mr. Perkins says.

"To what?" Mom flashes at him. "So far I haven't heard any evidence of wrongdoing. So what if Ricky came here last Saturday? I'm his mentor, and he had a problem he needed to discuss with me. I can't help it if Sandra has a vivid imagination."

"You do have to consider your appearance, Jackie." Mr. Perkins sounds like a patronizing teacher. "It is questionable for the pastor's wife to be in a car with a young man late at night in what looks like... a compromising situation."

"Compromising situation?" Mom's voice rises. "Right in front of my house? In full view of the neighborhood? Where Stuart or Harley or anyone could walk up? Just what kind of a tramp do you and Crystal think I am, Ted?"

Several of the men shift in their seats. Dad shifts and clears his throat.

"Jackie, just tell them it isn't true," he says. "That's really all the session needs to hear at this point, right fellas?"

"Well, we are also concerned about a non-repentant spirit," Mr. Perkins says. "Refusing to hear the church's discipline..."

My eyes narrow. I might be furious at Mom, but now I hate Mr. Perkins. He knows exactly what he's doing. And how those words will affect her.

"A non-repentant spirit?" Mom's voice is sharp. "And for what am I being disciplined exactly? So far all I've heard is a bunch of misguided innuendo."

"Jackie," Mr. Bryant's deep voice brings a much-needed calm to the room. "We're not trying to falsely accuse or insinuate anything. We know you. We know Stu. If you can assure us nothing's going on and agree to... modify your behavior going forward, we can put this behind us."

Mom's green eyes are sparking. I know her too well. Mr. Bryant is trying to give her an out, but his choice of words is like pouring water down a cat's back. He's allied himself with Mr. Perkins and stupid Mrs. Perkins and all her years of jabs and petty remarks.

"I'll have to discuss this with Stuart," Mom says evenly. "I'm not sure I'm ready to accept those terms."

"Jackie—" Dad starts.

She looks at him. "Stuart."

My dad looks down and then rises from the couch. At that the five men also stand and make preparations to leave. Mr. Perkins adjusts his waistband and makes some comment about getting back to the wife. I can just imagine Mrs. Perkins waiting at the door for the full account of what happened. She's probably holding her breath, too. She's finally found something that might stick, something that might put her stupid husband in charge and get rid of my mother for good.

The last elder to leave is Mr. Bryant. He tries one final time.

"I know this can be frustrating, Jackie," he says. "But it's just part of shepherding a growing flock."

Mom doesn't even look at him, and I can't stop staring at her. What has she done? What is this going to mean? By tomorrow everyone will know they came here and presented her with the story, and she didn't say a thing to contradict it.

Dad returns from seeing Mr. Bryant out and sits in a chair. He leans forward and rests his chin on his fists looking straight ahead at the fireplace.

"I'm sorry, Stu," Mom says quietly. "I just couldn't listen to them saying all of those things anymore. A non-repentant spirit?"

Dad lowers his face and rubs his forehead. Mom drops to her knees in front of him and puts her hands on his arms.

"Stuart?" her voice breaks.

My eyes fill with tears. If the congregation believes she's having an affair and won't repent, she could be excommunicated. If she won't answer them, what other choice do they have? Why is she doing this?

Dad looks at her for a moment before pulling her into his arms and rubbing her back. "Is it worth it to you?" He asks softly. "Is this really worth that much?"

She doesn't answer him. I can't stop the tears. He's going to let her decide. Even if it means he might lose his job. Lose his church. I know he will. It's the way he always is with her. Whatever she wants to do, she does. He won't stop her.

"I just, I can't be something I'm not," she says leaning back and looking at him. "And I can't go back on my word."

He smoothes her hair away from her face. "This could turn into something. More than what it is now."

"More than nothing?" Her voice is rising again.

"Don't get angry with me," he says quietly. "I'm on your side."

Mom sighs and puts her head on his shoulder. I watch as he holds her a few moments, rubbing her back.

"I'm going to ask Paul to lead the service tomorrow," Dad says. "I'll take the day off and let this die down."

"I'm going to take a bath," Mom says, standing up.

I watch as she breezes past my room, and I hear her door click. Dad slowly walks to his study. I've been lying on my stomach in front of my door watching the whole thing and now I roll onto my back. My eyes are damp as I stare at the ceiling. Watching the two of them just then, the way they talk and interact, I can only think of one thing. I sit up and grab my phone.

Meet@creek? I type.
BRT.

No one even notices me walk out the door, get on my bike, and ride off into the night. I'm at the creek sitting beside our tree with Jason in less than ten minutes. It's dark, but it's early. And the sounds of kids playing in yards and dogs barking can still be heard off in the night. It's all so normal-sounding I can almost believe what just happened at my house is some crazy dream I had. Only it isn't.

"So? What happened?" Jason reaches forward and laces our fingers. I look up at him. He really does care. And after such a short period of time.

"My mom's actually going to let them kick her out of our church."

"What? What the hell are you talking about, H.D.?"

I suddenly feel exhausted. "Trent's mom called one of the elders at our church and said my mom is having an inappropriate relationship with Ricky."

"Trent's mom?" Jason looks confused. "What does that even mean?"

"I guess that they're having an affair or something."

Jason strokes my hand. "And they believed that? Haven't they noticed how she is with your dad?"

"I don't know," I say, looking down. "All I know is they all came to our house tonight to talk to her about it, and Mom got all mad and said she'd have to think about whether or not to deny it."

He's quiet for a moment, and then Jason says the words that are killing me. "Like she's going to let them think it's true?"

I can't answer. I sit there staring at our hands, listening to the sounds of kids playing, the currents trickling by, and I can't think of a thing to say. That's exactly what she's going to do. And in front of the whole church. We're all going to be publicly humiliated. And if that's not bad enough, Dad could lose his job or be reassigned. We'll have to leave Shadow Falls. All my friends, my home, Jason. I can feel my eyes start to burn as the tears spill over onto my cheeks.

"Whoa, H.D." Jason pulls me into a hug. "Don't cry."

But I can't stop. Especially with him being so sweet. If Dad gets reassigned it could be to a whole other state. I might never see Jason again.

A sob jerks me, and he kisses my head. He's holding me so that my cheek is pressed against his chest, and I can smell that citrusey-wood scent in his clothes. I pull closer to him trying to forget all this stupid drama. We stay that way for several minutes until I slowly sit up and push my hair back. I wipe my face with my hands.

"She's so selfish," I say. "She looked at those men saying those things and she just forgot all about us. Me and Dad and what she's doing to us."

"She just lost her temper—"

"But it won't change anything," I interrupt him. "It never does. She's going to stick to her guns and Dad's going to let her. He always does."

I look at Jason and fresh tears fill my eyes. I really am starting to care for him. It's amazing how fast being with him has become my new dream, and now it could all be taken away just as fast. I put my head in my hands again.

"Harley," Jason whispers. He reaches up and smoothes my hair back. "You're getting too upset about this. I'm sure your dad'll talk to her, and they'll get it straight."

"Right," I breathe. I sit there imagining the possibility. That would be a first. I turn away and lean back against the tree. I think about my mom. My nontraditional mother and her crazy ideas. Jason's beside me, and we both listen to the currents for several minutes. Finally I speak.

"Do you know why I'm an only child?"

Jason smiles and pulls my hair back. "They couldn't top you?"

"It's because Mom thinks responsible Christians shouldn't have more than one baby. She really thinks they shouldn't have *any* children. That they should adopt unwanted babies and then raise them in Christian households."

"That's pretty radical. But I thought having kids was one of those sacraments or something."

"That's for Catholics," I say. "Mom believes God told us to be fruitful and multiply and to fill the earth. But now that the earth's full, we should focus on being good stewards."

Jason raises his eyebrows and glances back at the creek. "I don't think that idea's going to catch on."

"The only reason they had me is because Dad really wanted to have a baby," I say.

"C'mon, H.D. Your mom loves you."

"Oh, really?" I hiccup a breath. "You think so?"

"I know so," he says. "I was there when she cross-examined me before the luau. She wasn't letting me take you anywhere."

"Maybe. But that's just one example."

"OK. Give me another."

"She likes to say God gave us the Bible, but he also gave us a brain."

Jason laughs. "That's awesome. I agree."

"Yes, but you're not a pastor's wife. She's never once cared what her wild ideas mean to Dad. What they could cost him."

"I think your dad loves your mom's wild ideas."

"Maybe before, but I'm not sure he loves them now."

"I bet he does."

"How can you say that?" I demand. "He's not leading the service tomorrow. He could lose his job."

"Your dad is in love with your mom. Like seriously in love with her." Jason pulls me, and I slide my back against him so he can wrap his arms around me. "And it's pretty obvious she feels the same way about him."

"She's selfish. She gets on these soap boxes of hers, and she doesn't care who gets hurt by them."

"She loves you and she loves your dad. And she's fierce. I think you're going to be proud of her before it's all over."

We're quiet for a minute. I'm afraid to say what I'm thinking, but I do.

"And what if Ms. Jackson's right?" I say quietly. "What if there is something inappropriate going on?"

"Harley." Jason pushes me forward. I turn to face him. "You don't really think your mom would do anything with that guy do you?"

I look at Jason and think about it for a minute. I think about how my feelings for Trent changed after Jason came into the picture. How after a year of dreaming in lavender, one week with Jason changed everything. What if the same thing happened to my mismatched mom?

Then I imagine tone-deaf Pocahontas pressing her lips to hairless Ricky's. *Ugh!* I can't even picture that.

No. There's no way. At least not under any normal circumstances.

But what if he showed up unexpectedly? If she let him in and then he threw himself at her? Would she cave out of pity? Or hormones?

"What are you thinking?" Jason ducks his head to meet my eyes.

"It's hard to imagine, but what if…"

"What if what?"

"Remember that night after the movies when I ran into the house?"

"Our one fake date."

"Right. The reason I jumped out of the car so fast was because Ricky was there. His car was parked right in front of our house. At ten o'clock at night."

"Why?"

"I don't know, but Dad wasn't there. And when I went inside, I could hear them in Mom's office."

"What did you hear?" Jason takes my hand again.

"He was pleading with her, telling her he needed to see her," I turn my head away. This is so humiliating. "She was telling him to give it time. And she said she would always let him in."

I can feel the tears burning my eyes again.

"Why didn't you tell me this before?" Jason asks softly.

"I couldn't. It's too embarrassing."

"But nothing happened, right?"

I shake my head. "I don't know. I don't think so. Not that night."

"I dunno, I mean she's his teacher. That could've meant anything."

"Anything? Them at our house? Alone? On a Saturday night?"

"I'm just saying. What if there's another explanation?"

"Like what?" I take my hand back and cross my arms over my stomach. "She put herself in situations, in places where it looked like she did. Like she might've."

"You're not supposed to judge things by appearances. You know that."

"You're not supposed to, but you do. Everybody does. And she knows that. It's one of Dad's favorite sermons. Guarding your appearance."

Jason presses his lips together and we're quiet. The currents keep moving, only this time I'm not soothed by the sound. This time I think of my dream and those currents pouring down my nose and my throat. Drowning me.

"And then there's that whole 'try something new' thing," I say, starting to feel angry.

"What?"

"Like you were saying about being loyal and trying something new."

"I was talking about you and me. Your parents are completely different." He reaches for my hand.

I look directly in his eyes. "Oh really? Shelly's dad wasn't so different."

"I don't know Shelly's dad, but I know your parents. I've seen them together and it's way past old or new with them. What they've got's real."

I look down feeling my eyes getting hot. "Real," I say softly. My chest clenches.

He pulls me to him again. "I think you're tired and you're hurt," he says. "I bet if you got some rest and maybe talked to your mom about it, you'd feel better."

I don't answer. I don't tell Jason I haven't been able to talk to my mom about anything in what feels like a year. That she's always too busy teaching Ricky or working with a client or dispensing herbal wisdom.

"I don't know." Is all I say.

Several minutes pass, and I realize the sounds of dogs barking and kids playing have stopped.

"I gotta get home." I stand and dust off my shorts. Jason stands beside me and takes my hand as we walk back to the street. I pick up my bike and glance at his car. He's in a newish-looking Volvo tonight. "I never asked you what your dad does. I mean, to make you all Shadow Creek material."

"Oh," he grins. "He's a doctor. Psychiatrist."

For some reason that's funny to me. "Oh my god," I breathe. "What's that like?"

Jason shrugs. "He's gone a lot. On call and stuff, but when Mom died, he knew all the right 'things you're supposed to say following the loss of a loved one.'"

He says it in a deep, fake-formal voice, and I wrinkle my nose. "Really?"

"Yeah. We made fun of how stupid they all were. He's kind of a good listener, I guess."

I look down. "I'm sorry. My problems must seem really dumb to you."

"No! This isn't dumb. It's actually pretty serious."

I get on my bike and pause. "Thanks. I think you're a good listener."

He smiles. "I like listening to you."

I study his lips. His white teeth and his smile. Then I look back at his eyes and notice his expression has changed. He steps forward and with his forefinger, he gently traces a line from my forehead down the side of my face, moving my hair back. Then his palm rests on my cheek and he leans forward and kisses me. It's the softest thing, just his lips touching mine, but it steals my breath. It's electric, and when he straightens back up, I'm sure he felt it too. His dark eyes are so deep.

"'Night," he says softly, dropping his hand.

I nod and turn the bike toward my house. I think about Jason the whole ride back. He always makes me feel better, every time we're together. It's so effortless. And that kiss… I get home and I know what I have to do.

But Dad's waiting for me when I walk in the door. They both are. Mom's in the living room with her hands on her hips and Dad's in the kitchen holding his keys. I can't believe it.

"Harley!" Mom says. "Where have you been?"

No one even noticed when I left, and the last thing I expected was them to jump on me the minute I got home.

I'm immediately defensive. "I rode my bike down to the creek—"

"You do *not* leave the house like that at night." Her voice is angry, and it sparks the anger in me.

"I'm surprised you even noticed!" I shout back. "All you care about these days is yourself!"

"Harley." Dad's voice is low and even, and I know it means for me to get control, but I'm shaking and not sure I can. I stare at the floor, trying not to cry, as he puts his keys back on the rack and walks toward me.

"A lot happened here this evening," he says in a calm voice, putting his arms around me. "We wanted to talk to you. But you were gone. We were worried."

"Sorry," I mumble, still fighting tears.

Mom sighs and drops onto the couch. Dad motions me to a chair.

"Sit down, honey," he says.

"I know what's going on," I say, my voice still shaky. "You don't have to tell me. I was listening."

"I want to be sure you understand what's going to happen tomorrow," he says.

"I understand. And I really just want to go to my room. I don't want to talk about it."

Dad puts his hand on my shoulder. "I know this is hard, but it's just one of those things. We'll get through it, and soon it'll be like nothing ever happened."

"Like nothing ever happened?" Can he possibly believe that?

"Yes," he says smiling.

I shake my head. I don't know what alternate universe he thinks I'm living in. Or what alternate universe he's living in, but it'll take something major for it to be like this never happened.

Thirteen

The next morning is like some weird out of body experience. Getting dressed, Mom threatens to wear red to the service, but Dad insists she be reasonable. Then at church we all sit together on the front row, Mom in beige and me in a spring pastel. Dad's associate pastor leads the sermon, and everyone acts like nothing's going on. But I can feel two hundred sets of eyes on the backs of our heads. The icing on this whole bizarre cake comes at the end of the sermon when Mrs. Turner's pipe organ goes straight into the song "Praise the Lord." And just like that, the Doxology tradition is broken.

When the song's over, everyone makes their way out the back doors, while Mom and Dad stand beside me. No one even approaches us to say anything. But there's nothing you can say if you believe the rumors, and if you don't, Mom's chosen not to address them.

I watch the crowd rapidly disappearing and then I see Trent standing in the back of the sanctuary facing me. I stand for a few seconds looking back at him with my arms crossed until he motions for me to come there. Dad's talking to the associate pastor, so I move into the aisle and walk back to see what he wants.

"Hey, Harley," he says. He seems embarrassed and won't meet my eyes. "Can I talk to you?"

"I don't know."

His eyes meet mine then, and I'm less impressed by their pretty color. "I guess you're mad."

"Good guess."

"Could I just explain what happened? Please?"

I think about it a moment. I *am* curious to hear what he has to say for himself.

"OK," I say, and he pushes the heavy wooden door open and holds it for me.

I walk past him outside, and when I glance toward the street, I see Jason leaning against a tree. He sees me and smiles. I smile back at him, but then Trent comes out and catches the elbow of my crossed arm. Jason looks confused. His smile fades, and I start to motion for him to wait. But Trent pulls me around to the side of the building.

"Is it okay if we talk over here? I'd rather my mom not see," he says.

I follow him, and once we're out of sight, he stops and turns back to me. We stand there for several seconds as he looks down and kicks the grass. His hands are in his pockets.

"Well?" I finally say.

"I just... well, I wanted to say I'm really sorry about my mom. I didn't know all this was going to happen."

"What did you think was going to happen? You told me yourself how she is, how she's so suspicious. And then you told her about Ricky's car?"

He glances up, and the sadness is back. "I never thought. I mean, I didn't know it would turn into this big thing."

"You didn't know *what* would turn into this big thing?"

"When Ricky was at our house, I said I liked his car and that I remembered seeing it at your house. Remember? Last Saturday night?"

"Of course."

"Then Mom starts asking me all about it. Next thing I know, she has me over at Mrs. Perkins', and she's asking me all these questions. And Mr. Perkins—"

"So you didn't know why they were asking?"

"No. I mean, Mom was really mad when I got home Friday, and she asked me if I ever saw him at your house. With your mom."

"Why was she mad?"

Trent shrugs. "I don't know. But, Harley. You've got to know I never meant to cause problems for your family. I never thought..." He lets out a big exhale. "Can't you forgive me?"

I look down again. I know I should say yes and accept his apology. It's what Dad would tell me to do, but this is totally different. I wonder if even he could forgive Trent so quick. Knowing Reverend Dad, he probably could.

"I don't know," I say.

"Why won't your mom just say it's not true? I'm sure everybody'll believe her."

I shake my head. "My mom can be a little stubborn about certain things."

And maybe that's the problem. My frustration with her is making it hard for me to accept his apology. I push a piece of hair behind my ear. This is so hard.

We stand there a few minutes in silence. I don't know what to say, but Trent doesn't seem ready to let me go. He looks up at a nearby bush. Then I watch as he reaches over and breaks off one of the blooms and hands it to me. It's small with thick white petals and dark green leaves, and the fragrance is sweet but strong like a magnolia.

"It's pretty," I say.

"Then it's for you."

I sort-of smile. Is this supposed to be a peace offering?

He puts his hands in his back pockets and looks down. "I kind of had another reason for wanting to talk to you," he says. "I mean, I wanted to apologize for my mom, and I hope you'll forgive me?"

"I'm thinking about it."

"Well, maybe it would help if I apologize about Friday, too."

Now I'm totally confused. "You want to apologize for Friday?"

"I'm really sorry about our date. The movie and all."

"Oh. Just forget it."

"It was supposed to be different, but I couldn't seem to do it."

"Do what?"

He shakes his head. "I mean, I want to do something to make all this up to you."

"You don't have to."

"What if we went out again Friday? Yeah?"

"Are you kidding?"

"No! I was just thinking, like I said. I could do something nice for you."

I look down and shake my head. "No. But thanks."

"Oh, c'mon, Harley." He says it like I'm being unreasonable. I don't know what he's thinking. "I know you're mad right now, but you said we could talk before, and I think... I'd like to talk to you."

At this point, I can't think of anything he might say I'd want to hear. And besides that, I've given him two chances. That's enough tries, and even if it isn't, there's Jason.

"Trent, I just don't —"

"Tell you what, we'll go for coffee. I know the perfect place."

There's only one place, I think as I prepare to refuse. But he quickly continues.

"Don't answer now. Just say you'll think about it, and we can talk tomorrow."

I look back at the flower, not sure what to say. After all that's happened, after his mom, after our two terrible dates and even worse kiss, after all that texting, after Jason... Why is he doing this? Why now?

"You want to go for coffee," I say.

"Yes!" He practically shouts, seeming relieved. "A coffee date."

"Wait. I didn't say date —"

"We'll talk more about it later." He squeezes my hand and pulls me back to the front of the church, but I'm still trying to explain how I didn't actually agree to go out on a date with him.

He smiles and steps away once we're in sight of everyone, like we weren't just having a conversation that ended with him turning meeting for coffee into a date. I look up and see my parents walking toward our car, but Jason's gone.

"I'll see you tomorrow," he whispers before going to his mother, who's standing in a small circle talking to Mrs. Perkins. I can only guess what that cluster's discussing.

I hurry to catch up with my parents. There's plenty of time before Friday to sort out whatever just happened. I reach Mom at the same time as Mrs. Bender who's hurrying over from her car.

"Jackie?" she's huffing as she joggles up to us, and I'm reminded of those ducks that return every spring.

My mom looks up and stops. "Lois."

"I just want you to know nobody believes that pack of lies Sandra's spreading," Mrs. Bender huffs out the words as she catches her breath.

"I don't know," Mom says, glancing in the direction of the Perkins group. "I think some people might believe it."

"Idiots. Pawns and idiots. You just need to set the record straight, and we can get back to our lives."

Mom smiles. "Thank you, Lois. But I'm not sure I'm ready to give up my work over idle gossip."

"You don't have to give up anything," Mrs. Bender says. "We'll support you. Tom and I are ready to do whatever needs to be done—"

"We're just taking it one day at a time," Mom stops her. "But thank you."

She reaches out and gives Mrs. Bender's arm a grateful squeeze and then walks back to the car. I watch as Mrs. Bender shakes her head and turns back to her vehicle. She jerks her chin away when Mrs. Perkins gives her a nod, and I decide Mrs. Bender can talk about diarrhea all she wants. I'll never make faces or laugh at her again.

As always, Ricky's at our house first thing Monday morning, and I'm especially annoyed that he's whistling some tune like he's the happiest person on the planet. I go in the kitchen and start loading my lunch bag, and as usual, he walks over to smooth his hands over my hair.

"Just lovely," he says. I jerk my head away.

"I'm really not in the mood," I snap.

He crosses his arms and leans back against the counter, frowning. I give him the most disgusted look I can manage.

"You know, Harley, I've really only ever been nice to you. I wish for once you'd be a little less... like this to me," he says motioning with his hands.

"Mm hm. So how was your appointment with Ms. Jackson?"

His expression changes only slightly, but he hides it with a smile and starts stretching his arms. "She's an interesting client."

"I'm sure," I say turning back to my lunch.

"You know, this whole angry teen thing you're doing?" He motions again. "It's not the most attractive look for you."

I glare at him. "No?"

"No," he says. "You're much prettier as the sweet ingénue. And all that frowning's going to give you premature aging. Even less attractive."

"I really don't care if you find me attractive," I say. "In fact, I wish you would pay more attention to girls your own age. In Glennville. And leave my family alone."

He laughs. "Your family?"

"Yes."

"What's that supposed to mean?"

I look at him for a second. I've never really confronted Ricky about the way he carries on with my mom, but we're going on a year now. No time like the present.

"It means you're causing a lot of problems here, and I'm sick of it."

"Problems?" he repeats. "Like what, princess?"

"Like Dad losing his job problems."

Ricky is instantly serious. "I don't know what-"

I cut him off. "You just showing up here at night? Running around half-dressed and showing up at basketball games and touching my mom and being all affectionate? People have noticed."

My voice is sharp and his face turns red, but I don't care. I want him to be embarrassed. I want him to be gone.

"Mom's really only ever been nice to you," I continue, using his words. "She's worked with you and given you lots of help. You'll be a real jerk if you don't set the record straight."

"What record?" Ricky's voice is earnest. "Harley, I don't know what you're talking about."

I hear Shelly's horn beep outside. "I've got to go. Be sure and ask Mom what's going on at church."

I leave him standing in the kitchen with a dumb look on his face. Adrenaline's pulsing through my body, and I feel like I could run all the way to school. If that conversation doesn't change things around here, nothing will.

Shelly's excited as always when I get in the car, and for once I'm glad she doesn't go to our church anymore. It doesn't appear she has any idea what's brewing among the parishioners.

"So what'dja do this weekend?" She bubbles. "Friday was so great. I almost got Jason naked."

It's all too much. I actually laugh.

"What?" Shelly frowns. "I did!"

"Oh, I know."

"What do you mean you know?" She glances at me, and I remember she didn't know I was there Friday night, hiding in the creek.

"Sorry. I mean, I'm sure. How'd you do it?"

"Jumped out of the car at the creek. He chased after me, of course, and we almost went skinny dipping."

"Well, what happened? Why didn't you?"

"Oh some angry old man came out and started yelling at us," she giggles. "It was so great. I love stuff like that."

I look down. All the drama in my house has distracted me from my two other problems. Trent and Shelly.

"I'm hoping to do a little better this weekend," she continues.

"This weekend?"

"Yeah, I'm going to let him know I'm available. I didn't hear from him Saturday, and when I called yesterday, he seemed distracted. I figure I can drop some hints when we get to school."

I remember my weird Friday thing with Trent and bite my lip. I'm planning to explain that to Jason — and Trent, too, for that matter. It is not a date. I did not agree to go out with him. For whatever reason Trent needs to talk to me about something, and I guess I sort of said I'd listen. Now I can't remember how it happened exactly. It was all so fast, and I was still getting over that bizarre church service.

"You really think it's getting serious?" I ask. At some point she'll have to know about Jason and me.

"Well, so far we've had great chemistry."

I look out the window. I'm sure Shelly's doing her best to make that last statement true. What'll she say when I suddenly turn up with him? Maybe she'll give me another "assertiveness-pass"? For modeling her behavior? I bite my lip at the thought. Doubtful. I'm doing unto her what she's done unto me, and I know from experience it sucks. Things have gotten seriously mixed up.

At school, I can't decide who I should track down first, Jason or Trent. I see the Passat's already parked in Jason's space, and I wonder if the monster mobile's permanently retired.

"Still no Gremlin?" I ask.

"I think he says it's coming back this week. But I might have to flatten the tires."

I smile, thinking about our conversation Friday night. "He really likes that car," I say softly.

"I know. He's such a freak! Oh, well. I guess you have to overlook some flaws, right?"

I glance at her, thinking how his car-love is such a cute flaw, and she trots off in the direction of the building. I watch her go as I slowly walk toward the start of the week. I need to find Jason soon. And Trent. I have to clear up what's actually happening and explain it to Jason so he'll understand. I'd text him, but I need to see his face and be sure he doesn't read this wrong. I take a breath to calm myself. I can fix this.

But by the end of second period, I've almost decided to go to the nurse's office instead of algebra. I haven't seen Jason or Trent all day, and I'm feeling more and more queasy as I approach Mrs. Gipson's room. On top of all that, No one's said anything about the situation with my mom.

I jump into the bathroom to get my nerves under control before algebra, and of all people, there's Stephanie Miller. She glances at me as I stare in the mirror, wondering if I can fake a fever.

"Sorry about your mom. That must suck." she says between lip gloss swipes. "But at least Ricky's hot."

I glare at her. "It's not true."

She doesn't turn her head. She just continues smoothing her long brown hair behind her shoulders. "Well, it *is* hard to believe. I mean, your dad's a reverend and all, but your mom still looks at him like..."

Like he's a chocolate-dipped strawberry. I turn back to the mirror.

"So you're going out with Trent again Friday?" I jump, but Stephanie's looking at me now like she really cares about my answer. How does she know? And if she knows...

"No. Well, sort of."

"Sort of?" She fixes her take-charge, head-cheerleader brown eyes on me. "So are you his new girlfriend or what?"

"No. Why would you say that?"

"I'm just saying how it looks." She studies me a second longer, and then spins toward the door. "See ya, Harley."

I lean forward and press my head against the mirror. Now I'm truly freaking out. I've got to find

Trent and set the record straight. I've got to find Jason and explain what happened. And I'm about to get a tardy.

I take a deep breath and start for Mrs. Gipson's class. My throat grows tighter with every step I take closer. Just then Trent steps out. I jump and make a little *yip!* He's holding a plastic bag filled with tiny yellow and white flowers and a damp paper towel.

"Hey, I've been waiting for you," he says.

"I didn't know," I say, catching my breath.

"I thought you might like these." He smiles. I take the tiny bouquet but don't meet his eyes.

"It's honeysuckle," he says. "We have some growing along the fence at my house, and I thought of you."

"You did?" I frown, looking up at him. Why is he doing this? This is why everyone's so confused. Including me.

He shrugs and does a little smile. "It's your perfume," he says. "You always smell like honeysuckle."

I sniff the flowers. "You're right," I say softly. I can't believe it. He didn't seem to notice any of that on our real dates.

"You know you can pull them apart and there's a little drop of nectar inside?" He pinches a tiny blossom off a stem and then slides the green tip off the bottom. I watch as he pulls the thin white string through the flower and stops at the end. A clear drop appears on the thin strand. He looks at me and smiles.

"Yeah, I've done that before," I say, thinking. "You know, about Friday —"

"I'm looking forward to it!"

"Right. We're meeting for coffee. Meeting."

"That's the plan!"

I study his white smile thinking how there was a time, like a *week* ago, when I dreamed of a moment like this. Of Trent giving me flowers, chatting, noticing my perfume. Now all I wish is that he'd stop. Soon. Before Jason comes around the corner.

"Well, anyway, I just wanted to make it clear that it's not really a date. Just friends meeting up to chat."

"Good friends."

"Um… sure. So you want to meet at the Shadow Java or something?"

"Great idea! They have this really great macchiato. And a decaf skinny latte —"

"So we're all clear then?"

"You bet," he smiles. "How does seven sound?"

I bite my cheek not entirely convinced he's clear. "Let's make it six-thirty." Somehow earlier seems even less date-ish.

"Okay. And I'll see you later?"

"I guess. Oh, and thanks for the flowers."

He smiles and does a little wave. I head into class. I've done my best to establish that we're not going on a date, but the whole Friday night part has me worried. I need to get Jason alone so we can talk in person, but my throat goes dry when he walks in the room. He looks so great, and he's just in his usual faded jeans and t-shirt. His hair's messy, and I think of pushing my fingers through it. But he doesn't even look at me when he sits down. Worry twists in my stomach.

Mrs. Gipson closes the door and walks forward to start the lecture. I glance over to see if I can catch his eye, but I can't. He continues taking notes and listening. The whole class he's like that, as if an invisible wall has dropped between our desks and he's not even aware of my presence. I feel my eyes getting hot. He's heard what they're saying. And clearly he believes it.

The bell rings, and it's time for lunch. I stand slowly, wondering where to begin, but he stands up right next to me. He looks at me, and it's like a light's been switched on and he finally sees me.

"Braids again?" He asks, lifting one and then letting it drop. I nod. "Those flowers from Trent?" He points at them with his pen.

"Jason..." I say, still not sure how to start.

He waits, looking at me.

"Is something wrong?" Maybe if he goes first, I'll know where to begin.

"Nope," he says.

"There's been sort of a misunderstanding..." I can *not* believe I'm using that word.

His brown eyes narrow. The next class is filing in, and just as I'm starting my next words, Shelly sticks her head through the entrance.

"Hey, kids," she grins. "Jason! I've been looking for you everywhere. Come with me."

247

She grabs his hand and pulls him out into the hall. He doesn't look back as he allows her to drag him out. I slowly follow them, and when I reach the door, I turn toward the cafeteria. Looking back, I see Shelly slipping her hands into his back pockets and smiling, moving in close.

Jason won't even look at me, and I turn away, trying not to cry. I can't believe this is happening. Clearly he thinks I'm going on a real date with Trent. Somehow the whole dumb school does. And clearly he thinks it means something to me, which it doesn't. Shelly's right. I've seriously got mental problems when it comes to guys.

My eyes are damp, and I wish I could hit my own self over the head with my books. I should've told Trent no on Sunday. I should've told him no today. Forget the coffee, I don't want to talk. Why is he so persistent? What could he possibly have to say?

After school, Shelly's bouncing in her seat again. "Fri-day!" she sings. "We're going out on Fri-day!"

"You and Jason?"

"Ye-ah!"

"Great," I say looking down, feeling those tears again.

"So what's the deal, Harley? You didn't even tell me about this weekend."

I jump. Did Jason tell her I was at the creek?

"I'm sorry. It was just a coincidence."

Shelly frowns. "Coincidence?"

"I didn't know he was going to be there."

"Well, I figured that. I mean, what was he doing? Begging her to run away with him? I mean, sure he's hot and all, but your dad's a reverend. There's such a thing as boundaries. That's one of the first books Mom got after—"

"Hang on. You're talking about my mom?"

"Who else? Stephanie said there was some big deal about Ricky being at your house Saturday night. Did they bring up him running around in a towel, too?"

"No." I rub my forehead. I've got the worst headache.

"So what happened? And why didn't you tell me?"

"It all happened so fast, and I didn't know what to say." I can't tell her I discussed the whole thing with Jason instead.

Jason, who'd listened patiently and stroked my hair. Who'd held me close and kissed me. That kiss... I want to die. I have to make him understand what's really going on with Trent. That I don't care about him anymore, and it's *not* a date.

"Stephanie says they were in the car together late at night, and your mom didn't deny any of it."

"Yeah," I say, thinking maybe I can go to his house.

"Well? What do you think?"

"About what?"

"Harley! About the whole thing! I mean, Ricky's really hot, and they *are* all into yoga and massage and stuff."

"No," I say. "The answer is no. Nothing happened."

"I know. Your mom is totally into your geeky dad, I get it." Then she pauses. "Actually I don't get it."

I shake my head. "It doesn't matter. It's not true."

"What if they were like doing some yoga move." Shelly's voice gets this mysterious tone. "Like tantric. And he accidentally... you know... fell on her. And his hand—"

"Shut. Up!" I shout. My chest feels like it might explode. "You've got the dirtiest mind. And it's seriously pissing me off!"

"Harley! I'm only kidding," she says, reaching out to stroke my hand. "It's okay, you can talk to me. I've been there. Remember?"

"I'm not *there*. My mom is not your dad!"

Silence fills the car, and despite my anger, I feel a tinge of guilt. As much as her words hurt me, it's cruel to bring up her dad like that. I remember how she cried, her broken heart, how much it changed her.

We're quiet a moment longer. Then we both speak at once.

"I'm sorry," we say. Then we both look down.

"It's not true," I say quietly.

"But if it's not," she says. "Then why won't your mom just deny it?"

"That's just my mom..."

I think about Saturday evening and the way Mr. Perkins questioned her like it was the Salem witch trials or something. I remember his words... *behavior modification*, a *non-repentant spirit*.

"Well, the next time something like this goes down, you'd better tell me," Shelly says. Then she smiles slightly. "You have to let me be there for you. You know, return the favor."

We're in my driveway, and I smile. Then I lean across and hug her. For a moment it's like nothing's changed and we're still little girls. Not teenagers dealing with major life problems.

"Hey," Shelly stops me as I got out. "So you're going out with Trent again Friday?"

I shrug.

"You don't seem as excited as before. Is it all this stuff with your mom?"

"No. I mean, I guess." I can't explain to her about Jason. Not since she's apparently going out with him on Friday. It just makes everything a jillion times worse.

"Maybe you'll get some more of those something-like-spark-ie kisses. Yes?"

I look down, and Shelly smiles. "It's going to be okay, you know."

"Everybody keeps saying it is."

But when I walk in the house, it's all worse. The Benders are here and Dad's waiting in the kitchen.

"Harley, there's been another incident," Dad says. "I have to go to the church for a meeting. It seems, well, Ricky had an appointment with Ms. Jackson this afternoon. And... she says he threatened her."

"What! How? I can't believe it."

"I know. It sounds ridiculous, and not at all like Ricky," Dad says. "But your mom is talking to him, and I think he wants to speak to the session himself."

Mrs. Bender walks over to me and places her hand on my arm. "I know this is hard, but your mother is a virtuous woman," she says.

I stare at her speechless.

"You don't have to go if you'd rather stay home," Dad says. "The Benders have kindly offered—"

"No," I interrupt. "I want to go."

He nods, and I go to my room to change. I want to be present this time. Maybe if Mom sees me and my dad sitting there, she'll realize this is about more than her pride. It's about more than some personal philosophy or individual protest. Or even protecting her job.

When we get to the church, it looks like a Sunday morning service. The grapevine must've been smoking this afternoon because everybody's turned out to hear what Ricky has to say. I walk inside and see my mom on the front row beside her co-defendant. She looks serene. I take a seat behind them, and she doesn't even acknowledge my arrival. She just continues looking straight ahead at the empty pulpit as if my father's standing there delivering one of those sermons she always finds so inspirational. All of the elders and their wives are across the center aisle in the first two rows.

Dad goes and sits on Mom's other side, and I watch as she takes his hand. The Benders are beside me, and I know they're ready to stand up and defend her. Vigorously if need be. Mr. Bowden walks to the center of the room.

"I apologize for the sudden nature of this gathering," he says. "I didn't realize there would be so many interested parties."

He clears his throat and looks down. "Earlier today, we learned that Ricky Marino wanted to address the session about a recent matter. We thought it best to meet here. Of course, since this involves the pastor, members are welcome to be present."

Ricky's jaw is clenched, and he has a strange expression on his face. Mom looks down.

"Mr. Marino, would you like to come forward?"

Ricky stands and goes to Mr. Bowden's side. Mom glances up at him then, and her face is pleading. He turns away from her quickly, and I feel panic tighten my chest.

"I thought I'd just be talking to you men," he says. "I didn't know everyone would be here."

There's a low murmur in the crowd. I look around and see Mrs. Perkins sitting next to Ms. Jackson. They both have smug expressions on their faces, as if they're eagerly awaiting some major dirt. I feel ill at the sight of them.

Trent is nowhere to be seen, and I wonder if he even knows what's happening. I wouldn't know if Dad weren't the pastor. At least, I hope I wouldn't.

Mrs. Turner is sitting in the side pew looking pained. It appears her lips are moving, and I think she's praying quietly. A few of the parishioners who I recognize as Mom's clients are here seeming curious. Several other non-involved, regular members are here. I'm trying to remember if there's ever been an incident in our church of this magnitude. Nope. This is the biggest. The pastor's wife accused of adultery.

Ricky continues speaking. "I just learned this morning that Jackie had been accused of... well, that it had been said she and I were..."

His voice trails off, and I realize he's nervous. My stomach starts to burn. If he's about to clear their names, he should be eager to announce the truth, and he doesn't seem so eager to me.

"The statement was that your relationship is inappropriate," Mr. Bryant says from where the elders sit. "That is all you have to address."

Ricky looks at him. "Jackie said there was more to it than that." Then he looks down. "She says there was some suggestion that her position as an instructor might also be in jeopardy."

I hear throats clearing and Mr. Perkins speaks.

"There was some debate over whether it gives an improper appearance," he says. "With the two of you working so closely together. And in such an intimate field."

I hate him. And his stupid wife. And their stupid insinuations.

I glance in front of me and see my mother look down again. Dad slides his arm around her shoulders.

"Right," Ricky says. "Well... I think I can put all of your minds at ease and clear Jackie at the same time."

I watch as a calm comes over him and wonder what he's about to say. His brow relaxes and he sets his jaw as if he suddenly doesn't care that almost a hundred people have come out to hear his public statement.

"Jackie is a talented teacher, and I've learned so much studying under her," he says. I glance at Mrs. Perkins. She has an evil grin on her face.

"But even more than that," Ricky continues. "She's a compassionate friend, and her heart is so warm."

I watch as Ricky looks down and clears his throat. "It's been a difficult year for me, but she's always been available to talk and give me advice. I'm not sure I would've made it through these past weeks without her." He looks at Mom, and she smiles at him. "And she's so beautiful," he says, like he forgot where we are.

Mrs. Perkins' eyebrows rise. He quickly adds, "But I would never do anything... I couldn't."

He pauses and glances around at all of us. I notice his eyes rest on Ms. Jackson. "You see, I'm not interested in Jackie like that," he says directly to her.

Then he looks at Mr. Bryant. "I wasn't planning a public announcement, but well, the thing is... I'm gay."

Fourteen

The moment Ricky says the two words that clear my mom's name, relief hits me so hard, I nearly laugh out loud. Instead I shoot a glance at Ms. Jackson. Her face has gone red and her eyes are as wide as a cartoon character's. But beside her, Mrs. Perkins is just the opposite. Her eyes are little slits like a snake's, and I imagine she's silently cursing the fact that once again my mom has slipped through her clutches. When Mr. Bowden stands to dismiss the congregation, she jumps to her feet.

"That is *not* the end of this," she shouts. My eyes fly to my mom. Her jaw is set, and now she looks ready to fight. I look at Ricky, and his face says this is exactly what he expected to happen.

"I think we can discuss how to handle this in executive session, Crystal," Mr. Bowden says, clearing his throat. "Since clearly nothing inappropriate was going on."

"Nothing inappropriate!" Mrs. Perkins cries. "Every bit of this is inappropriate! From her sexually charged avocation, to this. Jackie's brought this sin into our midst. She opened the door to this perversion, brought it around our children! And as our pastor's wife, this cannot go unaddressed."

"Unaddressed?" Mrs. Bender jumps to her feet. "And just how do you want it addressed, Crystal? Jackie's done nothing wrong, and this young man doesn't even attend our church. But you've just been waiting for a reason to attack her, haven't you? To put Ted in charge."

"If Ted were in charge, *nothing* like this would have ever occurred," she says. "Now we have this blemish on our church."

I glance at Mom. She's looking down and her eyes have closed, but Ricky simply smiles. My throat feels all tight and painful. I mean, sure, Ricky doesn't go to our church, and I guess some people here think how he lives is wrong. But he's always been sweet around me. I don't feel like I've been subjected to anything.

"If you ask me, she's the blemish," Mrs. B. mutters.

"Ladies," Mr. Bryant's voice cuts through them all. "The issue has been resolved, and everyone is free to leave. Now."

He fixes his eyes on Mrs. Perkins. She presses her lips into a tight line as she sits down again, but her cover is blown. Now everyone knows she'd been out to get my mom, to replace my dad with her husband. She wanted Ricky to be the story of the night, but in the end, it's the truth about her that takes center stage.

The congregation rises and starts slipping out of the pews, making their way to the back amidst a low murmur. Mrs. Bender touches my arm and motions for me to come with her. I'll have to wait until tomorrow to find out what happens next, if Mom'll even talk about it.

The Benders drop me off at my house, and the only thing I can think about is telling Jason. I need to talk to him anyway, to make him understand how I feel and what happened with Trent. I grab my phone and send a text.

> *U there?*
> I wait several seconds, then a whistle.
> *What.*
> *Mom cleared. Ricky gay.*
> *No way.*
> *Way.*
> *Am glad. U OK?*
> *Need to talk. Creek?*
> *No.*

Pain tightens in my chest when I read his response.

> *Need to explain.*
> *Night, HD*
> *Tomorrow.*

I put my phone away and lay on my bed staring at the ceiling. Tears sting in my eyes as I imagine what he must be thinking. That I'm just some flaky chick who's been playing games with him since the day we met. I have to make him understand what's really happening.

But what *is* really happening? Why does Trent care so much about talking to me now, and why do I feel like I need to listen? Is it because he used to be my hottie-future-husband? My hero? I don't owe him anything. Do I? I bite my lip and remember us talking at the creek that night about his mom and her searching his room, his dad and him not feeling like he belonged. I can't just turn my back on him. Can I?

I breathe deeply and focus on tomorrow. Jason and I have talked about so many things before. I'm sure I can explain this to him as well. He just needs to listen to me. And now that this business with Mom is settled, there'll be no more distractions, nothing to get us off track.

Ricky's not at our house the next morning. I walk into the kitchen and look around, but for the first time in almost a year, he's absent. It's funny. I never dreamed I'd miss him, but now that I know the truth, that he was never a threat to my family, I wish he was here. He was funny and sweet to me. He was brave, and he set the record straight for Mom, even thought it meant a big, public display in front of a bunch of strangers—a few of which were hostile. I feel bad for being so mean to him yesterday morning, and I wish I could say I'm sorry. I didn't know it'd be the last time I'd see him.

I see the door to Mom's office is open, so I walk over and look inside. She's sitting in a chair holding a cup of tea.

"Mom?" I ask stepping around the door. "Hey."

She glances up and gives me a small smile. "Hi, Harley," she says softly.

I smile back and sit beside her. She doesn't speak, but she reaches over and smoothes my hair. The last time I spoke to her, we were shouting, too.

"I didn't hear you come in last night," I say. "Dad came in, but he was alone."

She nods and sips her tea. "I needed to discuss how we'd finish the semester with Ricky."

"It's weird not having him here. What's going to happen now?"

"He'll probably just do his last few sessions at the school in Glennville. It's a little awkward for him coming here now."

I nod and give her a grin. "Mrs. Perkins really showed her true colors last night, didn't she?"

Mom doesn't smile. "A lot of people agree with her."

"But you didn't do anything wrong."

"It's a very divisive issue, Harley," she says, smoothing my hair again.

I'm quiet a moment, and I think of Dad reading that *Issues* book. I look at her sitting there, legs crossed, hair swept back in a long pony tail.

"Why didn't you just tell the elders Ricky was gay?"

She smiles at me like I'm very young. "He asked me not to tell anyone."

"Why?"

"Oh, he had his reasons." Then she laughs softly. "I think he didn't want to cause any conflicts for your dad at church if it could be avoided."

"That really worked out." But I'm not satisfied with her answer. "You could've told them it was a secret—just to get yourself off the hook."

Mom shakes her head. "Ricky was struggling with telling his own family. I couldn't betray his trust like that."

I look down at the floor. "But by not telling, Dad could've lost his job. And we might've had to move-"

"Daddy wouldn't have lost his job." Mom sighs. "And I'm sorry you were worried. But there are some things you're too young to understand, Harley."

That makes me angry, and I look straight at her. "You say that, but it's not true. I understand a lot. And you did choose him over us."

"I didn't choose anyone. Your daddy and I were trying to decide what was best."

"Whether it was better that people thought you were having an affair? So being gay's worse than adultery now?"

Mom just looks at me. Her expression is weary, and I don't want to argue with her. But I still don't understand her staying silent.

"Ricky only had a few weeks left in his training," she says softly. "And then he'd be gone."

I can tell by her tone she's trying to diffuse our disagreement, but I'm not finished.

"You could've told me," I say. "You never tell me things."

"Oh, Harley," she sighs. "It would've been unfair to burden you with all that. And I do tell you things."

I hear Shelly's horn beeping, and I give up this round. But her words aren't true. She's kept me at arm's distance since Ricky arrived, and I feel like there's a lot I still don't know. We aren't finished here, but I have to get to school.

Shelly's pouty when I got in the car. I flop into the seat and pull my bag onto my lap wondering if she's heard the news. I would think it'd be all over town by now, and I half expect her to be excited, ready for me to fill in all the details.

"What's wrong with you?" I ask.

She breathes loudly. "Jason."

"What about Jason?"

"He cancelled our date Friday." Shelly pokes her lip out and drives slowly. I try to think of something to say. Other than *Yay!*

"Did he say why?"

"Just… he thinks things are moving too fast."

"Well," I search for something reassuring. "At least you only went out a few times. It's not like you were super serious, right?"

"I guess," she sighs. We're at school, and Shelly's slowly circling the parking lot. "Now what'll I do Friday?"

Just then Reagan walks by with her little brother Aaron. As they pass, I think about how Aaron always used to hang around when we went to Reagan's house as kids, and how he always made me laugh. He's only a sophomore, but he's got a fall birthday so he's closer to our age. We've lost touch, and watching him, I try to decide if he's gotten taller. Something's changed. He seems more confident or something, and as we climb out of Shelly's car, he looks back and smiles at her. My eyebrows go up, and I look at my friend. He's no Jason, but that's a great smile.

Shelly perks up. "Who's that?"

"Aaron? You remember. Reagan's little brother?"

"I thought he had braces."

I do a double-take. "That's what's different! He must've got them off." I remember that feeling—*freedom!*

"See ya later, Harley!" She skips ahead to catch up with Reagan and her newly transformed little brother.

"Assertiveness, pass," I quietly note as I follow them toward the building. "And that might be a record."

Just then I hear someone hurrying to catch up with me and turn back. It's Jason, and my heart does a flip.

"Hey," he says, slowing down to walk with me.

"Hey," I say, remembering to breathe.

"So Ricky's gay," he says. "Wow."

"I know! I feel like, so blind."

"Well, I never expected it, but I know you're glad it's over."

His eyes meet mine, and my knees go weak.

"Yeah," I say.

We walk a little further in silence. Now I feel so awkward, but I can't be weird around Jason. I have to talk to him about everything. I look up and see Trent going into his building and wonder if Jason sees him, too.

"So you're really going out with him again?" Yep. Jason sees him too.

I shrug. "It's not like a date or anything."

He stops and catches my arm. "Then what is it?"

He's frustrated, and that pain is in my chest again. I don't know what to say, and standing here with him, I don't want to be with anyone else ever. Not for any amount of time, like we agreed way back on that very first day at lunch.

"It's nothing," I stammer. "I mean, it was so confusing. He said he needs to talk to me."

"About what?"

"I don't know. I was super-mad at him after all that stuff happened with Mom, but he apologized. Then he gave me this flower..."

Jason's eyes narrow, and I can't believe I just said that. Trent giving me a flower is like the worst thing I could say. It sounds like I still care about him, and I *so* don't. At least not the way I care about Jason.

He turns and we start walking again. He doesn't say a word, and I can't think of a thing to say either. So much for no weirdness.

"I'm not going out with Shelly anymore," he finally says.

"She told me."

We walk a little further in silence. I see his jaw clench, then he finally speaks again. "OK, well, I gotta get to class."

"Wait." I catch his arm. "It doesn't mean anything to me."

"Then don't go."

I hesitate. "But it seems really important to him."

"Then do what you want, Harley." He shakes my hand off his arm and turns to leave. "Go out with him."

"Jason. Wait!"

But he doesn't look at me again, and it hurts so bad to see him walk away. I hug my books tighter against my stomach. My reasons are all stupid and lame, and if I can't explain to myself why I didn't tell Trent no, why should I expect Jason to understand? He's just understood so much. I guess I thought he would again. And I guess that's my problem. Assertiveness fail.

Jason disappears around the corner, and when I blink down, two tears hit my cheeks.

From the start, my coffee *non-date* with Trent is like all our other actual dates. We meet up at the coffee shop, and he's extremely polite as always. He apparently comes here a lot because he knows exactly what to order and even picks out a caramel macchiato for me that he says will make me camp out for the shop to open tomorrow.

"I never knew you were such a coffee bean," I say, as I sip the creamy drink. It really is delicious, and I just don't even want to know how many calories are in it.

"Good coffee is like good... um—"

"Ultimate Frisbee?"

He laughs. "Better. And by the way, I really like that about you."

"What?"

"You're funny." He looks down, then he looks at me more serious. "But more than that. You care about other people and helping them find a way to belong."

I don't know if that's true, but okay. I glance around the shop. It's very snug and full of yellow light. Several skinny-legged tables and chairs are arranged by the window in the front, and in the back are several large, velvety armchairs with smaller tables positioned around them.

It's more a place where college kids hang out, as all our friends tend to go to the Shadow Freeze, the ice cream and burger joint a half-mile up the road. Trent orders a skinny latte for himself, which doesn't seem fair since guys have much higher metabolisms than girls, and then he takes my arm. He escorts me to a plush, velvet couch in the back that has a long table in front of it. I sit on the couch, and he pulls up a stool to sit across from me.

"This better?" he smiles.

"It's great," I smile back at him. And not so long ago it would've been a dream come true, but now all I can think about is Jason.

He studies the menu, and I study his face. He really does have a sweet little mouth. It's kind of shiny like he uses lip gloss or something. And as usual, he's dressed just so. I like the shirt he's wearing. Most guys don't go for madras, but Trent looks very fashionable in it with his jeans.

"You always dress really well," I say.

"Hey, thanks," he smiles. "You too. I like the braids."

I can't believe he actually noticed for once. "Thanks."

"Your hair's so shiny," he says. "Do you use a special conditioner?"

"No. Just whatever's on sale."

We're quiet again, and a barista stops at our table. She asks if we want any biscotti or muffins, but I shake my head emphatically. Trent gets shortbread, and I watch as he breaks it into small pieces. I'm ready to get to the bottom of whatever he has to tell me, but first I excuse myself to go to the restroom.

As I walk back, I notice he's texting again. He's all happy like before, and whatever he's reading must be super-funny because he's almost snorting.

"Hey," I say.

He jumps and puts his phone away. "Hey."

"Who was that?" I ask. He'd better not start with all the secretive texting, or I'm taking off.

"Oh… it's just… I get this joke of the day thing. I hadn't checked it today."

"Really."

"I'm sorry," he says. "I'll put it up."

I remember running into Stephanie in the bathroom at school and her asking about us dating. I wonder if she's the mysterious texter. If she's been sending him messages all along. Whatever he claims, he looked really sad when they broke up, so it's possible she's trying to get back with him. Every few minutes I hear the whisper of his phone vibrating. He ignores it and tries to make small talk.

"I'm glad all that stuff worked out with your mom," he says.

"Yeah," I say, distracted by his humming phone.

"And I really do feel bad my mom made all that trouble. It wasn't cool."

"It's not your fault, and you said she'd kind of put you through it."

He nods, looking embarrassed. "Right. I forgot."

"You can't help how your parents act."

He looks at me, and for a split second it seems like he's about to say something. Instead he takes a bite of shortbread. I sip my rich drink. Then he laughs and reaches across the table.

"You've got foam."

I jump and wipe my nose with one of the paper napkins on the table. "How embarrassing."

"Happens to the best of us!"

I smile and watch him dunk a piece of cookie in his latte. He puts it in his mouth and smiles back, raising his eyebrows. I study his perfect hair, his ideal fashion sense, his great taste. All at once, I have the strangest thought about my former-future-husband. What if Trent isn't anybody's former-future-husband? At least not in the way you'd expect.

I shake my head and look at my drink. The caramel clings to the edges of my cup, and I think of how he and Stephanie had always looked way intense. I remember them holding hands and leaning against her locker, her smiling up in his face, their noses almost touching. It was a sight that used to make me ache with longing.

Stephanie Miller would never spend that much time in a platonic relationship. At least, I don't think she would. I take another sip and look back up at him. He's finished the shortbread and almost his coffee, too. Then he glances up at me and smiles.

"What?" he says.

I realize I'm staring and look down. "Back on Sunday you wanted to talk," I say. "What about?"

He swirls his cup a few seconds then puts it down. "I wish we could go somewhere else first."

I study my half-drunk beverage and decide I'm finished. "This was really good, but I feel full all of a sudden. Or I've had enough."

His blue eyes move from my hand to my face, and then meet my eyes. Something is very open and vulnerable in his expression. He's like a little boy who just saw something super-scary or something he really wants to do. I can't tell which it is. Maybe both?

He reaches across the table and I take his hand. We walk out to our cars, and he says he'll follow me to my house. I shrug and agree, and once we're there, he meets me on our front steps.

"Would you walk with me?" he asks. "This is a nice neighborhood for walking."

I glance up the street at the quiet sidewalks and dim yellow streetlights. I've never really thought about it, but it's true.

"Sure," I say. We start walking in the direction of the newer houses, in the direction of the creek. He never takes my hand, so I cross one arm over my waist as I look ahead. His phone buzzes again softly.

"You think that's something urgent?" I ask nodding toward his pocket.

"Huh?" At least he pretends not to know what the strange sound is. "Oh... No. It's just a friend."

"The same friend who was texting you at the movie?"

"You saw that?"

"Mm hm."

We're quiet again, walking, but I'm growing tired of this. "So is it a girlfriend?"

"Huh?"

"The texting?"

"Oh, no. No," he looks down. "It's just this guy." In the dim light I swear I see his face turn pink. "I mean... yeah," he continues, like he's just learning to speak English. "This guy. He's always forwarding funny jokes and stuff."

"A guy?" I ask. "Is it somebody I know?"

"Uh... no." Trent seems nervous for the first time all night, and I feel that wave of something coming. The same something I felt in the coffee shop.

"I like jokes," I say, trying to ease the tension. "Read me one."

"Oh, well... it's not something you'd get."

"Too dirty?" I smile.

"No, it's not that. It's just inside stuff. You know."

I don't, but I don't question him.

———

"I thought maybe it was Stephanie."

"Stephanie? Why would she be texting me?"

"Oh you know, because you guys dated and… well, she asked about you."

"What did she say?"

"Nothing, really." I try to remember what she did say. "She just asked if we were going out again. That's all."

He seems to relax at that. We'd turned while we were walking, and now we're back at my house again standing by his car.

"Harley," he starts then stops. He reaches forward and lifts the door handle, holding it open for me. "Can I talk to you just a little bit more?"

"Sure." I shrug and get in the car. He runs around and gets in, too, but he doesn't start the engine. Instead he faces me. Then he turns away again. Then he takes a deep breath and faces me again.

"You know that thing about your mom?" he starts. "What did you think about that?"

"What?" His behavior is so bizarre, I don't understand the question.

"I mean the thing with Ricky and all. What did you think?"

"You mean about whether my mom and Ricky were having an affair? I was humiliated. And scared. And mad—"

"Not that," he interrupts. Then his voice drops. "I mean, about him saying he's gay."

I shrug. "I don't know. I haven't really thought about it."

It's true. I've thought a lot about my mom, and I've been angry with her for choosing loyalty to Ricky over Dad and me. But I haven't really thought much about the other part of the story. Other than how Ricky's revelation also outed Mrs. Perkins.

"What if..." Trent's voice is so quiet I have to lean in close. "What if someone you know is like that?"

"Well, I know Ricky. I mean he's been at my house for almost a year—"

"I mean, what if it's someone..." he looks up at me then, and his lavender-blue eyes are serious. "Like me."

He's staring at me, watching my every move, waiting for my reaction.

"Trent," I feel like I'm waking up from a dream, but not a completely unexpected dream. Still, I'm not sure I'm hearing it right. "Are you saying you're—"

"Like Ricky," he says.

I just stare at him. "You're gay?" I whisper.

He looks down. "Yes. I mean, I think so."

"You think so?" I don't want to make him feel weird, but it seems like that would be something you'd know.

He nods.

"But you dated Stephanie for so long."

"Yeah," he sort of laughs. "She probably knows. I mean, because I never... I never wanted to—"

"But why would you think that?" I interrupt. For some reason, a part of me can't accept this so fast. Not about my one-time Mr. Right, hottie-future-husband. As far as I know, he's only dated Stephanie. And me, sort of. I guess. Of course, he's only been in Shadow Falls eighteen months, but still. It's too soon for me to accept he's on the other team.

"You just know," he says.

I shake my head. "But... how?"

"I don't know. You just do," he says again. "Like, well, look at you. You're really beautiful and sweet. And I should want to kiss you, right?"

"I guess." I feel self-conscious that he said I'm beautiful and that he's thinking about kissing me. Then I remember our one awful kiss. "But that wasn't... maybe you just need more practice."

"But I don't want to practice," he says looking at me. "At least, not with you."

I feel my face get hot. "So was I like your last try? Did I make you decide—"

He starts to laugh. "No! That's not how it works."

He laughs a little more, then he stops and leans his head back. He takes a deep breath and turns to me with a smile like I'm somebody new. Somebody he's just met for the first time and not Harley Andrews who he's known since sophomore year.

"I can't believe I just told you that," he says. "That I just said it out loud to you."

I can't believe it either. Even if I almost guessed it, I'm still not ready to believe it.

"Why did you?" I ask.

"I don't know," he says. "You're just... you've always been so nice to me. Like after class and stuff. You always seem to care. And you have the sweetest smile."

Wow. Talk about backfires.

"And that day outside the gym, remember that?" he asks.

I nod. How could I forget? I've been living on that day since it happened.

"I saw you were different from them. From Stephanie," he says. "I knew you'd understand what it's like to feel afraid, or like you don't fit in."

I remember our conversation the night of our one awful kiss, and him talking about his dad and being on the football team. I glance up at him, and realize how much he's saying to me now. Like he's finally getting a chance to speak.

"Then when I saw how your mom was with Ricky," he says. "I figured if he was safe with her, if he could trust her…"

"Then you could trust me." I finish softly.

"Can I trust you, Harley?" He looks at me, and again, his eyes are so earnest. He's just told me what might be the most important thing in his life, and I'm not sure I deserve to know it. I suddenly feel very protective of him.

"Yes! Of course," I say. "But what does that mean?"

"I just… I'm still figuring things out," he says, looking down again. "And I'm not ready for everybody to know yet."

"But you just told me."

"I know, but that's because, well, with the texting and the kissing, I couldn't keep lying to you."

"You could've just not asked me out again." It seems the most obvious solution to me.

"I know. But," he hesitates. "I needed to tell somebody. And I like talking to you."

He likes talking to me? This is the most he's said to me in like, ever.

"So you didn't tell Stephanie?"

"I couldn't tell her this. And my mom has no idea," he pauses. "If she knew…"

He doesn't finish the sentence, but I have a feeling I can guess what she'd say. After what he's told me about her and what she tried to do to my mom, I feel like I can understand him not wanting to tell her. At least not until he's ready.

"So I'm the only person who knows?"

"And Ricky."

"Ricky!"

"Yeah. I kind of asked him for his advice."

That makes sense, I guess.

"And now he's gone," Trent says softly.

I glance at him and the sadness is back in his eyes. It reminds me of how I feel about Jason. I miss him so much.

"Jason's dad's a psychiatrist."

"What's that supposed to mean?" His eyes flash in a way I've never seen before.

"I mean, Jason just said he's a good listener."

"It's his dad, Harley."

I want to die. I feel like the biggest idiot on the planet. "I'm sorry. I didn't mean…"

"I don't have mental problems."

"No! Of course you don't."

I'm quiet then. I look down at my hands and wonder if I should get out of the car now. We sit a moment in awkward silence, until Trent chuckles.

"You're not so good at this," he says.

I exhale in relief. "I know! I just... I don't know what to say. I'm sorry."

"It's okay," he says, reaching over and tugging my braid.

I smile, relieved. "But I won't tell anybody. You can trust me."

"Thanks."

"I'd better go now." I reach for the door handle.

It doesn't make sense, considering how I feel about Jason and how my feelings for Trent have evolved, but I really want to go inside and cry. Not because my heart is broken exactly, but because I spent so much time dreaming about a future husband who never really existed.

But before I can go, Trent leans forward and this time, instead of a peck on the cheek, he pulls me into a hug. It's warm and grateful, and as I hug him back, I realize it's all okay. I'm not angry or hurt or anything. I'm glad he told me. And so I spent a year daydreaming, praying, and obsessing about a guy who has absolutely zero interest in me that way. Or possibly any girl for that matter. I'm not the first female in history to do it.

Then I realize what else just happened. I just sat in a car outside my house, alone, with a boy who just told me the biggest secret of his life. A secret he asked me not to tell anyone, and I agreed. And then he pulled me into a long embrace, which I suppose to anyone outside probably looked like we were making out. And boy, would they be wrong.

I turn and stare at my house for a few seconds and consider running inside to wake my mom. I want to hug her and cry and tell her I understand now. But I don't. It's late, and I'm exhausted. We can talk in the morning, and after that, I can't wait to find Jason. I close my eyes, picturing his face. Tomorrow I'll find him and kiss him and tell him we can be together, and we'll be so happy.

Fifteen

I open my eyes the next morning to the sound of my phone. It's a text from Shelly.

Party 2night. David's. U in?

I think about it. A party at David's is perfect. Jason's sure to be there.

Sure, I text her back.

Then I quickly type in Jason's number.

Party 2night. David's. U going?

I wait a few seconds, but there's no reply. I roll onto my stomach and look at the clock. It's later than the morning when he took me to breakfast. I lean my head on my hand and exhale. I shake my phone, then I nearly throw it across the room when it whistles.

Yes.

I squeal, I'm so excited to see the word. It's like he's standing here saying it in person. My fingers tremble a little when I type back.

CUthere?

Dunno. Maybe.

That isn't exactly what I hoped to read, but it'll have to do for now.

OK! :o) I type back and immediately start planning.

So he's still a little mad, that's understandable. I'll spend the day getting all fixed up, and then tell him the good news tonight in person, face to face, looking my absolute best. Once he knows what's really going on, he'll understand. Then he'll smile and lean forward... I close my eyes and lie back on my bed imagining his soft lips touching mine. Mmm.

I'm still smiling when my phone whistles again. I flip over and grab it, but it's Trent.

Party 2night. David's. U going?

I stare at the phone and think about last night and all he told me. Everything's changed between us, but somehow I like it better. I wonder if this means we'll talk more now or what exactly our relationship will be like. I guess we're just friends. Just really good friends. I smile.

Yep. I text back. *CU there?*
U bet!

So it's Saturday morning, and Mom's sitting in her office drinking tea. I go straight in and drop to my knees beside her, wrapping my arms around her waist and hugging close to her. She sets her mug down and drapes her arms across my back. Then she leans forward and I feel her kiss my head.

"What's this all about?" she asks.

"I love you very much," I say. "And I'm sorry."

"What?"

"You were right. I really didn't understand anything."

She's quiet a minute and then she starts rubbing my back.

"It's okay," she says. She slides her cool palm over my forehead and smoothes it over my hair. "I hope at least you've seen how destructive it is to make snap decisions about people. To set your mind on things being on way or the other and then locking people into roles and stereotypes."

I sit up and nod. "Right. Stereotypes."

I'm pretty sure she's not talking about me at this point, but then her eyes meet mine. "I love you, Harley. And I've been thinking a lot about what you said."

"Which part?"

"About me not telling you things." Her eyes move around my face before returning to mine. Then she smiles. "You're a young woman now, and I should include you more."

"It's okay," I say. "I'm learning to trust you."

I lay my head on her lap again and let her stroke my cheek. I think about what Jason said that night when I told him about Ricky and my mom. That I might be proud of her before it's all over. I'm not quite ready for that to be the case, but it's possible.

"Mom?" I hesitate before continuing.

"Yes?"

"The church, Dad, is against who Ricky is." *And Trent*, I think. "So how'd you... I mean, what did you say to him?"

She's quiet a minute, her hand still on my head. Then I hear her sigh.

"God can do amazing things," she says. "It's not our job to put Him in a box and decide what He can do or with whom. It's our job to encourage and pray and love."

I sit up and look at her. I don't know what to say, but I feel like I understand what she means. "So you didn't say anything to him?"

"You know," she becomes thoughtful. "Jesus met people where they were. He didn't make them come to him."

"He got called names for it, too."

"It's true," she smiles and tucks a piece of hair back into my messy braid. "But it's the best way to live your life. It's a cliché now, but the philosophy was around long before the T-shirt."

"Right." I nod, ready to say it with her.

"You have to be the change you want to see in the world," she says.

I snort and then giggle.

"What?"

"Gandhi," I say.

"So?"

"I was expecting 'What Would Jesus Do' or something."

"Oh." Her face relaxes and she smiles. "Well, of course. That goes without saying."

I look at her a moment. I don't want to fight, but I know I have to get things straight with her. I have to finish telling her how I feel, even though I'm way less angry about it all now.

"It felt like you chose him over me," I say. "Like as soon as Ricky showed up, he was all you were interested in."

She's quiet a moment, and then she looks down at her hands. "You're right," she says. "I did get distracted by Ricky's problems. And I'm sorry."

I can't believe it. I've been so angry, but that's all I ever wanted her to say. I put my head down on her lap again. I'm not really crying or anything, but my eyes are wet.

"Oh, Harley," she sighs. "You mean more to me than anything. You just... you didn't need me as much then."

I take a deep breath and think about her words. "I was just so worried."

She smoothes my hair back. "I know. And I'm so sorry for making you worry. I really am." Then she smiles and lifts my chin. "Forgive me?"

I meet her eyes and my frustration releases. I nod, and I feel like smiling now, too. I *am* proud of her.

———

"So last night," her voice lightens. "Was the do-over date any better than the first one?"

She starts pulling out my leftover braid, and my hair falls in crimped waves around my shoulders.

"It was... different." I wonder if my promise to Trent includes not telling my mom. It probably does, but I wish she could know how similar our situations are.

"Well, he's very cute at least. And a sharp dresser."

"Yeah, but it's not going to happen."

"No?" she frowns.

"I just... well... I really like Jason. A lot." I say. And that's the truth.

"Oh. Well, if that's what it is," she smiles. "There's just no explaining attraction."

"Yep. Sometimes it just crashes right into you."

The rest of the day is devoted to party-prep and Operation Get Jason Back. I'm wearing the dress I had on when he asked me to the luau. He always liked that one. And the two little braids just at the top. Again, very *Vogue*. Everything's perfect for when I see him tonight. My heart actually rises at the thought. I'll tell him how I feel, and then we'll sneak away and do some make-up kissing. I smile as butterflies fill my stomach. Hopefully a lot of make-up kissing—I mean, we've been apart almost a week!

I tell Mom I'm heading to David's for a little while, and she doesn't question me. She's known

David's parents since forever, but I'm pretty sure they don't talk much. Of course, I leave out the part that they're out of town and his older brother sneaked a keg for the party. I feel bad about that since we've just gotten back on track, and I don't normally go to keggers. For one, Pete would be so disappointed if he had to arrest me, and for two, I'd be grounded for life. But this is an extremely special case, and once I find Jason and straighten things out with him, we'll ditch the party and run to the creek.

I love that thought.

I decide to walk because it's such a great night, warm and a little breezy. David's place is in the older part of our neighborhood, but it's one of the few larger homes in that area. Trent's getting there just as I'm walking up, extremely well-dressed as always. It's funny because now that I know his secret, he acts like we're the best of friends. You'd think we grew up together, he's so relaxed and chatty.

Everyone's in full party-mode when we walk through the door. David has rainbow disco lights shining everywhere and music is blasting. I look around trying to spot Jason, and I notice Trent looking around as well.

I lean over and shout in his ear. "So when you get to a party, you're just like me?"

"What do you mean?"

"You're checking out all the guys, too?"

Trent looks at me strangely for a second. Then he laughs and throws an arm around my neck. He pulls me close and kisses the top of my head in such a way that a few people hoot at us. Then he lets me go and smiles, and it's the first time I've seen him look genuinely happy.

"I'll see you in a minute." He shouts, and I watch him disappear through the bodies.

I push through the crowd in the opposite direction. Jason has to be around here somewhere. I see Shelly and Aaron dancing with their foreheads pressed together. Shelly glances at me, and I give her a little wave. I keep walking and looking around. Finally I see him leaning against the low wall beside the keg. He looks up and our eyes met, and for a moment, I can't breathe. I want to run up to him and tell him how awful everything is without him, tell him he never has to worry about me getting mixed up with Trent again and that we should go to the creek or at least run outside and start making out right away.

Instead I stroll over acting casual. He looks so great wearing jeans and a maroon t-shirt, his brown hair's a little shaggy around his face. It's funny how he looks amazing to me in anything now.

"Hey," I smile. My heart is that little hummingbird again.

"Hey." He looks away, and my smile fades. He's still mad at me, and I watch as he pours himself another drink.

"Beer?" he offers.

———

"No, thanks."

"Right. You don't drink, curse. You make all the right choices."

I press my lips together. I let that go because he's still mad, and I know he doesn't mean it. "I was looking for you. I hoped we could talk."

"Another talk?" He frowns and shakes his head. "You're going to have to find a new talk-buddy, H.D."

"No. Jason, it's more than that." I reach forward and touch his arm, lowering my voice. "Let's get out of here."

He shakes his head and pulls his arm away. I watch him lift the cup to his lips, and I start to feel very frustrated. This is not going how I'd planned it.

"Why not?" I ask. "What's going on?"

"Just got a lot on my mind tonight." He looks down and leans back against the wall. I step forward and slide my hand into his, lacing our fingers. It feels so nice.

"What's on your mind?" I ask gently. "Your mom?"

"No. But thanks for reminding me."

"I'm sorry. I just… I was hoping—"

"Look. I'm done with that. I'm not playing games anymore."

I start to speak, but a loud voice from behind cuts me off.

"What's up, Harley?" It's Stephanie. She pushes herself between Jason and me, removing my hand from his and replacing it with her own. "What are you doing with my date?"

"Your date?" I blink. "You're—"

"With Jason." She finishes, and her tone says back off.

"I didn't know." This time when Jason glances up at me, my eyes are stinging with unshed tears. He's going out with Stephanie now?

Shelly and Aaron walk up to the keg and for a second the three of us listen as they argue over whether Shelly stood guard while David stuffed Aaron into a locker freshman year. I might be funny, but I can't laugh. I feel like my heart's breaking, and I just wish they'd go away.

"You're wrong," Shelly argues with her eyes closed as she pours a drink.

"I'm *not* wrong." Aaron leans toward her.

"It wasn't David, it was Brian," she giggles.

"I think I'd remember—" Aaron starts.

"Well, even if it was David," Shelly cuts him off. "Here. Let him buy you a beer." She grins and holds up a cup. He smiles and leans forward to plant his lips on hers.

"So where's Trent?" Stephanie's loud voice cuts through the commotion.

Shelly turns her face toward us and frowns. My throat's tight, and I don't think I can speak. I can't believe I've lost Jason. And to Stephanie of all people.

"So that's it," I say to him softly, trying not to cry. "You don't want me…"

I can't finish. His eyes catch mine, and for a moment it's just us.

But Stephanie isn't through. "Have you kissed him yet?" she asks loudly. I glance at her and see she's starting to giggle. "Are you and your mom doing some special outreach to gays now?"

It's like the room went silent just at that moment, and her words echo through David's house. Shelly freezes and my eyes widen.

"Trent's gay?" Shelly asks, and her voice feels very loud to me. Then she starts to giggle, too. "Oh my god! Of course! That totally explains—"

"Shut up, Shelly."

"What?" I hear Aaron's loud voice. "Trent's gay?"

The news travels like a hot potato from person to person through the room, and I see Jason remove his hand from Stephanie's and take a step toward me. But none of it matters when I hear the voice behind me.

"Harley?"

It's Trent.

I spin around and see him standing there, staring at me. The look on his face is pure betrayal. My heart slams to the floor.

"Trent!" I step forward.

"I thought you said you wouldn't tell." His expression makes my stomach hurt. "I thought I could trust you."

"You can! I didn't..."

But before I can finish my sentence, he turns and starts pushing through the bodies. It only takes me a second to wake up and start pushing after him. But he's too fast for me. He's out the door and gone before I can catch up to him. I follow, but by the time I make it to the sidewalk, he's already pulling his car away. I watch as the Accord pauses at the corner before exiting the cul de sac and turning toward the main street through the neighborhood. And then he's gone.

I pull out my phone and try texting him.

Talk to me.

I wait several seconds. No response.

PLS.

No response.

I start to feel panicky. I have to find him and tell him Stephanie simply guessed it. I didn't tell anyone. But will it even matter? He didn't want anyone to know. He trusted me and now everybody'll know. It'll only be a matter of hours, if that long.

Oh, please help me… Please let me find him.

I keep walking in the direction of my house. I decide if I don't hear back from him by the time I get home, I'll ride my bike to his house. It's out of the neighborhood, but it isn't far. I try again.

I didn't tell! I text. *She guessed!*

More seconds pass. Silence. I let out a frustrated scream and want to throw my phone, but I look up and see I'm almost at my house. I run the rest of the way, toss my shoes on the porch and set off on my bike, riding back the way I came. David's house goes by, then the entrance to Shadow Falls. I pass the hydrangea bush at the corner of Main and Spring, down the highway to the newer development. Cars keep whizzing by. I hate riding on the highway, outside the safety of our neighborhood, but I have to find Trent. I have to find him and tell him what happened. The look in his eyes at David's... I push harder. He has to know the truth.

As I get closer to his house, I slow down. I can see the porch light on in the driveway, but the car isn't there. He didn't come home. Well, of course he didn't. It isn't like home is the most welcoming place in his life. It isn't like he'd go running there if he were hurt and betrayed. *Oh, God.* I pray again, chewing my lip. *Where is he?* I try again.

PLS. I text. *Talk to me.*

No response.

Then I call. The phone rings and rings, but he won't answer.

I sit there several minutes and look around, trying to think. I don't know what to do, so I turn back toward Shadow Falls. I slowly pedal back to the neighborhood, past the party, past the quiet church.

I'm getting closer to home when I consider one last possibility. I'm not sure he'll go there, but it's worth a shot.

When I get closer to the creek, I feel my heart jump as I see it. Trent's car.

I stand in the pedals and push as hard as I can to close the distance faster. I jump off and run up the small hill, and there he is, sitting beside the tree, looking out at the dark water. I drop to my knees beside him, panting from the ride and from running. After a few moments I start to catch my breath. Soon, the only sound is the constant movement of the creek. The nonstop musical trickling that continues, regardless of what's happening up here on its banks.

Several long minutes pass. Trent never looks at me, never acknowledges my presence. And then he speaks.

"This really is a nice spot," he says. "I remembered it from that night we came here."

"I've been looking for you everywhere," I say. "I called… you didn't answer my texts."

He motions to the car. "Left my phone."

I watch him in silence until eventually he looks back at me. It isn't a look of anger or even betrayal now. Just a question.

"Was this about your mom? Is that why you did it?"

"No!" I gasp, near tears. "Trent, you have to believe me. I didn't tell them. I didn't…"

He looks down.

"It was Stephanie," I continue, my stomach in knots. "She was there with Jason, and I guess she got mad at me for talking to him. And I think she was drinking. She just said it, and..."

He nods but doesn't respond. Then he sort of laughs. "I guess I expected that," he says.

"What do you mean?"

He looks up at me again. "I was so relaxed and happy. I thought it was all going to be okay. But I was still lying."

"But it can be okay," I say. "Why can't it? So what if they know. It doesn't matter."

"It does here," he says. "It does to my mom. And to some people..."

"No. It's just... you know how it is. You're just the latest gossip. It'll blow over."

He shakes his head. "You don't understand, Harley. You don't know what it's like to be... a blemish."

It hurts to hear him say that. *Stupid Mrs. Perkins.*

"You're not that. You're a wonderful, kind person," I say, thinking how this possibly puts me against Dad. I don't know how I feel about that, but I know I'm not wrong. Trent's not a sin or an abomination, and I won't let anyone say that about him.

He exhales deeply before looking away at the creek again. "I hate this place," he says.

I don't know what to say. I've never heard anyone say they hate Shadow Falls. Everyone I know loves it here. It's so clean and safe, with sidewalks and streetlights. And the adults are always saying how our neighborhoods are so well-manicured, and even though some of the newer residents in Shadow Creek have house alarms, it's mainly for show. Ours is the kind of town where you can leave houses and cars unlocked most anytime and nothing will happen. People are always moving here to get away from whatever bothers them about the city, and they all agree it's perfect. At least, it's always seemed perfect before.

"What will you do?" I ask softly.

He shrugs. "Tell my mom."

"You will? Are you scared?"

"Not as scared as I was to tell you."

"Why were you scared of me?"

"I don't know." He looks back at me. "You were always so nice to me. I guess I thought if you couldn't take it, nobody could."

I look down. It's the second time he's said that, and I have to come clean.

"I wanted us to be together," I mumble. "Like boyfriend and girlfriend. That's why I acted that way."

"I know," he smiles. "Ricky told me."

My jaw drops. "Ricky told you?"

"Yeah. He really wanted me to tell you the truth that first night."

I think about Ricky and Trent at his house that afternoon. Then I remember his sad eyes when we talked about Ricky being gone.

"Were you and Ricky..." I hesitate. "Together?"

Trent smiles and his cheeks turn a little pink. "No," he says. "He's too old."

"He's not that old," I say. Shelly had a crush on Ricky. Then again, Shelly's had a crush on almost every guy.

"Well, he says he is." I watch Trent pull a blade of grass.

I can't believe it. All this time I thought Ricky was *Dad's* big rival. "So you wanted to date him?"

Trent shrugs. Then he shakes his head. "I guess he's right," he says. "There's no way. But I liked talking to him. It made me feel… not so alone."

I frown at that. I don't want him to feel alone. I want to help him. He's trusted me and we're friends now, but I don't know what I can do. He's right about being different. No matter what the grownups say, people do put you in boxes and label you. And they do gossip and say mean things. And it does matter. Maybe not to everyone, but it will to Trent's mom. And it will to other parents, to other kids.

He starts to get up. "Well, I'd better do it now," he says. "Before I change my mind."

I watch him stand and gaze out at the water one more time.

"Do you want me to come with you?"

"No," he says.

"You can call me."

He looks back at me and smiles. "Thanks, Harley."

I watch him leave and the urge to cry comes over me again. I lean against the tree and wish Jason were here. I want things to be right between us so badly. I want him to put his arms around me and kiss me. I want him to smooth my hair back, and I want to smell his warm, citrusey scent. Then I remember Stephanie, and what she said, how angry he was. I look back at the creek and bite my lip. It cannot end this way. I have to fix this. Operation Get Jason Back is still in effect, and this time it's not based on a dream or a childhood list or a silly head-injury rescue outside the gym. I know Jason, and I know how it's been between us. He cares about me, and I care about him. How we feel is real, and I'm not flaking out this time. I'm going to be assertive, and I'm going to win.

Sixteen

Dad's sermon is on forgiveness. I can't believe it. I've heard him talk about this before, of course. About how choosing not to forgive someone is like putting you and that person in chains. It ties you together and drags you both down, and even if you can't forget, you can always choose to forgive.

I look at my mom, and think about how good it feels to forgive her. How hopeful I am that things are back on track with us. As usual, she's looking at Dad like he's saying the most amazing things, and I'm certain that she's formulating her own philosophical spin on his sermon. Something they'll discuss over lunch while I think about everything that happened last night and the night before.

The Doxology comes, and as I sing, I scan the room. Stephanie isn't here. Trent and his mom aren't here. Of course, Jason isn't here. I think about the time I complained to Mom that it never seems like the people who need to hear what Dad is saying are present when he says it. She said something like God knows who's going to be here before the day even comes. I'd said I wished God paid closer attention to what's going on in the present.

I sing out the Amen, and on cue everyone stands and surges toward the back doors. I descend from my perch and quietly follow them out. I feel a flicker of hope as I reach the exit remembering last week. Jason was outside waiting by the tree. But he isn't there today.

I think about him the whole ride home and wonder if I can skip lunch and go see him. But when we get to the house, I see Ricky's car.

"I've got to get those forms signed for Ricky," Mom says, reaching for the door handle. "It'll only take a second and then we can have lunch."

Dad gets out and goes inside. Mom walks over to the car, and I watch her talking to him. Then she says something, and he gets out and follows her into the house.

He's alone in the kitchen when I enter. Mom isn't here, and he's at the counter looking out the window. He seems relaxed and not at all uncomfortable. It feels like old times, but so much has changed.

I'm happy to see him.

"Hey, princess."

"Hey, Ricky."

"You look beautiful as always."

"Thanks." I feel a little embarrassed. That's what Trent said, and I wonder if the two of them discussed me.

"I wanted to thank you for what you did," I say. "For Mom. You were really brave standing up like that. In front of everyone."

"It wasn't that much," he shrugs. "I'm just glad you told me or I'dve never known."

We're quiet again.

"Your mom's a really amazing person. I know you don't get that now, but she is."

I nod. I get it a little more than he thinks I do.

"Anyway," he continues. "It's like I said. I'm glad you told me. She probably wouldn't have said a word to me, and I'd have never gotten over it if something bad happened."

I walk over to the bar and pick up one of the forms he's brought. It's his graduation paperwork.

"It's been strange not seeing you every day," I say. "I've missed you."

As I say the words, I realize I mean them very much.

"Yeah, I've missed you, too." I glance up and he smiles back at me.

"I talked to Trent," I say. "He says you were really nice to him."

"He's a sweet kid." Ricky looks back out the window for a second like he's remembering something. "It's hard being that age and going through all that... *stuff.*"

"He says you told him to tell me right away."

"Ho, yeah," he laughs. "When I realized who he was, I had to get you off the hook. I did not want to see you get hurt like that. Especially after all that concentrated effort."

"Thanks," I say, glancing up at him again. "It's funny because I guess I knew we weren't supposed to be together or something."

"Yeah? How so?"

"I don't know." I sigh, remembering how much I thought about Jason on my dates with Trent. How much I want to see Jason right now. The nonstop longing that crept in unexpectedly. "There was just... somebody else."

Ricky grins. "J.J.?"

I bite my lip and look down.

"It's okay! The heart knows what it wants."

I wrinkle my nose. "You sound like a greeting card."

Ricky laughs. "I've been hanging around your mom too long."

"No doubt."

"Well, I kept texting him possible ways he could tell you," he says. "But I guess he had to do it in his own time."

"That was *you* sending all those texts?"

"Yeah." Then he looks surprised. "Did it cause a problem?"

"Oh!" I shake my head and exhale a laugh. "I couldn't figure out who kept texting him on our dates is all." Then I remember how happy Trent was when he got them.

"I'm sorry," he says. "I was just trying to be encouraging."

"No worries." I go to sit down at the table. "I mean, it doesn't even matter now."

"I guess not."

"He really likes you, you know," I say. "He says you told him you're too old."

He glances at me then, "I am too old, Harley." His voice is serious.

"Still, if you like him..."

Ricky walks around the bar and leans against the side closest to where I'm sitting. "You've met his mom, right?"

I raise my eyebrows and nod.

"After all that happened. Then all that stuff with your mom... I could see her happily having me arrested."

We're quiet a moment before he speaks again. "Either way, it wouldn't be right," he says. "You guys are just kids."

Just then Mom comes back in the room carrying that silly magnets and menopause book.

"I'm sorry. I misplaced it," she says.

"Thanks." He puts it in his bag. "Well. I guess this is it!"

"Yeah," Mom says. Then she pulls him into a hug. "Keep in touch. And if I can help you with anything, let me know."

Ricky smiles at her with so much warmth. It's funny because before I'd interpreted that look as passion. Now I realize it's something else entirely. He turns to the door, and just like that, Ricky's gone.

At lunch Mom and Dad are engrossed in their discussion of Dad's sermon. It's nice to see them back to normal with each other, as if nothing ever happened. I can't believe Dad was right about that, but I'm glad.

When I finally finish eating, I run back to my room and grab my phone. I'm not sure if Trent will respond, but I have to try.

U OK? I text.
After a few seconds, I get his answer.
Yes.
How'd it go?
Not gr8. Not bad.
What now?
Leaving SF.
What?
Moving to G'ville.
No! :(
Yes! :)
Really?
Yes. Big :) Hate SF.
I know. :| Talk soon?
OK.

I lie back on my bed and breathe. I don't even realize I'm tired, but when I open my eyes again, the sun's going down. I jump up and grab my phone. I meant to do this earlier.

You there? I text.

I wait several seconds. Nothing.

I don't know if he'll respond after last night or what he'll even say, but I have to try. I need to see him. I can't wait any longer. Not one more second. Finally my phone whistles.

What up?
Crk?
Hmm.
Pls?
OK.

It takes less than five minutes to get there. I ditch my bike at the road and run to where he's standing by our tree on the bank. I only half-notice his car parked nearby.

"Jason," I pant when I finally reach him. He just stands there, watching me as I catch my breath. My heart's thrumming.

"Sorry I didn't make it for church," he says. "I kind of needed to sleep a little longer this morning."

"The head?" I ask.

He shrugs. "Somebody was a little hung over today."

"You really are a bad influence," I smile.

"I try not to be."

"You'll have to try harder."

I'm finally breathing normally again, but this small talk has to stop. I want him to kiss me. I take a step closer, but he doesn't respond. He either isn't getting the hint or he's decided to make me work for it, which I guess is only fair after how hard I made him work.

"So why'd you want to meet?" He asks, sliding his hands into his pockets. I watch him thinking how those hands need to be out of those pockets and pulling me close to him.

"Well, I was thinking," I hesitate. I know why I wanted to see him, but my carefully planned speech has gone out of my head at the sight of him.

"What?" he asks.

I look around. He isn't making it easier for me. "So how about that," I start. "With Trent, I mean."

He shrugs. "No biggie," he says. Then he looks at me a second. "I guess that makes me, what? The consolation prize?"

"No! I wasn't thinking that at all," I say, reaching for his arm. "I wanted to see you the other night at David's party. I want you to…"

But he catches my hand and holds it back. "Uh uh," he says. My stomach clenches.

He shakes his head. "I'm not here for that."

"But… I was hoping—"

"I'm not some yo-yo, Harley."

"I know you're not, but I just thought—"

"That I'd be waiting for you? Just like always?"

I look down and shrug. "I guess." My eyes are starting to burn again, and I'm afraid I might cry.

"I'm sorry your plans with Trent didn't work out."

I hesitate too long fighting tears, and he frowns, turning to go. "Like I said, no more games."

Then I remember the party. "But what about Stephanie? I mean, I don't understand. Why her?"

It's a dumb question. Anyone can see why guys want to date Stephanie, but Jason knows about me and her.

He shrugs. "She's nice enough."

"But she's just like them, the people you said you hated."

He puts his hands back in his pockets. "She's actually not," he says. "And at least she knows how to be real."

He looks straight into my eyes when he says it, and my stomach hurts. I have no response, no arguments. He's right. There's nothing I can say to change what I've done or how I've treated him. I've been playing games since the first day I met him, and it isn't fair to expect him to wait around for me to make up my mind. He's picked Stephanie, and no amount of assertiveness is going to change that.

"See you around, H.D.," he says and starts walking back to his car. I watch as he gets into the Passat and drives away. Then I slide down against the tree and put my head on my bent knees as the tears stream down my face.

The next morning I try to think of any reason to stay home, but it's no good. Mom's as tough about attendance as she is about facing my problems.

"It hurts too much," I whisper, staring into my coffee mug. "There's no way I'm learning anything today."

Mom's at the bar stirring honey into her tea. She presses her lips together and walks over to place her hand on my shoulder. "I'm sorry things didn't go the way you hoped," she says softly. "But you never know what can happen. Things can change in a day."

I shrug, and she starts combing my hair back with her fingers. "Want me to do a braid?"

I shake my head. "It doesn't matter anymore," I say.

She slides her fingers through the sides of my hair anyway and starts wrapping the strands from left to right, over and over. "From where I was sitting, it looked like Jason really liked you," she says. "I bet if you give him a little time, he'll come around."

I sigh. "No way, Mom. It's over," I say. "You should've heard him. He says I was playing games and the only reason I want him back is..." My voice trails off.

I haven't told Mom about the whole Trent thing yet. It's just too much to deal with all at once, and she can't help with that anyway. Not with the way Trent's mom feels about her.

"Is what?" I hear her frown as she continues braiding.

"Just because it didn't work out with me and Trent," I say.

She doesn't answer as she finishes my hair. Then she walks around to sit in front of me at the table. I continue looking at my coffee mug, but she reaches across the table for my hands. I slide mine into hers and look up, meeting her eyes.

"Tell you what," she says. "Just be yourself, and I bet things change quicker than you expect."

I don't roll my eyes at her although I want to. Instead I just smile and nod. Mom always has wild ideas.

In the car Shelly's completely distracted. I can't believe she didn't call me yesterday demanding I tell her everything about Trent, but I'd been sure this morning she'd be bursting. Instead she's strangely quiet as we drive the few blocks to school. She pulls into the first empty spot without even trying to find something closer and kills the engine. Then she just sits quietly for several moments. Now I'm starting to get worried.

"You okay?" I ask.

"I'm in love with Aaron," she says, looking straight ahead.

I catch myself before I laugh out loud, and instead I do a little cough. Then I clear my throat and turn in my seat to face her.

"Love?" I don't want to state the obvious, but I confess my problems are completely forgotten at this. "Is your mom trying a new self-help theory?"

"No," she says, still in zombie-mode, looking out the front window. "I know. It seems... really fast."

"It *is* really fast. You've only been out what, twice?"

She turns to look at me then, and I can tell by her expression this isn't a joke. "He said that, too. That it seems fast—"

"Wait," I interrupt. "So you've discussed it with him?"

"We sort of talked about it after the party." She looks down at her lap.

"What happened exactly?" I can't believe this.

She's quiet a moment, then she starts. "Well... after the Trent thing, the party kind of ended. So we went back to his house and we were all making out and stuff. You know."

I shrug, "Okay."

"Then I just... said it."

I stare at her, waiting. But she's stopped again. "And?"

"And he said that about it being fast, and I nearly died," Her hands go to her face, and she squeezes her eyes shut. "It just slipped out, Harley."

I reach over and rub her arm. "That's okay," I'm trying to make her feel better, but *ouch!*

"I told him I had to go," she opens her eyes and looks at her hands in her lap. "I pretty much stayed in my room all day yesterday just thinking about it. About him. He kept calling, but I couldn't answer the phone."

"So you haven't talked to him since?"

I watch her squirm. "I couldn't."

We're quiet. I want to be encouraging, but I'm still trying to recover. I know how she feels about things like falling in love and commitment these days.

"You know, I always thought you and Brian might get back together," I say. "Eventually, I mean."

She shakes her head. "Brian's a jerk." Then she adds in a quiet voice. "But Aaron's... different."

"Well?" I smile. "That's good. Right?"

She looks away, out the window. Several moments pass before she says anything again.

"I'll never forget the night my dad sat at our kitchen table and signed those divorce papers," she says. "And then he walked out the door like we never even mattered."

My eyes get warm. It's the same night I held her hand as she cried.

She turns back to me and kind of smiles. "But I can't keep making everyone else pay for what he did, right?"

I nod and she exhales.

"I told Aaron about that," she continues. "The divorce, I mean, and how it felt. How I felt."

"What'd he say?"

She looks down, smiling. "He said my dad's a jerk and he wants to kick his ass."

I reach for her hand and squeeze it. "Now *I* love Aaron. I mean, he's kind of a kid, but not really. Right?"

"He's different," she says softly. "I mean, when we're together, it's... I don't know. It's fun."

Our eyes meet and we smile just as there's a tapping on her window. We both turn to look, and then she opens her door fast. I lean forward and catch a glimpse of Aaron as her door closes again and my friend's back is pressed against it. I grab my door handle fast and stand up to see Shelly's arms clutched around Aaron's neck. I grin and lean back into the car for my bag before heading to the building. Everything feels happy and optimistic all of a sudden. People can change. Even if for a while they seem very determined to be angry and to not give other people a second chance. I set off for class smiling and ready to see Jason.

In our texts, Trent told me his mom is keeping him home from school now. Somehow she's blaming our school for him being gay. For him "thinking he's gay," which is what he told me she says. He and I agree that's idiotic, but a few times I catch the whispers of my fellow students discussing what happened at David's party. Half the female population is saying it's a vicious rumor and the other half is claiming they knew it all along. I hate it, and I'm glad he's not here, especially since I know how he feels about all the gossip. On the way to algebra, I think about how I used to rush to see him before class every day, and then I realize in just a few minutes I'll see Jason. My optimism abandons me, and I duck into the bathroom to check my hair and makeup. Stephanie's there. I narrow my eyes when I see her. She's looking in the mirror with one of her newest little Shadow Creek minions by her side, and they're talking and applying lip gloss.

"Hey, Harley," she says, glancing at me. "You know Ashley Lockett?"

I shake my head. "Hey," I say to the typically pretty, blonde-haired, blue-eyed girl standing next to Steph. There's always another one coming up.

She smiles at me. "Hey."

"Ashley's a freshman, but she's a cinch for the cheer squad next year," Stephanie continues unfazed. "Keep an eye out for her at tryouts this summer, okay?"

I don't respond. She's got a lot of nerve asking me for a favor at tryouts.

"Look." Stephanie puts down her gloss and turns to me. "I'm sorry about what happened at the party. With Trent. I was drunk and stupid, and I guess I sort of blew his cover. Or whatever."

My eyes widen. *I'm sorry* is something I never expected to hear from Stephanie Miller, and it leaves me fumbling for the proper comeback.

"Everybody says stupid stuff they regret," I mutter. Then I frown wishing I were brave enough to say what I really thought about her big mouth.

She turns back to the mirror, but she's looking down. "I really liked Trent," she says. "I thought we might get back together if... well, I hope he isn't too mad at me."

I manage to keep my expression neutral, but you could knock me over with a feather right now.

"I think they're moving to Glennville," I say. "And he's happy. He never liked it here."

"I can understand that," she says under her breath, looking up again and flipping her dark hair behind her shoulders. I watch her smooth pink gloss over her perfect mouth and refuse to picture Jason kissing it.

"I don't think it's going to work out with me and Jason," she says, as if she's just read my mind.

Our eyes meet in the mirror.

"Oh, really?" I say as if I couldn't care less. Right. I'm dying.

"I mean, he's hot and all." She smiles in a way that actually seems friendly. "But he's too distracted. I think he's still got a thing for somebody else."

I'm speechless. Stephanie Miller is not the type of person I'd ever expect to go out on a limb for anybody. Or to back down from something she wants. Now I really don't know what to say.

She does an exaggerated exhale and spins to face me. "Look, Harley. Here's fifty cents." She spreads both hands at my face. "Buy some backbone and go get what you want."

And with that the senior, head-cheerleader, hottest girl at school who's about to leave for college in California walks out, her pet freshman right behind her, leaving me standing there with my mouth open.

I quickly shut it and look at myself in the mirror. I glance at my hair. I didn't think about it at the time, but Mom gave me that same braid I was wearing the day Jason derailed my luau date with Trent. I'm even wearing a similar dress. My heart's thumping and with shaking hands, I smooth a few flyaway strands back and then touch up my lip gloss. Assertiveness. Break the Cycle. Backbone.

I have no idea what I'm about to do.

Seventeen

The bell's ringing and Jason's already in his seat as I sneak into class. I can't look at him. Stephanie's words are still swirling in my head. She didn't exactly say he's still interested in me but what else could she have meant? Something must've happened.

Mrs. Gipson's droning on about some formula or the order of operations, but I can't follow her right now. All I can think about is him just inches away from me and trying to figure out what he's thinking. I have to sneak a peek at him. My book and notebook are open on my desktop, and I lean forward in my seat so that my hair falls sort of past my face on the side. I raise my hand to my cheek and carefully turn my head just enough to glance in his direction. His brown eyes lock on mine and I jump, sending my textbook sliding off the side of my desk.

Wham! It hits the floor, and Mrs. Gipson stops speaking and turns to look at me. My cheeks are flaming red, and I quickly bend down to pick up my book. As I sit up again, I glance at Jason. He's looking at the teacher, but I can see him struggling not to laugh. *Great.*

When Mrs. Gipson turns around again, I hear him whisper. "You okay?"

I nod, but I don't look at him. At this point, the only cycle I've broken is the one where I have any dignity left.

Finally the bell rings, and I don't move as Jason stands and collects his things. He pauses for a moment beside me, but I continue making pretend notes in my book. I'm too flustered, and all my confidence is gone. I can't say anything to him right now.

After another moment he starts walking to the door, and I peek after him just in time to see Stephanie waiting in the hall. They walk off, and I turn back to picking up my things confused. They still seem to be together.

I sit with Robin and the other cheerleaders at lunch, watching Jason next to Stephanie at the other end of the long table. They aren't talking, at least not the way he and I always do.

"He was too perfect to be straight. And the way he dresses," Robin's discussing Trent with Meg and one of the other senior girls. Then her voice lowers. "I can't believe Stephanie dated him so long. That means she never…"

She raises her eyebrows and tilts her head toward the other end of the table. The girls snicker. I glance at Stephanie and Jason again, wishing I knew could tell what she's saying to him, if she's telling him they shouldn't go out anymore.

Brian's approach interrupts my thoughts. He puts his tray right between Robin and me and sits, scooting us apart. I roll my eyes. He's been a big goon since kindergarten, but Robin and the other girls giggle. I notice a few playing with their hair, suddenly blinking and smiling, and I feel like I missed a memo. Shelly and Brian were together so long, I never thought of him as a potential love interest. I glance at him and decide I still don't think of him that way.

"God, Brian. You're so rude," Robin complains, but when she pushes his arm, I notice her hand lingers before she takes it back.

"I figure this is the only safe table these days," he says, leaning back to open his drink. Meg picks up the conversation like nothing's changed.

"David says there's a For Sale sign in front of his house now." She slides a perfectly highlighted strand of hair behind her ear. Brian watches her, and I can tell he's looking for a way to impress her.

"I heard his Mom threatened to throw him out," Robin continues.

Brian groans loudly. "It's the great fag invasion of Shadow Falls," he says. "Shit. I'm just glad he never joined the team. I can't be worrying about *that* at my backside."

My teeth clench, and I stand up, sliding my tray off the table. "You're an idiot, Brian," I snap.

All eyes fly to me, but I don't care. I don't care if Brian's just trying to impress Meg. I can't sit and listen to this anymore. Shelly is totally right about him. Jerk.

Robin shoots me an apologetic look, but I keep walking. Maybe it isn't much, but I can at least walk away from them, not sit by and pretend to agree with their ignorance. I catch Jason's eyes as I pass. He can tell something's wrong, and as I push through the heavy cafeteria door, I see him frown.

The rest of the day's pretty quiet, and by the time the final bell rings, my anger's subsided. Shelly's beaming rainbows and sunshine in the car. It's nice she's having such a breakthrough in her personal life and all, but it just reminds me of Stephanie and Jason.

Was she serious about breaking it off with him? And if so, then what? Will he be all hurt and need a recovery period? No. They only went out once. But it only took me once to be hooked on Jason.

"Okay. Frown police," Shelly glances at me while turning onto my street. "What's going on?"

I sigh. Since the whole Aaron-love thing, I figure it's safe now to tell her. "I was just thinking about Jason."

"Jason? I thought you got over him weeks ago."

I chew my lip. She technically was going out with Jason during all our encounters at the creek.

"Well…" I'm not sure how to say it.

"Well, you've finally realized what a super hottie he is?" she smiles. "I told you that the first day, but you were so into Trent."

"I guess. But I can't stop thinking about him now. And he's all with Stephanie." I exhale, hoping it'll ease the pressure in my chest.

Shelly turns into my driveway and kills the car. "Okay, I'm going to tell you something." She turns in her seat to face me. "I should've told you weeks ago, but I didn't think it mattered."

"What?" I frown, and she reaches across and presses her index finger between my eyebrows.

"Piece of tape right there," she says. "Supposed to break the frown-habit."

I bat her hand away. "Just tell me."

"Don't get big-headed, but the whole time we were dating, I could tell he was still into you," she says. "You could *so* get him back if you wanted, I just know it."

My heart jumps. "But what if he really does like Stephanie?"

"Too soon," she says. "And have I taught you nothing, Grasshopper? If you want him, go get him! Assertiveness. Break the Cycle!"

I fall back against the seat. "I tried that," I say. "I texted him and asked him to meet me at the creek."

Shelly's eyes widen with her smile. "Now we're getting somewhere!"

I shake my head, looking down. "No we're not. He thinks I'm only into him now because of what happened with Trent."

"Ew." Her smile fades. "Gotcha."

"Tell me about it," I sigh again.

I watch her thinking a few moments, then she jumps. "Go to his house," she says.

I shake my head and reach down for my bag. "I can't do that."

"Old Harley can't, but Assertive Harley can," she says. "Go there and stand in his driveway and tell him how you feel. It's in all the movies. The ultimate romantic gesture."

I think about it. He *did* come to my house that night—and the next day—to ask me not to date Trent. And he did at least show up to meet me at the creek the night I texted him.

"But what will I say?"

"Just say what you feel."

I walk back to my room after dinner. Mom's washing the dishes. Dad's in his study reading as usual. My conversation with Shelly is the only thing on my mind. I go over and sit on my bed, pulling open the little drawer under my lamp where my old list is hidden. Also stuffed in the drawer is my copy of the police report from the day Jason hit me with his car. I wonder for a split second if I should've given this to mom, but more importantly, I see written on the top right side Jason's address. I know exactly where his house is. I can do it, I can go there tonight. But how can I get out of my house?

I walk back to Dad's study. He glances up at me and smiles. "How's it hanging, biker-chick?"

"Missing the open road."

He chuckles. "Kids at school behaving?"

I nod. "For the most part. There's been some gossip, but I just ignore it."

He puts his book down, smile disappearing. "It's hard, I know," he says. "I'm sorry if the gossip hits home sometimes."

"It usually doesn't bother me," I say, looking down. "I mean, we've all grown up together. We all know each other."

"But when it's your mom—"

"Oh, it's not that. Ricky killed all that with his big reveal. It's just... this other friend. He didn't get so lucky."

Dad frowns, but I don't have time to get into it with him now. I have something else on my mind.

"Would you mind if I rode my bike for a few minutes? Just around the neighborhood?"

He's still serious. "It's a little late, honey. And cars don't always expect bikes at this hour."

"I won't leave the neighborhood. I just need to clear my head."

He glances at the clock and hesitates.

"I'll be careful," I say. "And honestly, I won't be gone more than just a little bit."

"Don't leave the neighborhood," he says.

I nod and start to leave, but then I stop. "Hey, Dad?"

He looks up at me again. "Yeah?"

I study the door frame, running my fingernail down one of the lines in the wood. "How did you know... I mean, when you met Mom. How did you know she was The One?"

Concern crosses his face, and he sits forward in his chair. "Well, for starters, we were both adults, Harley. College graduates."

"I know. But I was just wondering, like if God told you or something. Or like if there was some sign."

He smiles. "Your mother's very beautiful and she liked me, so that was a big neon sign when I first met her."

"C'mon, Dad, you know what I mean. Did you like, maybe have a dream about her? Or maybe you read a scripture or you made a list or something?"

He gets serious again. "I met your mom when we were undergrads, and we liked each other very much," he says. "Then we graduated and I left for seminary."

"Right..."

"I was gone several years, but when I came back and saw her again and we could still talk and our interests had converged rather than grown apart," he pauses. "We had found ourselves first, what we wanted to do with our lives and who God wanted us to be. And then we were able to find each other."

I look back at the lines in the wood, thinking about his words.

"Why are you asking me this, Harley?"

I shake my head. "I just had this thing. It's really stupid. I thought God had brought someone here, this guy, just for me. But I was wrong."

Dad's face grows thoughtful, and he picks up his pencil. "You know, God can bring people into our lives for reasons other than romance."

I glance back at his blue eyes, then I looked up at his blonde hair and feel like such a dork. Of course nine-year-old me made a list describing my Dad. He was the only example of an ideal husband I knew.

I smile and step forward to kiss his cheek. "You know, you're really good at your job."

"You'd better scoot. And don't be gone long."

"OK," I say as I dash out the door.

In less than five minutes I'm approaching Jason's house, but when I see the place, I almost lose my nerve and keep riding. It's huge, with a big stone entrance and bronze lanterns hanging at the door with real flames. I feel like I'm walking up to a small castle. And it takes me a few seconds to find the doorbell.

This is a mistake, I think as the door starts to open. Then right in front of me appears what has to be Jason's dad. He looks a lot like Jason, only with little lines around his eyes and gray hair at his temples.

"Hey," he says in the same casual-friendly manner as his son. "Are you from the school? Jason didn't tell me he was expecting—"

"Oh, no," I shake my head. My whole body is trembling for some reason. "I mean, I'm sorry. He isn't expecting... I mean, I'm Harley."

I try to smile and appear normal despite my completely psychotic behavior meeting him for the first time. I hope he can't see me shaking.

He smiles and opens the door a little wider. "I think he's mentioned you," he says. "Come in?"

My cheeks feel hot at the idea of Jason discussing me with his dad. "Oh, no," I say, looking down then shoving my hair behind my ear. "I was just thinking,"

I swallow a hard lump in my chest and try to get a grip. "Maybe I'll just come back another time."

I turn to leave when I hear Jason's voice from just inside the house. "Hey, Dad," he says. "It's okay, I got it."

I glance back and see Mr. James smile at his son. "It was nice meeting you, Harley," he says as he leaves the doorway and goes inside again. I nod, still moving away, toward the drive. Jason takes a step toward me and closes the door behind him.

"What're you doing here?"

Seeing him melts all the confidence I was feeling. I stop moving back, but I'm not sure I can form a coherent sentence now. It reminds me of that first day he appeared in church and I had to sing. Only tonight I just had dinner, so there's no way this is low blood sugar.

"I really wanted to see you," I manage to say.

He takes another step toward me. "News travels fast," he says. "So you heard Stephanie called it off?"

"No... When? What'd she say?"

There's a hint of his old smile in the corners of his eyes. "Something about going away to college," he says. "And not wanting a long-distance relationship."

I almost laugh, and I feel the smallest bit of hope, like I can actually do what I rode over here to do.

"I'm sorry." I clear my throat and try to act sympathetic. "I hope you're not too disappointed."

"I'm not," he says, watching me.

I'm quiet again, and as I search for the right words, I realize I'm not very good at saying how I

———

322

feel. I think about what Shelly said, and I think about Stephanie, too. They both say he still has a thing for me. I think about everything that's happened, and I know this is it, time to make my assertiveness move — only this time with the right guy. Fifty cents. Break the Cycle.

"Jason," I blurt. "I know I acted stupid and you're mad. And you're right to be mad. But..." I close my mouth and breathe, trying to slow down, to be cool. "I really do want us to be together. And it has nothing to do with Trent."

He crosses his arms over his chest, still watching me. I step forward and reach out to touch him. I'm actually doing it, and I feel like I'm going to be sick.

"I think you do, too," I say, looking directly into his brown eyes. My stomach is completely clenched.

He looks at me for a beat longer and then slides his arms down. "You think so?"

I nod taking another step toward him. "I mean, we did have fun, didn't we?" I steal his question from the night we played Truth or Dare. Only it's my turn now to get the truth. "And aren't you just a little sorry we're not together anymore?"

He doesn't answer, but I still see that little smile lurking in his eyes. "I don't know," he says. "I kind of enjoyed watching you not look at me in class today."

"Are you saying I'm not very sneaky?"

He reaches up and slides that stray piece of hair out of my face. "Not even a little bit," he says softly. I lean my cheek toward his hand, closing my eyes for a moment. And in that brief space he leans forward and brushes his lips against mine.

It's the same tiny kiss as that last night at the creek, our lips barely touching, but my knees get weak and all the feelings I've been holding for the last three days go rushing to my head. I catch the front of his shirt for balance as he opens his arms, and in one movement I'm back in them again, warm and strong and not giving up. We're quiet for a moment, and I can feel my heart beating so fast.

"I guess you're right," he says. I look up at him, and he smiles back. I study his face, his brown hair, then I start to giggle.

"What?" he smiles.

"Dark chocolate with milk chocolate highlights."

"Shelly," he groans, rolling his eyes.

"She was seriously hoping something would happen with you two."

"No shit. Talk about an octopus."

I slant my eyes, and he quickly changes it. "I mean, yeah. Tell me about it."

I pull myself close to him again and feel him inhale at the top of my head. "Mmm," he breathes. "Missed that."

"What?"

"You always smell like... like little flowers or something," he smiles. Then he leans close and lowers his voice. "It's very distracting in class."

The butterflies zoom through my stomach. "It's honeysuckle," I say, lifting my chin for a kiss. He pulls me close, sealing his lips over mine, warm and perfect.

"I wish we were at the creek." I move my head to his shoulder and think of the currents that would be trickling downstream right now.

He holds me, and I feel his fingers playing with the ends of my hair. I think of our first dance all those weeks ago at the luau.

"So is it our turn to come out now?" he asks. "We're officially together? For real?"

"Yes," I say, nodding. "For real."

He leans back, eyes twinkling. "If that's the case, does that mean skinny dipping?"

I glance at him, biting my smile. "No."

"I promise not to steal your clothes."

"Jason."

"At least I get to kiss you."

I kiss him again, and at that moment, I feel like I can stay and kiss him all night. His soft brown hair in my fingers, his arms around me. It's heaven. Then I remember Dad.

"Gotta go!" I give him a squeeze. Our fingers lace as he follows me down to my bike, waiting at the street. But before we get there, I notice a familiar shape in the driveway. The Gremlin.

"Oh, no," I groan. "The monster mobile's back."

"Doesn't it look awesome?"

"Seriously?"

"It took a little longer in the shop because they had to special order a part to fix the A/C," he continues. "For you."

"How thoughtful."

He pulls me back into his arms and smiles. "You really hate it?"

"Yes." But his disappointed expression makes me cave. "Still, I could probably get over it. Every now and then."

He leans forward and presses his soft lips to mine again. Good answer.

The hydrangea bush on the corner isn't blooming anymore, but I think of Trent whenever I see it. Not long after David's party, he and his mom moved to Glennville, but we still keep in touch. He texts me and lets me know how much he loves being in the city, even if they're living in an apartment now. He also says his Mom blames my mom and our church as a corrupting influence. I'm sure Mrs. Perkins agrees, but her power's gone. Dad's position is safe.

Trent's mom has stopped searching his room, he says, and he jokes it's because she's afraid of what she might find. I can tell he's happier, and that makes me happy for him. At school nobody gossips about him in front of me anymore, and I'm getting better at saying how I feel about things as they happen.

Mom and Dad are back to their routine of alternating work, philosophical debate, and then sending me out to pick up dinner. But I'm glad to go because it gives me an excuse to run down to the creek with Jason, where I'm also getting better at Truth or Dare.

Prom arrives, and Reagan and her crew's "Once Upon a Time" theme seems a fitting end to a year of surprises. The witches have been exposed and their evil schemes foiled, truth has been revealed through acts of bravery, the cycle I was stuck in has been broken, and even Shelly has learned to believe in love again. I suppose in fairytales it's a bad omen for the prince to take you to the ball in a Gremlin. But I've stopped playing games and living in fantasyland.

Jason and I are officially together, and while I'm no longer trying to spot my future husband, my very real boyfriend is gorgeous in a tux. My little black prom dress is just a bit longer than my cheerleader uniform, and as we dance, he plays with the ends of my hair. I smile, he steals a kiss, and I assert that next year will be blissfully crash-free. No faking.

The End

Acknowledgments

With first books, it feels like there's an entire universe of people to thank—from my mom, who always insisted I'd write a book, to my first readers, Richard, Kim, Jenni, Melissa, Rebecca, and Allyson—my first "fans." You have no idea how much your excitement meant to me.

I've been blessed with many, many supportive people in my life, too many to count. But I would be remiss not to acknowledge the ones who helped me with this book in its early stages, Carolyn Snow Abiad, Tami Hart Johnson, Anne Kenny, Odessa Toma, Jen Daiker, and Kate McKean. Thank you for your great ideas and encouragement.

I was lucky to have ongoing support to make this book available to readers regardless of format, most notably from Susan Quinn, Jolene Perry, and Brent Taylor. You guys rock!

To the blogging community, Matt, Jessica, Sheri, Laura, Lydia, Sarah, Old Kitty, Stina, Katie, PK, Janet, Elle, TJ, Mary, DL, and so many others—I have to stop naming names. You've always supported me. You've always been there for me. I'll always be grateful.

14495655R00189

Made in the USA
Charleston, SC
14 September 2012